Highlander Forbidden

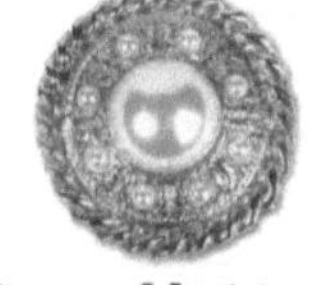

Stolen Highland Hearts
Book Three

JAYNE CASTEL

Forbidden love tastes the sweetest. He should hate her—instead, she becomes his obsession. Rivalry and passion collide in Medieval Scotland.

Jaimee Mackay wants to remain unwed, but the time is coming when she must choose a husband. As a laird's sister, it's her responsibility to strengthen clan alliances. But when her brother holds a gathering in her honor, she is shocked as her clan's greatest enemy joins the warriors vying for her hand.

A man she hasn't been able to stop thinking about since a chance meeting months earlier.

Alexander Gunn has been brought up to hate the Mackays. A clan-chief's son, he intends to continue the feud that the Scottish king has done his best to end. Yet the words he and Jaimee shared earlier in the year have resulted in an obsession.

He has to have her.

The connection between Jaimee and Alexander ignites as soon as they meet again. **But will the hostility between their clans keep them apart?**

Steamy, emotional, and steeped in Scottish history, Jayne Castel's new series set around the lives and loves of three Mackay siblings will steal your heart.

Historical Romances by Jayne Castel

DARK AGES BRITAIN

The Kingdom of the East Angles series
Night Shadows (prequel novella)
Dark Under the Cover of Night (Book One)
Nightfall till Daybreak (Book Two)
The Deepening Night (Book Three)
The Kingdom of the East Angles: The Complete Series

The Kingdom of Mercia series
The Breaking Dawn (Book One)
Darkest before Dawn (Book Two)
Dawn of Wolves (Book Three)
The Kingdom of Mercia: The Complete Series

The Kingdom of Northumbria series
The Whispering Wind (Book One)
Wind Song (Book Two)
Lord of the North Wind (Book Three)
The Kingdom of Northumbria: The Complete Series

DARK AGES SCOTLAND

The Warrior Brothers of Skye series
Blood Feud (Book One)
Barbarian Slave (Book Two)
Battle Eagle (Book Three)
The Warrior Brothers of Skye: The Complete Series

The Pict Wars series
Warrior's Heart (Book One)
Warrior's Secret (Book Two)
Warrior's Wrath (Book Three)

The Pict Wars: The Complete Series

Novellas
Winter's Promise

MEDIEVAL SCOTLAND

The Brides of Skye series
The Beast's Bride (Book One)
The Outlaw's Bride (Book Two)
The Rogue's Bride (Book Three)
The Brides of Skye: The Complete Series

The Sisters of Kilbride series
Unforgotten (Book One)
Awoken (Book Two)
Fallen (Book Three)
Claimed (Epilogue novella)

The Immortal Highland Centurions series
Maximus (Book One)
Cassian (Book Two)
Draco (Book Three)
The Laird's Return (Epilogue festive novella)

Stolen Highland Hearts series
Highlander Deceived (Book One)
Highlander Entangled (Book Two)
Highlander Forbidden (Book Three)

Epic Fantasy Romances by Jayne Castel

Light and Darkness series
Ruled by Shadows (Book One)
The Lost Swallow (Book Two)
Path of the Dark (Book Three)
Light and Darkness: The Complete Series

All characters and situations in this publication are fictitious, and any resemblance to living persons is purely coincidental.

Highlander Forbidden, by Jayne Castel

Copyright © 2021 by Jayne Castel. All rights reserved. No part of this publication may be reproduced, stored in a retrieval system, or transmitted in any form or by any means—electronic, mechanical, recording, or otherwise—without the prior written permission of the author.

Published by Winter Mist Press

ISBN: 978-0-473-56793-4 (paperback)

Edited by Tim Burton
Cover design by Winter Mist Press
Cover photography courtesy of www.shutterstock.com
Brooch image courtesy of www.pixabay.com

Visit Jayne's website: www.jaynecastel.com

***

This book is dedicated to Juno—our sweet and spirited beardie-cross, who passed away recently. Goodbye, June-bug. You will be missed.

November 2008—April 2021

***

I love you as certain dark things are to be loved,
in secret, between the shadow and the soul.
—Pablo Neruda

1

REPUTATIONS

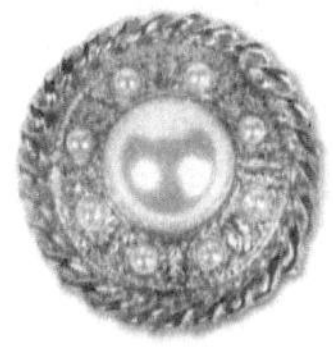

Inverness, Scotland

Spring, 1427

SHE SHOULD HAVE known better than to stare at him.

Seated in the great hall of Inverness Castle, as the din of rough voices echoed off the pitted stone walls around her, Jaimee Mackay surveyed the warriors amassed in the cavernous space. Never had she seen so many of the Highland clans together in one place. And so many who hated each other.

Jaimee didn't want to look at the Gunns, the sworn enemies of her people. Yet she couldn't help herself.

Her gaze settled upon Alexander Gunn—the Gunn chieftain's first born.

Like his father, who sat next to him, he wore his clan sash. The Gunn plaid was a dull, dirty green in comparison to the more vibrant Mackay shades of sea-blue and emerald. Even the threads of red in the cross-hatching did little to enliven it. However, the drabness of the sash he wore couldn't dim Alexander Gunn's presence.

Jaimee had already noticed him the evening before, upon their arrival in Inverness, yet like a moth to a dancing flame, he drew her attention once more.

Everything about the clan-chief's eldest son screamed danger. There were many tales about Alexander Gunn circulating the Highlands. Folk said that his father was a vicious brute who'd beaten all his sons regularly when they were wee, although he'd been hardest on his first-born. He'd brought Alexander up to be just as tough and merciless.

Certainly, the grim look upon Alexander Gunn's face made Jaimee believe the rumors.

But she couldn't fail to note that despite the semi-permanent scowl that marred his forehead, the man was handsome. He was big, with wild black hair, storm-grey eyes, and a short beard. A thin silver scar marred his left cheek, but instead of detracting from his good looks, it just gave him an even more roguish edge.

It wasn't wise to watch him so intently—the man who'd dealt her brother a grievous injury in battle. Connor had revealed recently that the dirk wound he'd suffered during the Battle of Harpsdale—the battle that had claimed the life of their father—had been at the hand of Alexander Gunn.

Gunn brute. Jaimee's gaze narrowed as her attention remained fixed upon him. *Someone should return the favor.*

Alexander Gunn looked her way then.

The impact of their gazes locking was a punch to the gut. Stifling a gasp, Jaimee went rigid in her seat. Next to Jaimee, her brothers, Morgan and Connor, were deep in discussion about something, but she paid them no notice.

Alexander Gunn had trapped her gaze with his—and he wasn't letting go.

Those eyes, almost purple-grey—like a stormy sky—held her fast. And as the stare drew out, she watched his gaze widen, his handsome, scarred face tense.

He knows who I am, she realized.

Jaimee's spine stiffened. Few men intimidated her. She'd grown up with two elder brothers, and of late had gotten proficient at swatting away potential suitors. But this man was different.

Her skin prickled from the power of his gaze; it stripped away her defenses. To Jaimee's surprise, her palms grew sticky, her pulse beating a panicked tattoo at the base of her neck.

The wail of a Highland pipe rent the air at that moment, cutting through the rumble of conversation.

Jaimee jerked her gaze away from Alexander Gunn. Suddenly, she felt oddly light-headed and breathless.

However, she had no time to dwell on her reaction to the hated Gunn warrior, for at that moment two regal figures, clad in flowing red surcoats, glided into the great hall of Inverness.

King James and Queen Joan had arrived. Now the parliament that would decide the fate of the northern clan-chiefs would begin.

Jaimee's thoughts were troubled when she took a walk alone in Inverness Castle's walled garden two days later.

A light drizzle fell, yet she paid it no mind. After all the things she'd seen and heard since her arrival at Inverness, she felt in need of some peace.

It was all so unfair.

Those blasted Gunns had escaped punishment, while King James focused his attention on the Mackay and Ross clans. Niel Mackay, the clan-chief's only son, was to be locked away at Bass Rock, while the Ross clan-chief was to lose his head, along with two other clan-chiefs.

The aftermath of the sentencing still shook the castle, for the Mackay clan-chief had sacrificed his son to save his own neck. The king had threatened to have Angus Mackay beheaded, and Angus had offered up Niel instead. An awful scene had ensued. Niel had leaped up and tried to throttle his father.

Jaimee ground her teeth, reliving the memory of the altercation while she walked the paths of the garden, amongst neatly trimmed yew hedges that formed a maze. Her booted feet crunched on the fine pebbles while a light, misty rain fell silently around her, coating everything. It was a good time to take a walk here, for few others would bother venturing out in the rain.

The devil take those Gunns. If they hadn't goaded the Mackays for so long, Angus Mackay would never have gathered the forces of Strathnaver and marched against them. But the king didn't care—his focus had been on the fact that the Mackays had been the aggressors at Harpsdale.

The Mackay clan chief had brought dishonor upon his clan. And now Niel was going to be locked away in some foul prison.

Jaimee's belly churned guiltily at the thought of the Mackay clan-chief's son. Niel had flirted outrageously with her over the years, had even murmured to her once that although he was not yet ready to take a wife, she'd be his choice if he ever did. She'd rebuffed his attentions, although the haughty attitude she adopted with him only seemed to encourage the man further.

Niel Mackay would no longer pester her though.

Deep in thought, she walked the narrow paths, losing herself in the maze. Emerging at the far side of the garden, where budding roses climbed the high walls, Jaimee lifted her chin, taking in the heavy clouds that hung over Inverness.

The weather had been gloomy since shortly after their arrival, and she longed to feel the sun upon her face again.

The crunch of booted feet upon gravel behind her made Jaimee spin around.

Her gaze alighted upon a tall dark-haired figure clad in leather, a black woolen cloak hanging from broad shoulders.

Alexander Gunn was standing just a few feet behind her.

For a moment, Jaimee merely gaped at him. Where had he come from? And more importantly, what was he doing in this garden?

Frowning to mask her fluttering panic, Jaimee drew herself up. "Did ye follow me in here?"

It was a bold, rude question—not to mention arrogant. But she was so surprised by his appearance she decided to go in for the attack.

The Gunn heir merely stared back at her for a moment, before his sensual mouth twisted. "I'm taking a walk, My Lady, like ye."

"In the rain?"

"Aye. I enjoy the scent of honey-suckle as much as the next man."

Their gazes met squarely then, and like two days previous, Jaimee's breath rushed out of her. And just like that day, she saw his grey eyes widen. The air in the walled garden changed then. It felt heavy, charged—as if a thunderstorm loomed overhead.

Alexander Gunn walked toward her, a slow, stalking tread that made fear coil in the pit of Jaimee's belly.

Hades, he's tall. She was used to tall men: her brothers both towered over her despite that she wasn't a short woman. But this warrior was huge and brawny. He stopped just a couple of steps back, his gaze searching her face.

"Jaimee Mackay, isn't it?" he rumbled.

Heat flowered across Jaimee's chest. She just prayed it didn't creep up her neck to her face.

"Aye," she replied coolly, glad her voice remained steady and didn't betray her racing pulse. "But I think ye already knew that, Alexander *Gunn*."

His mouth lifted at the corners, the barest hint of a smile. "I see we are already acquainted with each other's reputation."

Jaimee arched an eyebrow. She shoved down the urge to take a step back from him and fold her arms across her chest in an effort to put some distance between them. Standing so near was disconcerting.

This close, she could smell him: leather and warm, spicy male. The scent did strange things to her belly.

"So, I have a reputation?" she asked, injecting an icy edge to her voice. She couldn't let this man sense weakness—she guessed he thrived on it.

"Aye," he said softly. "The bonny Mackay woman who thinks she's too good for any man who courts her ... I've heard of ye."

Heat did rise to Jaimee's cheeks then, although it wasn't a flush of embarrassment but anger. "And yer reputation precedes ye, Gunn," she ground out the words. "Warmongering and traitorous bastard that ye are. Ye nearly killed my brother."

His gaze widened once more, and she could have sworn she saw his pupils dilate. Jaimee's already galloping heart beat faster. Of course, a beast such as him would enjoy being insulted. Heat flushed through her once more.

This man had nearly robbed her of Connor. How she wished she carried a dirk on her this afternoon. She'd have loved nothing more than to stab Gunn in the guts with it.

"Connor Mackay lives, does he not?" Alexander Gunn replied, his voice low and emotionless. "Perhaps I showed him mercy at Harpsdale?"

Fury pulsed within Jaimee in a hot, red haze that obliterated all fear of this man.

Mercy? Alexander Gunn wasn't capable of it. He was the devil's spawn, if not Satan himself. He'd sat there smirking while the Mackays had been blamed for the Battle of Harpsdale. His father had told lie after lie without even blinking. How dare this savage even speak to her?

Jaimee's lips parted as a blistering response rose within her.

But the crunch on the pebbles behind them made the words catch in her throat. Turning, Jaimee saw a small dark-haired woman standing there.

She recognized her instantly. Maggie Munro—a widow who'd accompanied her uncle, a chieftain, to Inverness—cast her an apologetic look.

Swinging her attention back to Alexander Gunn, Jaimee struggled to gather her thoughts. What would he do now? Insult her again? She balled her fists at her sides. She wanted to lash out at him, to flatten his nose into a bloody pulp.

Alexander Gunn's handsome face shuttered. The fact they were no longer alone had doused the goading look in his eyes.

Stepping back, he favored both women with a curt nod. Then he turned on his heel and strode from the garden without another word.

2

MY FUTURE IS NO GAME

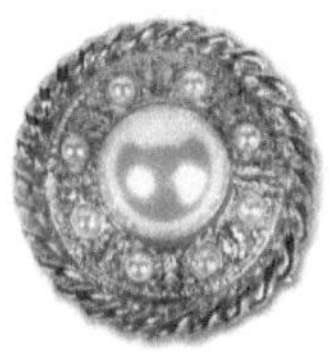

Farr Castle
Strathnaver, Scotland

Six months later ...

JAIMEE SOMETIMES HAD the urge to throttle her brother.

Now was one of those times.

She loved him, of course. Connor Mackay, laird of Farr Castle, was a big-hearted, kind man. But he could be incredibly aggravating.

"I've already sent word out to all our allies," he informed her across the table. "Ye won't wriggle out of choosing a husband this time, lass."

They sat in the chieftain's solar, high up in Farr Castle. Every morning, the chieftain and his kin broke their fasts together in this room. Connor and Keira—and their three-month-old bairn, Rose—sat at the head of the rectangular table, while Morgan and his wife, Maggie, sat down one side. Jaimee, her cousin Kennan, and his wife, Cait, had taken their places opposite.

Jaimee lowered her spoon, abandoning her porridge. "Cease speaking to me like I have the wits of a fowl," she replied. "Haven't I already told ye that *if* I take a liking to one of the men at the games, I'll wed him?"

It grated on Jaimee to make this assurance. She wouldn't choose just any man, just to please her brother.

Perhaps sensing the rebelliousness that still bubbled beneath his sister's calm demeanor, Connor frowned. "That's not good enough. I've called over two dozen warriors to our gathering at Halladale. I need ye to promise me that ye *will* settle on one of them."

"Connor." Keira, Connor's wife, spoke up then. The warning note in the woman's voice made the chieftain stiffen. Keira sat next to her husband, their bairn swaddled against her breast, as she buttered a piece of bannock. "Please stop heckling yer sister."

"She's right, brother," Morgan agreed from farther down the table. "Keep nagging like this and Jaimee will take herself off to Iona."

Jaimee pulled a face, even if she appreciated Morgan taking her side. They all knew she wasn't suited to a nun's life. Apart from the fact she wasn't remotely pious, she chafed at being told what to do.

Jaimee's willfulness had always been her problem. No doubt Connor was wishing he'd been given a meeker sister.

The chieftain's mouth thinned, his fingers tightening around the cup of milk he held. He cast his wife a hurt look, as if he'd expected her to support him. He then frowned at his younger brother. "Stay out of this, Morgan."

Jaimee heaved in a deep breath, quashing rising irritation. Aye, she appreciated Keira and Morgan speaking up on her behalf. Yet she could fight her own battles. This argument with Connor had begun shortly after he'd taken up their father's place as chieftain of the Mackays of Farr. Although her brother had never admitted such outright, she sensed he thought Rory Mackay had overly indulged his only daughter.

At two and twenty, Jaimee should have been wed with at least two bairns by now. A chieftain's daughter, or sister for that matter, needed to marry well to forge alliances and strengthen relationships. Jaimee knew that, yet she'd fought against the fate that had already been set down for her.

Over the years, she hadn't liked any of the men her father or brother had brought before her—not one.

Frowning, Jaimee let her gaze travel to the solar window. It was open, letting in a cool morning breeze. A grey dawn filtered over the sea. Summer had ended, and September had brought overcast days. The nights were now drawing in, and the dawn broke increasingly later. The harvest was done, and the cold weather had yet to arrive.

It was the perfect time of year for a clan gathering—and a popular season for weddings.

Gaze focused on the monochrome sky, Jaimee's throat tightened.

I want what Ma and Da had.

In a vulnerable moment, Jaimee had once revealed to Keira that she desired a love match, like her parents. Rory and Rose Mackay had been inseparable. Indeed, they had died just months apart. Although Jaimee hadn't voiced her desire to Connor—for it seemed a silly, sentimental thing to admit to her brother—the happy marriages surrounding her at Farr Castle only made her more determined to wait.

They've all been lucky, but what if I'm not?

Both her brothers and cousin were all blissfully wed, yet Connor expected her to pick a husband from this gathering as if she were selecting material for a new gown.

"Jaimee?" Connor's voice, laced with impatience, intruded. "Will ye take these suitors seriously?"

Blinking, she shifted her focus from the window, back to her brother, and met his eye.

No, it wasn't marriage itself she railed against, but the fear she'd be locked in a loveless, passionless marriage for the rest of her life. And yet, she knew her obstinacy was trying Connor's patience.

"Aye," Jaimee replied stiffly. "But I can't promise that I will *wed* one of them. Until I meet the men, I can't know whether any will be suitable ... can I?"

Connor's jaw bunched. "Many of us are betrothed without even meeting our future spouse," he growled. "I think ye are playing games with me, sister. I know ye value yer freedom, but sometimes we must *all* do our duty."

Jaimee scowled back at him. Her fingers clenched around the spoon she still held. That was one of his favorite arguments, for although he adored Keira, she wasn't the woman he'd been initially betrothed to. Their parents had promised him to a lass he'd never even met when he was only eight. Just under a year earlier now, he'd gone off to the priory upon the isle of Iona to fetch his betrothed—but the woman he'd retrieved hadn't been Rhianna Ross, as he'd believed, but Keira Gunn. The two women had woven a deception and swapped identities. Things had nearly ended badly for Connor and Keira. However, Jaimee was relieved that once the lie had been unmasked, the couple had salvaged their relationship.

"My future is no game," Jaimee replied between gritted teeth. Aye, sometimes she longed to fling herself across the table and wrap her fingers about her brother's throat. "I have agreed to this gathering, Connor ... and ye shall just have to content yerself with that."

A tense silence fell across the table.

Jaimee dropped her gaze to her congealing porridge. She usually enjoyed this time of day, yet Connor's nagging had ruined it. He sensed her reluctance—but that didn't mean he had to push things.

Cait cleared her throat then, splintering the tension. Jaimee glanced up to see her friend cast her a sympathetic smile. "I wish I could accompany ye to the Strath of Halladale," she said with a sigh, before glancing down at her protruding belly. Cait's stomach was so swollen with the bairn she carried that she'd had to push her chair back from the table to be able to sit comfortably. "The bairn's not due till Samhuinn, but Cullodina tells me I shouldn't be traveling at this stage."

"And she's right," Kennan agreed gruffly. "I won't be going to the gathering either." He glanced over at the laird then. "Someone's got to look after things while ye are husband-hunting, eh Connor?"

Jaimee cut her cousin a reproachful look. He wasn't helping.

The meal passed in uncomfortable silence after that.

Abandoning her porridge a short while later, Jaimee went outdoors to check on the dogs. Morgan's hound, Gritta, had whelped a litter of pups during the summer, and spending time with the lively wee beasts was often a salve when her mood was low.

The dogs were housed in an enclosure between the stables and the forge. Belligerent shouts were coming from the latter this morning. Jaimee frowned. Farlan, the blacksmith, didn't get on with the lad he'd apprenticed. The pair often quarreled, and from the sounds of things, the two men were about to come to blows.

"Stop yer whining, old man." Gil's heckling voice carried out into the landward bailey. "It's only a blade."

"Useless clod-head!" Farlan bellowed back. "Ye have ruined it ... a halfwit could have done a better job!"

Jaimee's step faltered. She was tempted to stop off at the forge and try to break up the row. Yet she wasn't fond of Gil. His blatant stare and sneering face made her hackles rise.

Farlan will deal with him, she assured herself.

Leaving the bailey, she instead squeezed through the high wooden gate into the kennels. Excited barking met Jaimee as she pushed her way through the muscular wolfhounds that greeted her, tails wagging, to the pen where the puppies were kept.

"Hello lads and lassies." A smile crept over Jaimee's face when she let herself in and was immediately assaulted. The pups were growing fast. They were now weaned, and Gritta spent very little time with them. They were at a mischievous age, and Jaimee batted one of the pups away as it sank its needle-like teeth into her hand. "Ouch, Conn ... was that necessary?"

Perching on a stool in the corner of the pen, Jaimee let the puppies push against her ankles. Some of them greeted her briefly before tumbling off to play with their siblings. It had been a large litter of ten pups.

However, one of the puppies wasn't interested in playing with the others. A little bitch covered in soft grey fluff clambered up onto Jaimee's lap.

"Good morn to ye to, Milish," Jaimee murmured, caressing the pup's velvety ears. The wolfhound's name meant 'sweetie'. It was the perfect name for such a lovely natured creature. Jaimee had already asked the master of the hounds if the bitch could be hers—and of course, he'd agreed. Old Conry rarely denied her anything.

With a sigh, Jaimee watched Milish lick her hand.

I wish Da were here to see this litter, she thought wistfully. Like Morgan, Rory Mackay had been fond of his hounds. Old Conry said that this litter was the finest he'd seen in years. A sad smile curved Jaimee's lips then. Her father would have been proud.

Spending time with the pups often made her feel better if she'd argued with Connor—something that happened regularly these days—but even Milish's delightful company couldn't lift the weight from her shoulders this morning.

She'd agreed to wed, yet she dreaded the gathering—dreaded having to choose a husband from those competing.

What if I don't take a liking to any of them? It was certainly possible.

Another sigh gusted from Jaimee. She wasn't the sort to sulk or brood, yet of late she often sought solitude. When the other women—Keira, Cait, and Maggie—gathered in the women's solar in the afternoons to sew, weave, spin, and gossip, she found herself making excuses not to join them these days.

It wasn't because she disliked any of them. All three women were as dear to her as sisters—even Maggie, who'd only wed Morgan in the spring and hadn't resided at Farr Castle long. They were all warm and lively company.

Tension coiled in Jaimee's belly. An odd mood had descended on her over the summer, one that had little to do with dreading the upcoming gathering.

And whenever she tried to pinpoint when it had all started, panic curled up within her like wood smoke. She often tried to deny the truth, yet this morning she couldn't.

It's his fault.

No, not Connor—but someone else. Someone she wasn't related to.

Her enemy.

Alexander Gunn. How she wished she hadn't stared at him that day—if she hadn't, then perhaps he wouldn't have approached her in the garden. Even now, her breathing quickened at the way his gaze had speared hers across the crowded great hall of Inverness. And when he'd spoken to her in the garden, she'd been assaulted by warring emotions.

She'd wanted to kill the bastard, and yet at the same time, she'd been fascinated by him.

He'd lingered in her thoughts for days afterward, and whenever she recalled their brief exchange and the heat that had warmed the damp air between them, goosebumps rose on her skin.

"Why does that beast plague my thoughts?" she whispered to Milish. "Why can't I shake him off?"

However, the pup merely climbed up and licked her chin. Milish wasn't any help at all.

Jaimee's mouth flattened into a thin line. *Enough.* She couldn't let Alexander Gunn destroy her peace. Perhaps the man was a warlock as well as a warmongering brute. Perhaps he'd cast a spell over her.

She shook her head then, as if by doing so she could toss George Gunn's first-born from her thoughts. Two nights previous, she'd woken from a disturbing dream: a hot, sweaty dream, in which a man kissed her, before stripping her naked. *A man with Alexander Gunn's face.* The dream had gotten hazy after that, for apart from the occasional kiss with warriors at gatherings, she had little experience with men. She was still a maid.

Nonetheless, Jaimee had awoken tangled in bedsheets, disturbed, and restless.

The memory of that dream still haunted her.

Drawing a deep, steadying breath, Jaimee focused once more on the upcoming games and the decision that awaited her. She didn't enjoy dwelling on the gathering, yet she preferred it to thinking about Alexander Gunn.

Despite Connor's heavy-handed manner, she understood that he was only doing his duty—both as head of the family and her brother. A woman in her position was *supposed* to take a husband.

This was her responsibility, her role. She should do as her brother asked—let these men vie for her hand and be open to wedding one of them.

Jaimee exhaled sharply. She had to do her best not to disappoint her brother in the coming days. She'd try to keep her sharp tongue leashed and her fiery nature banked, although she was making no promises if any of her suitors proved themselves boorish.

Her jaw firmed then, stubbornness rising within her once more. *I will not marry a man I cannot love.*

3

ARRIVALS AT HALLADALE

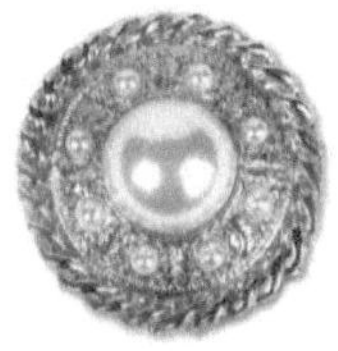

The Strath of Halladale
Strathnaver, Scotland

A week later ...

"I HOPE YE have yer dirk-blade sharpened, brother."
Will Gunn's voice cut through the wind. "Connor Mackay
isn't going to greet ye with a kiss."

Riding ahead of the party of eight warriors, two of
whom were his brothers, Alexander Gunn snorted. He
turned in the saddle, favoring William, the youngest of
his five brothers, with a harsh grin. He then patted the
dirk at his side. "If he gives me any trouble, he can kiss
this."

Some of the warriors riding behind his brothers
laughed. However, Tavish—the second-born of the Gunn
brothers—sneered. "So, we're here to shed blood then?"

Alexander inclined his head. "We're going to take part
in the games ... however, if blood needs to be spilled, it
will be."

Will barked a laugh, while beside him Tavish's
expression hooded. "What if Mackay and his friends
decide the only good Gunn is a dead Gunn?" Tavish
asked. "We'll be outnumbered, ye realize?"

Alexander's lip curled. "Being outnumbered has never worried ye before, Tav."

The comment was deliberately goading, but Alexander didn't care. That was how it was between him and Tavish. They had always been rivals.

Tavish's gaze narrowed. "We haven't ridden deep into Mackay territory to a gathering we weren't invited to before," he pointed out, his voice dropping to a growl. "Will's right ... ye had better get ready to draw yer dirk. They won't welcome us."

Alexander turned back to the direction of travel with a shrug. "They might," he replied, "The Mackays are bruised after Inverness ... diminished."

"Are they?" Tavish countered, a challenge in his tone now. "I'm sure Angus Mackay doesn't think so."

"Angus Mackay isn't hosting this gathering," Alexander reminded him. "Connor Mackay is ... and the new chieftain of Farr isn't as volatile as his clan-chief."

Indeed, Alexander had observed the chieftain during the recent parliament at Inverness. They'd once met in battle, and he'd dealt Mackay a nasty wound, yet the laird of Farr hadn't sought reckoning when they'd been under the same roof. In his place, Alexander would have.

"Connor Mackay is a *reasonable* man," Alexander continued. His mouth twisted then as if he'd just tasted something sour. He might as well have said: "Connor Mackay is a weakling and a coward".

As expected, both his brothers gave derisive snorts. Like Alexander, they shared the same view of those who didn't go looking for a fight.

War was in their blood. Belligerence was second nature.

Violence hummed in Alexander's veins like a nest of wasps seeking release. Aye, he hadn't ridden here for a fight—not exactly—yet there was a part of him that longed for it. He liked a challenge, and knowing that he traveled through enemy territory made excitement quicken in his belly.

The Gunn party rode across the sun-browned Strath of Halladale. Gazing around him, Alexander took in a wide valley framed by rolling hills to the south and a ridge of mountains to the north. Their destination wasn't far off now. Shortly, the river they followed would take them to the place of the gathering.

Alexander's stallion, a heavyset black, aptly named 'Destroyer', tossed his head impatiently. Alexander had slowed him to a trot so that he could converse with his brothers, and the beast chafed at the bit.

They were in the midst of Mackay territory, something which should have made any Gunn nervous. Indeed, Alexander had noted the way his warriors scanned their surroundings as they rode.

It was rare that a Gunn entered Mackay lands without the intention of conducting a raid or meeting their foes in battle.

They were supposed to be out patrolling the Gunn borders, but they'd met a merchant on the road out from Castle Gunn, who'd told them that the Mackays were gathering at Halladale. Apparently, warriors from all over the Highlands were traveling there to vie for the hand of Connor Mackay's sister.

That evening, as they'd sat warming themselves by the fire, Alexander had grinned across at his companions. "Fancy some games, lads?"

His warriors followed him faithfully everywhere and had agreed readily to go with him into Mackay lands. However, his brothers had been reluctant.

"How are ye going to explain this trip to father when we get home?" Will called, raising his voice to be heard over the wind that whistled across the exposed strath.

Tavish muttered something in response, although the wind whipped his words away before Alexander could catch them. Of course, George Gunn wouldn't be pleased that they'd ridden to Halladale without his blessing.

Alexander set his jaw, irritation rising. It was a familiar sensation of late, for his father sought to control him in all things and his first-born found it increasingly tiresome.

Today, however, Alexander was making his own decisions. The clan-chief would just have to swallow it.

"I'll tell him that the Gunns turned up at a Mackay gathering and bested them at every game." Alexander then cast his brothers another feral smile. "And if we slit a few throats afterward, all the better."

Jaimee swung down from her horse and pushed a lock of hair out of her eyes. The wind was blowing like a banshee today, whipping dust into her face. The Strath of Halladale was an exposed spot.

Tucking the errant hair back into her braid, she took in her surroundings. Encircled by mountains etched purple against a streaky sky, their gathering place sat on the rocky banks of the river that cut through a swathe of meadows. In spring, the strath was lush green. But now, as they began the slide toward winter, the grasslands had turned brown and sparse.

Jaimee knew this place well. It was a popular meeting spot for her clan. Over the years, Angus-Dow Mackay had held many gatherings here. A wistful smile curved her mouth then, despite the dread that lay heavily within her and the nerves that cramped her belly. Halladale brought back many good memories of when her parents had been alive. When life had been so much simpler.

Her cousin Kennan had finally professed his feelings for Cait here, at a gathering a few years back. Cait's father was Farr Castle's blacksmith. Farlan had been overprotective of his only child, but at the gathering, Kennan and Cait had forced him to let his daughter lead her own life and follow her heart.

Jaimee's smile faded, her belly clenching once more. Cait was one of the lucky ones. She wished Connor would let *her* be.

Turning back to her horse, Jaimee began to undo the gelding's girth. He was a stocky bay named Tor. Her father had gifted him to her as a colt.

Don't dwell on what's coming, she advised herself sternly. *Just grit yer teeth and get on with things.*

Laughter reached her, carried on the wind. Turning once more, Jaimee spied her brother Morgan and his wife, Maggie, standing together a few yards away. They should have been unsaddling their mounts, yet instead, Morgan appeared to be teasing Maggie. Morgan's faithful wolfhound, Gritta, sat behind the couple, scratching. This was the bitch's first trip away since she'd whelped. The puppies had been weaned, and no doubt Gritta was enjoying her freedom.

Morgan towered over his wife, for the woman stood at no more than five feet, and all of the Mackays of Farr—the men and the women—were tall. Maggie craned her neck up to meet her husband's eyes, her face alive with mirth. She then gave him a playful shove.

In response, Morgan pulled her into his arms and kissed her.

Jaimee gave an irritated snort and twisted away, focusing on unfastening the girth. Morgan and Maggie had a playful way with each other and were often acting the fool. And, as often, the game ended with a kiss.

They'd only been wed since spring—forced into the union after being found in a 'compromising situation' at Inverness. Maggie had been a widow and had come out of mourning not long before they'd met. Jaimee was aware that her sister-by-marriage had initially struggled to come to terms with her new life at Farr Castle. It warmed her to see how happy they were these days. However, in her present mood, their levity irked her.

"I thought we'd be some of the first to arrive." A female voice intruded then. Removing her mount's saddle, Jaimee turned to see Keira standing behind her. She carried Rose in a sling across her front. "But look, the Leslies are here already ... as are the Munros."

Flattening her mouth, Jaimee did turn to look. Her gaze swept over the clusters of hide tents that were going up a few yards from the river bank. Keira was right. Jaimee also spied Forbes and Ross clan sashes. Her brother had indeed sent word far and wide. However, as she surveyed the amassing crowd, her gaze narrowed.

The atmosphere here was odd, watchful. She spied a knot of Ross warriors then, observing the Mackays before murmuring amongst themselves.

News of a rift within the Mackay clan had clearly spread through the Highlands she realized.

Continuing to survey her surroundings, Jaimee's frown deepened when she recognized a few of the faces—some of the warriors were former suitors she'd already rejected. No doubt, they'd thought to try their luck once more.

Jaimee chewed her lip, trying to ignore the misgiving that gnawed at her insides. Hopefully, there would be some new faces at this gathering—a chance at least for her to meet someone she actually liked, someone she might grow to love.

"There's no sign of Angus Mackay as yet," she murmured in an attempt to distract herself.

"He'll come," Keira replied. "Connor made him promise when he visited him two weeks ago."

The women's gazes met then, and she saw that Keira's midnight-blue eyes were troubled. The Mackay clan-chief had gone quiet for months now. After the scandal at Inverness—in which he'd offered up his son, Niel, to be imprisoned, in order to escape the executioner's ax himself—he'd retreated from public life. The scene in the great hall of Inverness, as Niel attacked his father before being dragged away in irons, was still whispered of in the Highlands. Niel was now incarcerated in the island prison of Bass Rock, while his father had locked himself away in his cliff-top fortress of Castle Varrich.

This would be the first time he'd shown his face at a gathering since the incident.

Setting the saddle down upon its pommel behind her, Jaimee dug around in the leather backpack strapped to it, for the plait of straw she used to rub Tor down.

She expected Keira to move away then, to go to where Connor was overseeing the warriors erecting their tents. But she remained behind Jaimee.

Rubbing the straw plait over Tor's muscular hindquarters, Jaimee pretended her sister-by-marriage wasn't there. She adored Keira, but she wished to keep her own counsel this afternoon.

Ignoring, or perhaps oblivious to, her wishes, Keira eventually cleared her throat. "Ye know Connor won't insist ye choose a husband," she began softly. "Not if no man here truly interests ye."

Heaving a sigh, Jaimee didn't halt in her task. "No, but he'll give me that exasperated look ... and then when we return home, he'll continue to pester me ... to invite potential suitors to visit." She paused then, hoping that her sister-by-marriage didn't think she was acting like a spoiled chit. "I know what's expected of me, Keira," she continued softly, "but that doesn't mean I have to like it."

She turned back to her brother's wife, to see that she was observing her intensely.

"What is it?" Jaimee asked, tensing under the scrutiny.

Keira smiled. "I was just remembering what ye said to me last year ... about how close yer parents were." She broke off there as Rose gave a squawk. Soothing her daughter, she glanced up once more. "I don't blame ye for wanting that for yerself."

Jaimee's brow furrowed. "We both know that's not how it usually happens. Ye were prepared to wed my brother without even meeting him first."

Keira's gaze shadowed. "I was desperate, Jaimee," she murmured. "It was either that or remain on Iona for the rest of my life." Her throat bobbed then. "Ye know it's not a decision I'm proud of."

Jaimee glanced away. "Aye," she murmured, guilt constricting her throat. "I know ... and I'm sorry if I've a tongue like a boning knife today." She gestured to the gathering crowd around them. "All of this has put me out of sorts."

Keira nodded, her lips parting as she readied herself to answer.

However, the thunder of approaching hoof-beats interrupted the two women. Turning from Keira,

Jaimee's gaze shifted to where a knot of riders neared from the east.

Jaimee frowned. East? Where had these warriors hailed from?

And then, as the riders drew closer to the camp, Jaimee spied the sashes the men wore across their fronts.

Her breathing caught, and her heart lurched.

Just when she thought this day couldn't get any worse, fate had proved her wrong.

No ... it can't be.

But there was no mistaking the plaid of dull-green with red cross-hatching.

The Gunns.

4

I SWEAR

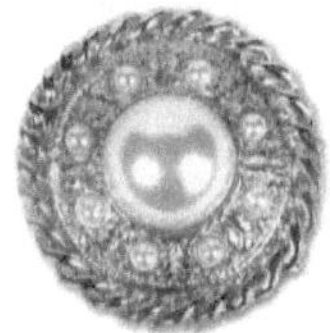

THE WORLD TURNED silent for a few instants—as if even the wind drew its breath—stilling as Alexander Gunn and his party of warriors reined in their horses at the periphery of the camp.

"Do my eyes deceive me?" Keira's voice had a strangled edge to it.

Cutting her sister-by-marriage a sharp glance, Jaimee wondered if the Gunns' arrival horrified her as much as it would everyone else here. She was a Gunn after all. However, Keira's face had paled, and she was staring at Alexander Gunn as if Beelzebub himself had just dropped into their midst.

"No," Jaimee replied, her voice cold and flat. "That's indeed the Gunn first-born."

"But ... why would he show his face here?" Incredulity filtered into Keira's tone now, as the initial shock wore off.

Jaimee's gaze went to where Connor had left overseeing the tent construction and was now stalking toward the newcomers. Likewise, Morgan now left Maggie's side and followed. The grim look on her brothers' faces made fear coil within Jaimee. This wasn't going to be pretty.

Tossing aside the straw plait, she stepped around Keira and went after Connor and Morgan.

Like them, she would face Gunn.

Approaching the new arrivals, hands clenched at her sides, Jaimee noted that Connor had stopped a few yards back from where Alexander Gunn had just dismounted. Gunn rode a huge black stallion, a fearsome-looking beast with massive feathered feet. Morgan halted just behind his brother. The rest of the Gunn party remained astride their coursers. The men's faces were stony, tense, as if they expected trouble.

In contrast, their leader seemed remarkably at ease. Alexander Gunn's body was loose, his shoulders relaxed.

Jaimee ground her teeth. Of course he would appear unconcerned. The man's arrogance and hubris knew no bounds.

"Lost yer way, Gunn?" Connor greeted him, his voice low and hard.

Holding the reins loosely in one hand, Gunn turned to Connor and flashed him a grin. However, there was no humor in the expression and not the slightest hint of softness. His storm-grey eyes were veiled. "I'm not lost, Mackay. I know exactly where I am."

"Ye aren't welcome on Mackay lands, Gunn dog," Morgan growled.

A beat of silence followed these words before Gunn's grin hardened. He then raked his gaze over Morgan Mackay, taking his measure. "Even if we're here to take part in the games?" he drawled.

Whispers of outrage and incredulity rippled through the crowd that had gathered, forming a semi-circle around them.

Jaimee wondered if she'd misheard the man. Surely, he wasn't serious about competing in the games?

However, Connor hadn't misheard Gunn. "Ye weren't invited," he replied, biting the words out.

Gunn arched a dark eyebrow. "Ye sent word throughout the Highlands, welcoming warriors to compete at Halladale." He paused then, his gaze fusing with Connor's. "And so ... here I am."

Standing behind her brothers, Jaimee couldn't see either of their faces. Nonetheless, judging from the tension in Connor's shoulders, he was now glowering at Gunn.

"What kind of trickery is this?" he snarled.

"No tricks," Gunn replied with infuriating calm. He turned then, gesturing to the two dark-haired warriors mounted behind him. "These are two of my brothers: Tavish and William. We're *all* here to compete."

"Send the shit-weasel on his way, Mackay!" Donald Leslie's gruff voice boomed behind them.

A chorus of "ayes" followed. Jaimee didn't need to glance behind her to know that the warriors, Mackays and their allies alike, would be reaching for their dirks.

Her belly cramped then. She couldn't bear the thought of Connor and Morgan being hurt. This scene could escalate into a bloodbath if something wasn't done.

"Cease this farce," Connor ground out. The cold violence in his voice made Jaimee shiver. She'd only ever heard her brother this angry once—when he'd fought their uncle Domhnall to the death after he'd challenged Connor's leadership. His right hand strayed to the hilt of the dirk at his hip. "Are ye trying to make me look a fool?"

All gazes settled upon Alexander Gunn, awaiting his reaction. His brothers both wore tense expressions and sat rigidly in the saddle. But the Gunn first-born appeared composed.

Jaimee watched him in morbid fascination.

"No, Mackay." Alexander Gunn's gaze never left Connor's when he finally answered. "I can't help it if ye are thin-skinned."

Connor made a disgusted sound in the back of his throat, while angry muttering rippled around them. "What reason does a Gunn have for attending a Mackay gathering," Connor demanded. "Unless it's to start a fight?"

A half-smile curved Gunn's lips. "Life has been all work and no play for me and the lads of late. We thought we'd enjoy a little sport … share a few laughs with our fellow Scots. Isn't that right, lads?"

A few 'ayes' behind him, and one or two snorts, followed this comment.

Connor muttered a curse, before spitting on the ground between them. "Ye'll get no entertainment here, ye shit-eating bastard." His voice was hoarse as he struggled, and failed, to rein in his temper. Connor did draw his dirk then, the sound of steel scraping against leather rending the air. "Enough talk. Draw yer blade and face me!"

Alexander Gunn's smile widened, a goading expression that made Jaimee's hackles rise. "I'm not here to brawl, Mackay … but to compete for yer fair sister's hand."

A heartbeat passed, and a sickly sensation washed over Jaimee before her brother roared his reply. "Over my dead body!"

Sweat bathed Jaimee's skin, and her heart lurched into her throat when Alexander Gunn's right hand moved toward the hilt of the dagger at his hip.

"No!" Jaimee's strangled cry cut through the cool air.

She wasn't sure where the cry came from, only that she couldn't let this continue. She'd lost her father to the Gunns. She wouldn't lose her brothers too. Alexander Gunn had nearly killed Connor once. She couldn't let him get another attempt.

Connor had spoken true: this visit was clearly an act of aggression. Alexander Gunn couldn't be interested in competing in the games—and although he denied it, he was just trying to provoke Connor into a fight.

But all the same, she couldn't let this end in bloodshed.

"No," she repeated, reining in her panic. She then strode forward, pushing her way through the fringes of the crowd and stepping up at Connor's side. "This gathering was called on my behalf. I will not have ye fighting each other."

She hadn't wanted Connor to hold this cursed gathering, yet now he had, she felt responsible for what happened here.

"Jaimee." Connor's voice was harsh and held a clear warning. Yet she ignored him. Instead, her attention settled upon Alexander Gunn.

Their gazes met and held.

He stared back at her, his storm-grey eyes glinting. Like when they'd stared at each other in that courtyard garden in Inverness, she saw his pupils dilate.

He's enjoying this.

"I need yer word that ye come in peace," she demanded. "That ye will merely compete in the games … that ye won't draw weapons against anyone here."

"Sister," Connor cut in. "Enough. Let me deal with this."

Jaimee tore her gaze from Alexander Gunn and stared her brother down. "No, Connor … I don't want Gunn here either … but if ye fight him, the king's parliament, and the punishment he dealt us all, will be for nothing."

"What punishment?" Morgan spat. Like Connor, his face was pale and taut, his green eyes glittering with barely suppressed rage. "George Gunn stood there before the king and *lied*." Morgan shifted his baleful gaze to Gunn. "Do ye deny it?"

Alexander Gunn stared him down. Jaimee watched him, in awe of just how implacable the man was. "No," he replied after a pause. "But my father did what he had to in order to protect his clan." His gaze then shifted back to Jaimee.

The impact made her breathing still, made the fine hair on the back of her neck prickle.

"I'm not here to discuss the past," Gunn said quietly. "It's dead. Gone. But I give ye my word that I come in peace. Allow us to remain, and I … and those who follow me … will not raise arms against anyone here. I swear."

A heavy silence followed these words. Even the muttering that had surrounded them died away.

It was shocking indeed, to hear Alexander Gunn make such a vow.

Jaimee stared back at him, reeling by the turn of events, by the fact that the man who'd haunted her thoughts and even invaded her dreams, now stood before her. He'd ridden here, challenged her brothers' wrath, and now boldly held her eye.

Moments passed before Jaimee cleared her throat. "Very well," she replied. "I accept yer word."

Heart racing, she then shifted her attention to Connor. Her brother wore a poleaxed expression, humiliation warring with rage in his pine-green eyes.

Their gazes fused. They both knew what she'd just done. A Highlander's pledge was his bond. In extracting a promise from Alexander Gunn, she'd effectively tied her brother's hands. Worse still, Gunn had sworn an oath before a crowd of onlookers; Connor couldn't pretend those words hadn't been spoken.

She'd weather his anger later when they were alone, but at present, all Jaimee could think about was preventing this situation from spiraling out of control.

Squaring her shoulders, she continued to hold Connor's eye. "Do *ye* also accept his word, brother?"

5

BLOOD WILL BE SPILLED

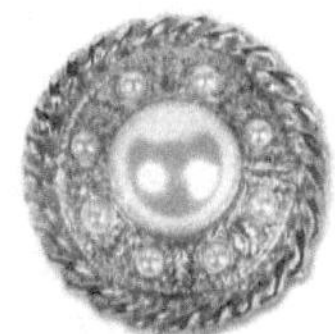

"WHAT. HAVE. YE. Done?"

Connor loomed over Jaimee. A nerve ticked under one eye, and his handsome face was contorted into severe, feral angles. The pair of them stood in the chieftain's tent, away from prying eyes. However, his voice, harsh with anger, carried.

Crossing her arms across her chest to ward off his rage, Jaimee held her brother's gaze. "I did what was necessary, Connor. Ye were about to start a fight."

"Aye," he growled. "With our clan's greatest enemy. Ye had no right to intercede. No right."

Jaimee swallowed. Her brother was intimidating, yet she wouldn't be cowed. "I did ... ye called this gathering for me. I couldn't let it turn into a blood-bath!"

Breathing hard, Connor shook his head. "The sight of Alexander Gunn ... on our land ... turns my stomach." His voice roughened then. "Why did ye have to make him swear an oath?"

Jaimee's chest constricted. "I'm sorry, Connor," she whispered. "I know ye feel manipulated ... but getting Gunn to make a promise was the only way I could stop ye from fighting him."

She understood her brother's anger, for she'd wielded his sense of honor against him, yet she'd been desperate.

Connor had growled out his agreement earlier, although she'd seen what it had cost him—what it was still doing to him.

Her brother was a good man, and she'd used his decency to trap him.

Jaimee unfolded her arms and let them fall to her sides. Her hands then clenched. She'd already been on edge before the arrival of the Gunns, yet now she felt as tense as a drawn bow-string. Her temples had started to throb, and the mother of all headaches was looming.

Aye, things were bad enough as it was—she didn't need Alexander Gunn stirring everyone up. But he would continue to do so while he remained at the gathering.

Jaimee's fingernails bit into her palms. *Gunn can't stay here.*

Somehow, she had to find a way to get rid of him—preferably without him drawing his blade on Connor. However, her focus right now was to make her brother understand that she hadn't betrayed him.

"I didn't want to undermine ye ... or to humiliate ye, Connor," she said huskily, "but I fear I did." Jaimee swallowed then as her throat thickened. "I just can't bear the thought of losing ye."

He stared back at her, the angry planes of his face softening just a little. Connor's eyes shadowed then. "Do ye have so little faith in my ability to best Alexander Gunn?" There was hurt in his voice.

Jaimee shook her head and took a step forward. Hesitantly, she reached out, her fingers closing around her brother's forearm. "I've seen ye fight ... and I don't doubt yer skill ... but—" She shivered then "—Alexander Gunn is a vicious brute. Did ye see how calm he was standing there? Does warm blood actually run through his veins?"

Connor snorted. "I have my doubts." He placed a hand over where hers still grasped his arm and squeezed gently. "I know ye were only trying to help, lass," he murmured. "But letting Alexander Gunn and his men attend these games is like inviting a fox into a fowl coop."

He scowled then. "Whether or not ye will it, blood will be spilled."

"I don't want the Gunns here." Angus-Dow Mackay took a draft from his horn of mead before casting the laird of Farr a thunderous look. "Get rid of them."

Connor heaved a deep sigh. "I intend to … as soon as Alexander Gunn breaks the promise he made my sister, that bastard is mine."

Seated across the fire, Jaimee tensed, her fingers clenching around the wooden cup of mead she'd been nursing. She thought Connor had accepted things, yet she could see the anger still smoldering in her brother's eyes. With a sinking feeling, she realized he was merely biding his time.

Jaimee's heart started to pound against her breast bone. *Goose-wit!* She'd been foolish to extract such a promise from their enemy. Of course, Connor knew that one of the Gunns would pick a fight soon enough. And when they did so, the oath would be broken.

She regretted interfering now. She'd damaged her relationship with Connor, all for nothing.

"The Gunns want a fight," Angus muttered. "And we'll give them one."

Jaimee's attention shifted from Connor to her clan-chief. The Mackay had arrived shortly before dusk with an escort of twenty warriors. The only kin he brought with him was his nephew, John Mackay of Aberach. Angus's wife, Estelle, hadn't joined him. The clan-chief's wife had been ailing of late and didn't feel well enough to travel. John Mackay, a tall, lean man with a mop of curly dark hair and serious blue eyes, sat next to his uncle this evening, listening intently as the conversation unfolded.

Next to Connor, Morgan's gaze glinted. "I look forward to it."

"The opportunity will present itself soon," Connor assured the clan-chief, his expression grim. "Don't worry."

The clan-chief glowered at Connor over the rim of his drinking horn. "Soon isn't good enough, Connor ... I don't want Gunns on my land. Not now. Not ever."

A snort to the clan-chief's left drew Jaimee's eye. Robert Mackay of Balnakeil sat watching Angus with a look of thinly veiled disdain. "Fighting words, eh? Reminds me of the speech ye gave at Inverness."

Silence fell around the fire. The Mackays were gathered about one of the many hearths that dotted the camp. Night had fallen, and the wind had died. Moths now danced above the flickering flames.

The headache that had plagued Jaimee all afternoon intensified when she saw the challenge in Robert's eyes. Her temples now throbbed in time with her thudding pulse. Since the mess in Inverness, Robert had been attempting to stir the other Mackay chieftains up. He'd even sent Connor a missive a few months earlier, requesting that they meet to discuss whether or not Angus-Dow Mackay was fit to rule the clan.

Connor had thrown the letter on the fire, although he and Morgan had visited Robert a few weeks later to ensure that the man wasn't causing more trouble. Robert had been quiet since then, although observing his face this evening, Jaimee had a sinking feeling that the matter hadn't been forgotten.

"Aye," Angus growled, meeting Robert's gaze. "And what of it?"

"George Gunn showed ye up, didn't he? Ye came across as a blundering oaf, Angus. And when things didn't go yer way, ye threw yer son to the wolves."

A muscle bunched in the clan-chief's bearded jaw. "Niel made a necessary sacrifice," he replied, his voice icy.

"One he didn't choose."

"Robert," Connor cut in, the warning clear in his voice. "Let's not—"

"I made the best decision for our clan," Angus Mackay rumbled, interrupting Connor as his face reddened in the firelight. "And I will not have the likes of ye question me over it, Robert Mackay. Remember yer place, man."

Jaimee excused herself early from the fireside. Murmuring that she had a headache—which wasn't a lie—she rose from Maggie's side and retreated. The aggression that crackled in the air tonight felt like an approaching thunderstorm.

Suddenly, she just had to get away.

As soon as Jaimee left the circle of firelight, the throb in her temples eased just a little. The rumble of conversation drew back, and she loosed a deep sigh.

The Gunns' arrival had only served to worsen the strain within her clan. She was glad that their allies all huddled around their own fires tonight. It was best the Leslie, Forbes, Munro, and Ross clans didn't witness such arguments. Even so, she'd seen the veiled glances earlier in the evening, the murmured comments between the invited warriors.

She wondered if some of them had attended the gathering out of mere curiosity. Did they expect to see the Mackay clan-chief row with his chieftains? Did some of them hope to benefit from the friction?

Jaimee moved through the tents toward her own. It sat behind Connor, Keira, and Rose's shelter and was much smaller. She would share the tent with her maid, Fern. It was much darker away from the hearth, and it took Jaimee's eyes a few moments to adjust. Flickering torches had been driven into the ground at intervals throughout the camp, illuminating the night.

Pausing outside her tent, Jaimee glanced up. There was a new moon tonight, which made the sky even darker than usual. The moon's absence highlighted the sparkling band of stars that stretched overhead. Looking north, she spied the familiar pan-shape of The Plough, before her attention settled upon the Pole Star—the star that revealed true north to travelers.

Jaimee's mouth curved into a sad smile. Staring up at the stars brought back memories of her father. Rory Mackay had taught her the names of all the stars in the night sky: Pegasus, Taurus, the Seven Sisters, and Orion the Hunter. He'd recounted to her all the old stories about how these names had come about.

Throat thickening, Jaimee tore her gaze from the sky. It was just over a year now since her father fell in battle. She'd lost her parents only months apart, for her mother had sickened in the spring and her father died in the summer.

She missed them both. There were still times when she entered the great hall and expected to see her father sprawled in his chair before the hearth, times when she entered the women's solar and glanced at the loom by the window as if hoping to see her mother seated there.

Ducking into the tent, Jaimee found it empty. Fern hadn't yet retired. She wondered where her maid was. The lass had gotten a little wild of late—ever since the arrival of Aileana, Maggie's vivacious maid. Lord knew what mischief the two of them were getting up to.

Jaimee checked her thoughts with an irritated frown. *Mother Mary, I'm turning into a bitter spinster.* The lasses were young and excited to be at the gathering. It also was too early for most folk to retire.

In truth, Jaimee wasn't sleepy—and her headache was starting to ease now she was away from her kin. She just couldn't stomach any more of the bickering around the fireside.

Not when her nerves were already stretched to breaking point.

Foreboding sat like a brick in her belly.

She didn't want to admit it, but Connor had the right of it. The Gunns never kept their word. How many oaths had George Gunn broken to Angus Mackay over the years? How many times had he agreed to stop his raids, only to continue as soon as the winter thaw ended?

Jaimee's temples started to pound once more. In trying to help, she'd likely made the situation worse.

I have to mend this.

Instead of crawling onto the sheepskin that Fern had laid out for her, she retrieved her woolen shawl and ducked outside once more.

It was no good. Something had to be done.

Connor had made it clear at the fireside that he'd take action against Gunn, as soon as the opportunity arose.

A sickly sensation swept over Jaimee then, and she drew the shawl tightly about her shoulders. It wasn't an overly cold evening, for the howling wind had died to a whisper, yet she suddenly shivered. It now felt as if someone were taking a hammer to her skull.

The last thing she wanted was to see Alexander Gunn again, yet she wouldn't be able to rest unless she faced the man. This was her fault. She needed to make a plea, needed to appeal to whatever shred of decency lay in that shriveled heart. She had to convince him to leave.

Straightening her shoulders, and trying to ignore her pounding head, Jaimee set off across the camp toward the eastern outskirts, where the Gunns had pitched their tents.

6

JAIMEE'S PLEA

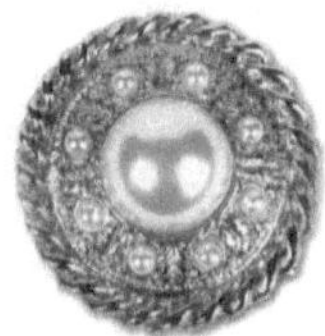

THE CLOSER JAIMEE drew to the Gunn tents, the slower her gait became.

Eventually, she came to a complete stand-still.

What are ye doing? Her heart now felt lodged in her throat. She felt shivery, and yet her palms were clammy.

It occurred to her then that she was afraid.

She feared Alexander Gunn.

Suddenly, the dread she'd felt at having to choose a husband at this gathering paled in comparison to confronting this man. She'd happily agree to wed the first man to cross her path tomorrow if it meant she didn't have to see Alexander Gunn again.

The realization made Jaimee's jaw clench. This was a new sensation, one that angered her. Gunn wouldn't cow her; she wouldn't let him.

Forcing herself on, she approached the cluster of hide tents that had been pitched a few yards away from the others. And as she drew near, Jaimee spied a handful of men seated around a flickering fire. Even at a distance, she saw Alexander Gunn among them. The warrior was easy to spot. His swarthy looks and hulking build made him stand out, even amongst his kin. His brothers were seated near him, and the three men looked to be deep in discussion.

Suspicion quickened within Jaimee. Were those cunning bastards plotting? Connor was right: they were already planning on how best to cause trouble.

"What do ye want, lass?" A rough male voice intruded then.

Swallowing a scream of fright, Jaimee whipped around to see a bulky shape emerge from the darkness. Of course, Gunn had set his men at watch around the tents. He didn't trust the Mackays, or their allies, either.

Drawing herself up, Jaimee faced the shadowy guard. "I'm Lady Jaimee Mackay," she announced, glad that her voice didn't betray her fear. "And I'm here to speak to Alexander Gunn. Take me to him."

The imperiousness of her command made the warrior before her draw up, his muscular body stilling.

Panic snaked up once more. They stood in the darkness here, unseen by the others. All the man had to do was clamp a hand over her mouth and drag her off somewhere, and no one would be any the wiser.

Jaimee's body grew taut, and she took a cautionary step away from the warrior. *Curse ye, foolish woman. Why didn't ye bring yer dirk?* Indeed, she'd left the weapon—which her father had gifted her on her fifteenth birthday—in her tent.

"Very well," he said, his voice surly. "Follow me, *Lady Mackay.*"

When they stepped into the circle of firelight, Alexander Gunn glanced up. For a moment, Jaimee had the satisfaction of seeing the Gunn heir caught off guard.

It was the first time she'd seen him thus. His broad shoulders stiffened, and those grey eyes that almost appeared purple in the firelight widened. His sensual lips parted.

An instant later, he uncoiled his big body and rose to his feet. "Lady Mackay ... this is a ... pleasant surprise." He inclined his head then. "To what do I owe the honor?"

The rumble of his voice washed over Jaimee, causing a strange warmth to settle in the pit of her belly. Resolutely ignoring the sensation, Jaimee raised her chin. "I wish to have a word." She paused then, noting the smirks on his brothers' faces. This wouldn't go well if they had an audience. "Alone."

Snorts followed this comment, and one of the Gunn brothers—the taller of the two—raised a suggestive eyebrow. "I didn't realize Mackay women were so forward, brother. Ye lucky dog."

To his credit, Alexander Gunn ignored the jibe. He merely held Jaimee's gaze before gesturing to the largest of the group of tents to his left. "Shall we, then?"

Spine stiff, Jaimee nodded. Then, swiveling on her heel, and ignoring the sniggers and lewd comments of the surrounding men, she marched across to the tent before ducking inside.

She entered a remarkably pleasant space. This tent was easily thrice the size of her own, and high enough for even a tall man to stand at full height without having to bow his head. The men had brought in branches from woodland to the south to use as tent poles. Sheepskins covered the ground, while a small hearth glowed in the center of the space, illuminating the interior in red-gold.

Her pulse beat an erratic tattoo as Jaimee moved near to the hearth and turned to face Alexander Gunn.

The moment he ducked inside the tent, it felt too small.

Even though she was a tall woman, he loomed over her. His presence seemed to suck the air out of the cramped space.

"What is it that ye wished to speak to me of then?" he asked.

Jaimee suppressed a shiver at the timbre of his voice. She'd never heard one like it: iron cloaked in lamb's wool. His voice was almost a drawl, however, his eyes were intense when they settled upon her.

Clearing her throat, Jaimee forced herself to hold his gaze. "I realize that I made a mistake today," she began. How she wished her voice didn't sound so brittle. Standing this close to Gunn completely threw her. She wished she could back up, could put more space between them, but there was nowhere to go. "I shouldn't have meddled. I shouldn't have insisted ye make a promise ye have no intention in keeping."

He quirked an eyebrow. "What makes ye think I intend to break my vow, Lady Mackay?"

"Ye are a Gunn. Such promises mean nothing to ye."

His mouth lifted at the edges, the barest hint of a smile, yet his gaze remained predatory. "I'm surprised," he murmured, "that ye seem to suppose so much about me … since we are virtually strangers."

Jaimee swallowed. "I know enough about ye, Gunn. I was only trying to stop a fight from erupting, but I should have let my brother deal with ye as he saw fit."

He continued to watch her. "But ye didn't … and thanks to ye, we can remain at Halladale."

Jaimee curled her hands into fists at her sides. "Aye … that was an error … one that I wish to rectify." She paused then, her gaze imploring. "Please, pack up before the dawn and leave."

Silence followed this request. It was a long, uncomfortable hush, broken only by the rumble of men's voices outdoors.

When Alexander Gunn replied, his voice gave nothing of his thoughts away. Likewise, his expression was inscrutable. But his gaze was hot, searing. "I don't want to leave, Lady Mackay."

Jaimee's heart started to race. She took a step toward him, angling up her chin so that she didn't break his stare. "Ye must. Yer presence here worsens an already tense relationship within my clan. This gathering was supposed to help heal relations, but that won't happen if ye remain."

"So, the Mackays are still hurting after Inverness?" he asked, an enigmatic smile curving those beautifully-molded lips. "Why aren't I surprised?"

Heat flushed through Jaimee, anger quickening within her. "I'm not here to discuss my clan," she replied, her voice clipped now. "But to ask ye to find it within yerself to show some *decency*." She paused then, attempting to rein in her temper. She wouldn't succeed in this if anger got the better of her. "I don't know what has driven ye to come here ... but it will only end badly if ye stay ... for us *all*."

He didn't reply; the man merely observed her. He was maddeningly still and unresponsive. Not for the first time, Jaimee wondered if a heart actually beat in his chest. He didn't act like other folk. No wonder he was such a formidable opponent on the battlefield.

"Please." The word came out in a whisper. Jaimee hadn't come here planning to beg, but Gunn was driving her to it. She'd made a terrible mistake interfering, and if it meant that she had to humiliate herself to get him to leave, she'd just have to bear it. Connor had once told her she was too prideful, but it was time to humble herself. "I'm making a plea now, Gunn. Just leave."

He didn't answer her immediately. Long moments passed, and then he stepped close to Jaimee. The heat of his body reached out to her, and the scent of him—leather, horse, and spicy male musk—filled her nostrils.

He was standing too near.

"I came here for *ye*, Jaimee Mackay," Gunn finally murmured.

Jaimee went rigid. Her heart suddenly started pounding so fast it felt as if it would escape her chest. What the devil was the man saying? He was deranged. He'd come to Halladale to stir up trouble, not to vie for her hand. The notion was ridiculous. He had to be mocking her.

Jaimee drew in a deep breath, readying herself to scold him. She needed to put an end to this exchange.

But Alexander Gunn wasn't finished. Instead, he moved closer still and leaned in, his breath feathering across the shell of her ear as he continued. "Very well ... I'll leave."

Relief rushed through Jaimee, the reaction so strong that her knees weakened. However, his next words destroyed her brief reprieve.

"If ye lie with me, I'll make sure we are gone by the dawn."

Jaimee froze, prickly heat flushing through her. "What?" she managed to croak. Had she heard him correctly?

"Aye, lass … if ye let me tear those clothes from yer delicious body, if ye let me lay ye down on these sheepskins, let me spread ye wide and sink into yer softness, yer heat … I'll go."

Jaimee's breath left her. For a few instants, she simply couldn't breathe, couldn't move. His words were fire and ice—they both heated her blood and chilled her body. They were rude, presumptuous, and dishonorable.

And so, Jaimee did the only thing she could in such a situation.

She hit him.

Her palm flew up and struck Gunn across the face, the sharp crack of the slap ringing through the tent.

Jaimee's body went rigid then, and she readied herself for his response. Such a brute would surely hit back. However, Alexander Gunn didn't move. He remained there, so still she wondered if he was actually breathing.

Taking the opportunity to escape, Jaimee fled the tent.

7

SO WRONG, SO WICKED

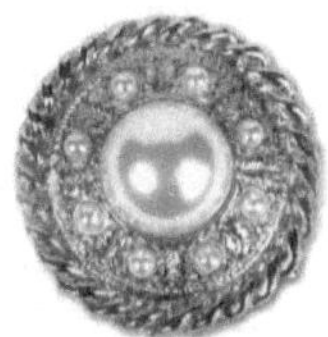

"BEAST. LETCH. *BASTARD*." Jaimee choked out the insults as she stormed away from the Gunn tents, back to the safety of the Mackay encampment. "How dare he?"

She couldn't believe that he'd said such things to her. The Lord strike him down, Gunn had been about to ravish her.

He hadn't touched her, yet the menace was there—a physical presence inside the tent.

And she'd fanned the flames by hitting him.

Jaimee's belly churned. She really was a goose-wit. Venturing into the Gunn lair had been an idiotic thing to do. She'd even forgotten her dirk, before demanding to speak to Alexander Gunn alone. One mistake after another.

She started to sweat then, her gaze darting from side to side before she glanced over her shoulder to make sure she wasn't being followed. *Connor can never know about this.*

She shuddered to think how her brother would rail at her for putting herself at such risk.

Reaching the Mackay tents, Jaimee slowed her pace. Surprisingly, the headache that had plagued her all evening had now gone. The sound of drunken singing filtered through the camp, coming from the Mackay fireside. At least her own people were no longer fighting. However, such was her turmoil, Jaimee could hardly bring herself to care.

Let me tear those clothes from yer delicious body … let me lay ye down on these sheepskins, let me spread ye wide and sink into yer softness, yer heat …

Jaimee gasped before she clasped a hand over her mouth. The sound was far too close to a sob for her liking.

The words were so wrong, so wicked. And yet in the instants following them, her body had utterly betrayed her. Fire ignited in her lower belly, and even now the tender flesh between her thighs ached. Hot and cold bathed her limbs, and her senses had heightened.

Her wits had returned moments later, and that was when she'd slapped him. But for a brief spell, her body had responded as keenly as if he'd been caressing her.

Muttering the filthiest curse she knew, Jaimee crawled into her tent.

"Jaimee?" Fern's sleepy voice greeted her.

Damn her to Hades, couldn't Fern have stayed out later with Aileana and given her some time alone? She wasn't in a fit state for company at present.

"Aye, it's me," Jaimee replied, her voice hoarse. She was grateful it was dark inside the tent, so her maid wouldn't see her flushed face. Even so, Fern had sensed something was amiss, for she sat up.

"Is something wrong?"

"No." The word came out in a gasp. "I'm just tired."

"Do ye want me to brush out yer hair?"

"No, let's leave it till the morning. Go to sleep."

Silence followed this command, and she could literally feel Fern's concern enveloping her. The maid was her own age and had served the Mackays of Farr for years. Jaimee sensed her hurt. However, it couldn't be helped tonight.

"Are ye sure nothing is amiss?" Fern asked once more. "Yer voice is odd … have ye been weeping?"

"No … I've just been arguing with Connor."

"Again? I thought ye'd patched things up?"

Frustration exploded within Jaimee. She couldn't bear being interrogated by Fern—not now.

"Aye, we have now," she rasped, crawling over to her sheepskin and collapsing upon it. Jaimee then rolled over to face the hide wall of the tent. "If ye don't mind, Fern. I'm exhausted. I just want to sleep."

Her maid ceased her questioning then, perhaps noting the pleading edge to Jaimee's voice.

Jaimee Mackay wasn't one to beg, yet she had done so twice this evening.

She'd humbled herself before Alexander Gunn, and he'd exploited her weakness by dishonoring her.

She was a laird's daughter. He had no right to speak to her thus. And yet he had. And there had been no remorse on his face after she'd struck him. His gaze had merely burned with lust.

Jaimee squeezed her eyes shut, cursing him—and cursing herself.

I wish Ma were here, she thought, tears pricking her eyelids. Her mother had been knowledgeable on many subjects. She would have known what to do in a situation such as this.

But Rose Mackay was no longer alive. She could no longer counsel her daughter.

Drawing in a deep breath, Jaimee waited for her racing pulse to settle. Despite her words to Fern, and her assertion that she was tired, there was no way she'd be able to sleep tonight. Instead, she needed to find a way to get through the coming days.

Her mother, Rose, had been a kind yet strong-willed and practical woman. She certainly wouldn't have let the likes of Alexander Gunn fluster or intimidate her. She'd also have made the best of her situation, however challenging she might have found it.

Jaimee's jaw firmed as resolve settled within her.

Enough of this, lass, she chastised herself. *Ye need to stop interfering in men's business. Ignore that Gunn beast ... and focus on the reason ye are here.*

The following morning a group of warriors would compete for her hand, and she would pay close attention to all of them—save Gunn, of course. There had to be a man amongst the group she could grow to love.

Jaimee's throat tightened, and she swallowed hard to ease the sadness that crept up from her chest.

It was time for her to let the romantic notions go. She wasn't a princess in one of those old tales, destined for the kind of love that shook mountains and threatened to bring the sky down. She'd tarried long enough.

Courage, Jaimee, she counseled herself, even as an ache rose under her breastbone. *It's time to grow up.*

Alexander's cheek still stung when he ducked out of the tent and rejoined his brothers at the fireside.

"Lady Jaimee made a swift retreat," Tavish greeted him with a wolfish grin. "Ye were yer charming self I take it?"

Alexander didn't answer. He merely sank down before the fire once more and reached for a skin of ale. His left cheek burned like the devil, although fortunately, his short beard would hide the redness from his brothers' prying eyes. He resisted the urge to reach up and rub it.

Jaimee Mackay had a powerful arm for a woman.

"What did she want?" Will asked after a pause. His youngest brother's eyes gleamed with curiosity.

"She regrets interceding on our behalf ... and wants us to leave Halladale before dawn," Alexander replied.

Will snorted a laugh. "Really?"

Tavish raised dark eyebrows. "And how did ye respond to that?"

"I refused, of course."

"Hence the way she fled," Tavish replied. "The woman looked as if she were running from a fiend of hell."

It was Alexander's turn to snort. *She was.* He unstoppered the skin of ale and took a deep pull.

That had been surprising.

He hadn't planned to say such things to Jaimee Mackay; in fact, he'd been shocked that she'd dared to wander into his camp, unarmed and unescorted. The woman either had nerves of steel or was utterly daft. Either way, he hadn't expected to see her.

And he hadn't thought she'd plead with him either.

Her demand that he leave with the dawn had amused him; she was the one who'd made Connor agree to let him stay after all.

But her entreaty had unleashed something—a wickedness had arisen within him that he hadn't been able to contain.

She'd looked lovely tonight, even lovelier than when he'd spoken to her in Inverness. Her red-gold hair was loose, save for two thin braids that pulled it back from her face. She wore a moss-green kirtle over a cream-colored lèine. The garments clung to her tall, lithe body, and the green kirtle accentuated the smoothness of her skin, the dark green of her eyes.

Jaimee Mackay had the face of an angel and the fire of a hell-cat.

Alexander's belly tightened then as he remembered her scent. He'd stepped close, indecently close, to Jaimee before he'd murmured the words that had earned him a slap across the face. She'd smelt of rosemary and sunshine.

It had taken all his will not to reach for her.

Considering her reaction to his words, it was just as well he hadn't.

"The lady didn't look as if she's taken a liking to ye," Tavish's voice intruded upon his heated thoughts. There was a jeering edge to his tone. "What did ye say to her?"

Alexander remained stubbornly silent.

"Surely, ye aren't hoping to win her hand?" Tavish continued. "I thought we were here for a bit of fun?"

"Father wants ye to wed Robina Oliphant," Will piped up. "He'd never suffer ye taking a Mackay bride."

Alexander frowned. He didn't want to wed Robina Oliphant. Their father had been trying to secure the match for years now. The woman in question was a shy mouse of a lass; Alexander didn't find her remotely appealing.

What he wanted was a strong, fiery wife—a woman who'd challenge him.

A woman like Jaimee Mackay.

"I'll decide whom I take as my wife," he said eventually. He meant it too; their father's insistence had been grating upon him of late. George Gunn sought to control his first-born in all things, but he wouldn't get his way with this.

"Aye, but Jaimee *Mackay*?" Will was watching Alexander with a bemused look. "Are ye trying to get the lot of us butchered in our beds?"

Alexander cocked an eyebrow. "Ye'd better sleep with one eye open while we remain at Halladale, Will."

"And the oath ye swore today?" Tavish was scowling now. "Surely, ye don't expect us to keep it?"

Alexander's mouth twisted. It was just as well he was the first-born. These two idiots weren't capable of lacing their own boots. He would have thought it was obvious he was playing with Mackay.

"Of course not," he replied, giving his brother a withering look. "Ye'll get the fight ye're spoiling for, Tav ... but let's enjoy a few games first."

8

URGES

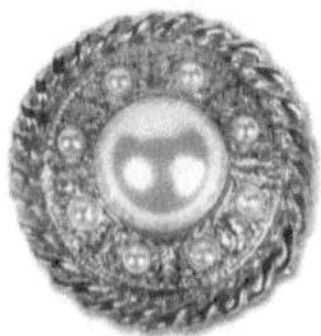

JAIMEE SHIFTED UNCOMFORTABLY upon her stool, before pulling her shawl closer about her shoulders. It was a grey, windy morning, and the 'gaoth a tuath'—the North Wind—had a bite to it. Seated with her kin, as the games began, she fought the urge to scowl.

This was the last place she wanted to be this morning.

After the encounter of the night before, she wanted to saddle Tor and gallop all the way back to Farr Castle. Only stubborn pride kept her sitting there—that and the decision she'd made.

Jaimee clenched her hands together upon her lap, fighting the instinct to break one of the promises she'd whispered to the darkness: not to look Alexander Gunn's way.

The bastard was out there this morning, warming up before he took his turn at the hammer throw. Today, the warriors would compete in a number of contests: the hammer throw, stone put, and the caber toss, among others. Then, on the morrow, the winners would begin rounds of wrestling. On the third day, the champion of the games would be chosen after knock-out rounds of mock swordplay.

Jaimee surveyed the large crowd competing. Connor had told her around two dozen men would be vying for her hand, yet she'd counted over thirty. Relief fluttered through her as her gaze swept over unfamiliar faces. Many of the newcomers were handsome, and some of them kept glancing her way, naked interest in their eyes.

Surely, one of them is suitable?

Tearing her gaze from the competitors, Jaimee glanced then at Maggie. The two women sat on the edge of the crowd of onlookers on the fringe of the competition field.

"Maggie," she began hesitantly. "Can I ask ye something?"

Her sister-by-marriage met her gaze, her mouth curving. "Of course."

"I know ye didn't love Morgan at first." Maggie's eyes widened at the directness of the statement, and Jaimee's cheeks warmed. She hadn't meant to be quite so blunt. "What I mean is … ye married him first … and love came later, didn't it?"

Maggie inclined her head. "Aye, it was lust that brought us together in the beginning." Her smile widened. "Although I quickly grew to like and respect yer brother."

Jaimee cleared her throat. "So it's possible then … to fall in love with someone ye were forced to wed?"

Maggie's smile faded. "I wasn't *forced* to wed Morgan. My options were limited, yet he let the choice be mine."

Jaimee let out an exasperated sigh. "Sorry, that came out wrong. I meant that it's possible to be happy with a man ye don't love straight away?"

Maggie held her eye. "It is." She paused then, her gaze turning thoughtful. "Real sentiment doesn't blossom overnight. Love that grows slowly is like the roots of a mighty oak: embedded deeply in the ground and meant to last."

Jaimee considered these words, a little of the tightness in her chest easing. Her mother had once told her she'd known the first time she locked eyes with Rory Mackay that there would be no other man for her.

But most people didn't experience an instant connection like that.

She looked away then, turning her attention once more to the competition unfolding before them.

And then, without meaning to, her gaze alighted upon the very man she'd vowed to ignore. Gunn had just stripped off his lèine and now stooped to pick up the large iron smith's hammer.

Jaimee stared, transfixed. Just like that, she forgot Maggie, forgot everything except the sight of the Gunn warrior's heavily muscled torso. Despite the dull day, his lightly tanned skin gleamed, highlighting a network of crisscrossed scars upon his back.

Jaimee's breathing hitched. Those weren't battle wounds. *He's been whipped.* Such scarring was distinctive. They were old scars, like the thin silver scar that marked his left cheek. How on earth had he gotten those?

As she looked on, Alexander gripped the blacksmith's hammer in both hands, whirled it around his head, and threw it hard.

Jaimee was spellbound. He was a big man, yet he moved with such grace and precision that she literally couldn't tear her gaze from him. His braies sat low on his hips, revealing the vee of hard muscle that led down to his waist band.

He was more beautiful than any man had the right to be.

And curse him, he'd thrown his hammer the farthest of any so far.

"Jaimee?" Maggie's voice intruded. "Does something ail ye ... yer cheeks are flushed."

Ripping her gaze from Gunn, Jaimee focused on Maggie once more. Curse *her*, why couldn't she stop staring at the man?

The knowing look in Maggie's eyes made the heat in her cheeks flame hotter. Maggie was too polite to say so, yet she'd seen the way Jaimee had just gawked at Alexander Gunn.

Jaimee swallowed hard. "I wish I hadn't interfered yesterday," she admitted huskily. "I've just made things worse."

She glanced over at where Gunn now strode back to his warriors, who were applauding him. Both Tavish and William Gunn were competing this morning as well, so neither of them was cheering. Instead, his brothers wore sour expressions.

"No, ye haven't ... I'm glad ye intervened," Maggie replied, her tone firm. "Connor and Morgan can't think straight when it comes to the Gunns. Both of them might be dead now if ye hadn't stepped up." She then favored Jaimee with a rueful smile. "I swear ye have nerves of steel, lass."

Jaimee tried to smile back and failed. How she wished she were as courageous as Maggie believed. However, thanks to her, Alexander Gunn was still here. He'd crossed the line the night before but had made his desire for her clear. She hadn't imagined the heat she'd seen in his eyes in Inverness. The man lusted after her.

Cold sweat beaded Jaimee's body. Surely, Gunn had been lying—he hadn't really come here to compete for her hand? Didn't he realize she'd never choose him? Even if he bested every man here, the final decision was hers.

Once more, without realizing what she was doing, Jaimee's attention gravitated toward the Gunns. Alexander was talking to Tavish, but then, as if he'd been waiting for her to look in his direction, his gaze snapped to Jaimee.

Heart pounding, Jaimee glanced away.

The devil spike her with a pitchfork, she had to control these urges. Maggie had just given her sage advice: she needed to look for a good man she could like and respect. Love would come later.

In the meantime, the last thing she needed was to be distracted by lustful thoughts about her clan's enemy.

Focus on the other warriors, she counseled herself.

Dragging in a ragged breath, she looked to where other contestants were taking their turn at the hammer throw. A Forbes warrior stepped up to the line a few yards away. He was tall and muscular and walked with an arrogant swagger. And as Jaimee looked on, the contestant swung the blacksmith's hammer around his head and let it fly.

Alexander took the drying cloth one of his warriors handed him and toweled himself off. He'd just knelt by the banks of the River Halladale, which flowed alongside the camp, and sluiced icy water over his sweat-slicked torso. It wasn't a hot day, yet the morning's contests had been tiring. They'd taken a break now, to eat—and the rest of the contests would resume in the afternoon.

The barest hint of a smile lifted the corners of Alexander's mouth. It was going well. He'd won nearly every contest he'd taken part in; there would be no risk of him being prevented from going through to the second day of the competition.

Reaching for his lèine, he pulled it on. "What's for the noon meal?" he asked the warrior still standing behind him. Fynn Gunn was the most loyal of all his men. Like the Gunn first-born, he wasn't one to waste two words where one would do. Alexander liked his silence and his dogged loyalty.

"Spit-roasted venison, by the smell of things," Fynn replied, glancing back at the camp behind them. "Yer brothers have already started without ye."

Alexander nodded. "Well, we'd better join them."

In truth, he wanted to keep a close eye on Tavish and Will. They'd spent most of the morning trading insults with any Mackay warrior who crossed their path. There had been an incident, after the hammer throw, when Tavish had hurled a slur at Robert Mackay of Balnakeil. The laird had snarled a reply and lunged for Tavish.

They'd have ended up brawling if two of Robert Mackay's warriors hadn't held their laird back.

Alexander's mouth twisted. He understood his brothers' desire to heckle the Mackays—the same instinct boiled within him too. Just over a year earlier, he'd faced these bastards in battle. However, now the games had begun, he found he was really enjoying himself. He wanted to beat his competitors. As such, he didn't want Tavish and Will causing too much trouble.

Not yet, anyway.

Striding into the center of the camp, Fynn at his heel, Alexander's gaze swept over the milling crowd. He didn't fail to notice that all the gathered clans sat apart. The Mackays might have called their allies here, yet Alexander had noted the rivalry between them during the day's competition. He'd also noted how they all watched the Mackays—especially the clan-chief.

Around Alexander, a number of men and women sat on the trampled grass, wooden dishes of flatbread and roasted venison on their laps. His belly growled at the toothsome aroma of the rich meat, and he approached the lads who were slicing up the venison and handing out dishes of food.

Taking a double-helping for himself, Alexander continued to survey the crowd.

There was one person he was searching for—a face that currently eluded him.

Where was Jaimee Mackay?

An instant later, he spotted her. She sat with her brothers and their wives, at the edge of the crowd.

Alexander's mouth thinned. He wanted to approach her, yet he couldn't with her bodyguards flanking her. Jaimee sat between Connor and Morgan, and he knew she'd deliberately positioned herself thus.

To avoid me.

Alexander carried his food over to an upturned wooden pail and settled himself down to eat.

It mattered not. He was a patient man.

Eating slowly, he let his attention travel over the rest of the crowd. Like his father, Alexander was an observer of others. One could learn much from watching one's enemies.

It didn't take him long to spot where the tension lay within this amassed group.

The Gunns aside—his brothers and the rest of Alexander's men wisely sat on the fringes of the crowd for the noon meal—there were other strained relationships at this gathering.

The Leslies and the Forbes for one. The clans in question sat far apart today, although some of the warriors had nearly come to blows twice during the morning's competition. However, it was the relations within the Mackay clan itself that interested Alexander.

Angus Mackay looked half the man he'd been at Inverness. The Mackay sat upon a stool, in the midst of his clansmen, his dish piled high with venison. No, he hadn't lost any of his girth, yet there were lines upon his bearded face that hadn't been there months earlier, and Alexander didn't remember his hair being so grey. The clan-chief sat with a slight stoop, as if wearied.

The cracks are starting to show, Alexander observed. Two of Angus Mackay's chieftains—Robert Mackay of Balnakeil and William Mackay of Dun Ugadale—deliberately sat apart from him.

Alexander noted the way Robert Mackay kept casting dark looks at his clan-chief's turned back.

Aye, things were strained. Alexander wouldn't have been surprised if a serious rift formed within clan Mackay in the coming months.

Father will be pleased to learn of this. The thought rose unbidden, followed by a surge of irritation. Sometimes he felt like one of his father's hounds, always looking for ways to please the old man. Did he not have a will of his own?

He did—and that was why he'd come to Halladale. He was doing something for himself, following his own instincts.

George Gunn wouldn't be his master.

A gust of wind whipped across the strath then, stinging Alexander's cheeks. He glanced up at where the sun was doing its best, and failing, to peek through the heavy clouds. Hopefully, the weather would hold up over the next two days.

Finishing his meal, Alexander rose to his feet, brushing crumbs off his braies.

His attention shifted, once more, to Jaimee Mackay, and he saw that she too had stood up. She was now moving through the crowd, toward the Mackay tents.

Alexander moved to intercept her.

9

THE PRIZE

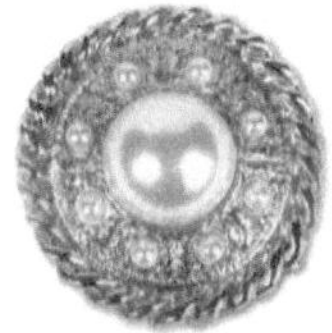

JAIMEE HAD NEARLY reached the fringes of the crowd when a man stepped before her, blocking her path.

Halting, she raised her chin and looked straight into Alexander Gunn's arrogantly handsome face. As always, his grey eyes held a challenge.

"Good day, Lady Jaimee," he greeted her, his voice a low rumble.

Squaring her shoulders, Jaimee faced him. This was intimidation. The warrior was enjoying this game of cat and mouse. After a shaky start, Jaimee had successfully ignored him for the rest of the morning, and she'd deliberately eaten with her kin to avoid their paths crossing.

But Alexander Gunn was determined, she'd give him that.

"Hello," she greeted him coldly.

"Did ye enjoying watching the hammer throw and caber toss this morning?" he asked, his tone mild.

"Aye ... I thought Robin Mackay and Blaine Forbes did brilliantly." It was true—she'd picked out both men as possible contenders for her affections.

Gunn arched a dark eyebrow in response. "*I* won both those contests," he pointed out.

"Did ye?" Jaimee folded her arms across her chest. "What do ye want, Gunn?"

His mouth curved. "Can't a man greet a bonny lass?"

"After what ye said to me last night, I'm surprised ye have the nerve to speak to me at all." Jaimee stood her ground and waited for an apology.

It didn't come.

She clenched her jaw so tightly that her ears started to ache. How she wished to slap his face once more.

Alexander stepped closer then, holding her gaze, a sensual smile curving his lips. He leaned in, so that no one but Jaimee could hear him. "I meant every word, Jaimee."

She remained still, although her body now quivered. "Then ye are even worse a brute than I took ye for," she croaked. This was why she had to avoid him: the man didn't have any boundaries, any respect.

His smile widened as he drew back. "Aye ... that's probably the case." He continued to hold her gaze. "But ye will still have to watch as I compete for yer hand." He paused then, letting his words sink in. "It's the stone put this afternoon ... a contest we Gunns excel at."

"How nice for ye." Sarcasm dripped from every word, yet Gunn was unmoved.

He flashed her a grin then, the expression so unexpected that Jaimee's breathing caught. "Aye." He leaned close once more. "Shall we have a wager, My Lady?"

Jaimee fought the urge to lick her lips, a nervous gesture that would give her away and allow him to focus upon her mouth. "No."

"I really think we should," he continued. "How about ... if I win the stone put challenge this afternoon, ye reward me with a kiss?"

Jaimee drew herself up, outrage quickening in her belly. "I will not!"

"It's agreed then," he replied, with maddening calmness.

"No, it's not. Do ye have cloth in yer ears? I said—"

"Gunn ... I do believe ye are hogging the lovely Jaimee Mackay all to yerself." A loud male voice intruded. Both Jaimee and Alexander glanced left to see a tall, broad-shouldered warrior with long brown hair approaching.

Duncan Mackay, Robert Mackay of Balnakeil's younger brother, stopped before them. He ignored Gunn, his dark-blue gaze settling upon Jaimee instead.

"Piss off, Mackay," Alexander Gunn growled. "I haven't finished speaking to the lady."

Duncan glanced his way before flashing his competitor a harsh grin. "I think ye have. Step aside, and let the rest of us speak to the prize."

The prize? Jaimee ground her teeth. She wasn't an object, for pity's sake.

Even so, Duncan Mackay's arrival gave her a chance to escape Alexander Gunn. An opportunity she would willingly take.

"Ye are right, Duncan," she greeted him with a bright smile. "Gunn can't have me all to himself, can he?" She stepped up next to Duncan and linked an arm through his. "I was going to rest for a short while before the games resume, but shall we take a stroll together instead?"

Duncan's grin softened into a smug smile. "A fine idea." He then cast his rival a look of victory. "See ye at the stone put challenge."

Alexander Gunn's lip curled before he raked a dismissive glance over his competitor. "Aye, ready yerself to have yer arse whipped ... again."

Duncan's smile vanished, and Jaimee felt the arm she held grow rigid. She became aware then that they'd attracted an audience. A number of Mackay warriors were watching—and there was no mistaking their hard expressions or the hostility in their gazes.

"Whoreson," Duncan growled. "I look forward to wiping that smirk off yer face."

Swallowing hard, Jaimee reminded herself of the vow she'd made herself the night before. She'd already caused enough trouble by interceding where she wasn't wanted. This time she would keep her mouth shut.

Aggression rippled across the crowd. Muttering followed when Gunn replied to Duncan with an obscene gesture. He bent his right arm up with the fist pointed upward, while his left hand slapped the bicep of his bent arm.

The *bras d'honneur*—arm of honor—was an emphatic French gesture that had grown popular in parts of Scotland of late. It needed no translation.

Jaimee went hot and then cold at the naked challenge in Gunn's stormy eyes as he stared Duncan Mackay down. The latter's face flushed as he sought to rein in his temper.

Jaimee slowly released the breath she hadn't realized she'd been holding. Aye, it wouldn't be long before the Gunns and the Mackays drew their dirks against each other. And this time, she'd let them.

Alexander Gunn won at the stone put.

Jaimee had feared he would, even if she'd whispered silent prayers to the contrary all afternoon. The men had all lined up and taken turns at hurling heavy river stones as far as they could muster. Each competitor was given three chances, and his best throw was recorded for the final score.

Even from the sidelines, Jaimee could see that Gunn's longest throw had bested all the others, including his brothers'.

Tavish and William Gunn had scowled as they watched their elder brother compete. However, their disappointment at losing to their brother at the stone put wasn't as strong as the reaction from some of the other competitors.

Duncan Mackay's face was thunderous as he stalked from the field.

Alexander Gunn remained there, turning to seek out Jaimee's gaze.

She refused to look his way, even as the heat of his stare burned into her. Like during the noon meal, she'd made a point of wedging herself between her two brothers this afternoon.

She wasn't about to give him the opportunity to corner her again.

Connor rose to his feet then, as the competitors and audience alike quietened.

One glance at her brother's face and she could see he wasn't happy. His eyes were hooded, and lines of tension bracketed his mouth and nose. Although other warriors had competed well today, it was clear that Alexander Gunn's performance put him out front.

Jaimee could feel the frustration that vibrated off Connor's tall frame. Not for the first time, she regretted putting him in this position.

"That concludes today's strength contests." The chieftain's voice carried across the field. "I give thanks to all who competed." Connor halted then, his brow furrowing. "The following eight men will go through to tomorrow's wrestling competition." He cleared his throat. "Duncan Mackay, Robin Mackay, Fergus Leslie, Blaine Forbes, Abel Munro, Fife Munro ... and Alexander Gunn." Connor's mouth twisted as he said this last name.

Muttering followed Connor's announcement, as the crowd rumbled its disapproval. However, when Jaimee chanced a glance in Alexander Gunn's direction, she saw his face remained impassive.

The fact he'd gone through to the next round didn't surprise her; the bastard had won nearly every game this afternoon. However, Jaimee was relieved that Robin Mackay and Blaine Forbes were also through, for the two warriors had continued to impress her.

"Some of ye did better than others today," Connor continued, his frown deepening to a scowl. "But tomorrow ye will all start from scratch with the wrestling."

"Are we having feasting, dancing, and drinking this eve, Connor?" Hugh Mackay of Loch Stach called from the sidelines. "We're all looking forward to seeing yer bonny sister dance with the lads."

Jaimee tensed. She'd been so focused on the games that she'd forgotten each of her suitors would have the chance to woo her in the evenings afterward. And, of course, that would include Gunn. Forcing her expression to remain neutral, for she was aware that all her suitors were now watching her, their gazes keen, Jaimee clasped her hands together upon her lap.

If she was serious about finding a husband here, the dancing would allow her to talk with Robin and Blaine. Or maybe one of the others would impress her. Both Abel and Fife Munro were handsome, brawny men, yet so far the brothers had given her the impression of being a bit slow-witted and vain. Perhaps she would think differently once she'd actually conversed with them.

Connor nodded, his scowl remaining. "Aye, as soon as supper is done with."

"Ready, sister?" Morgan flashed Jaimee a smile as he ruffled his dog's ears. Gritta sat nestled in at his feet. "Ye always did love a ceilidh ... almost as much as Ma." His gaze clouded then, for they both recalled how Rose Mackay had loved to dance.

"Aye," Jaimee murmured. "Only, this one is a little different, Morgan."

She knew what was expected of her, yet she was nervous all the same. Once again, she wished her mother were still alive to provide sage advice.

Night had fallen. She was now seated next to her brothers and Maggie as a piper began a jaunty tune. Keira had retired early with Rose, leaving the rest of her kin to enjoy the dancing.

"It'll be fine," Maggie soothed. "Just a short dance with each of them, and ye will be done."

Jaimee nodded, her thoughts turning inward as she went through the questions she intended to ask her suitors. Hopefully, it wouldn't take her long to tell who would make a decent husband, and who wouldn't.

She glanced down at her skirts and brushed the dirt off the fine wool. Fern had insisted she wear something pretty for the evening and had dug out a pine-green kirtle. She'd brushed out Jaimee's hair, so that it fell in heavy red-gold waves over her shoulders, and pinned Jaimee's favorite brooch to her breast.

It was one her mother had given her at Yuletide, a year before her death. Made of intricately wrought silver, with mother of pearl studding its center, and framed by glittering specks of crystal, the brooch was a lovely piece of jewelry.

Gunn will want to dance with ye too. The intrusive thought popped up, yet Jaimee firmly pushed it aside. She'd deal with that brute later. Right now, she needed to focus on her other suitors.

As she rose to her feet, Jaimee caught Connor's eye. The eldest of her two brothers had been quiet all evening. He wore an introspective expression, as if he too was lost in his own thoughts.

Brother and sister's gazes held for a moment, and then Jaimee gave Connor a nod. She wanted him to know she was taking this seriously. She wouldn't let him down, not this time.

The strains of the Highland pipe lifted high above the gathering, joined shortly after by the voices of men and women who sang along.

Feeling the weight of gazes upon her, Jaimee moved to the center of the space that had been cleared. Relief fluttered through her when other men and women joined her. She'd feared that she'd be forced to dance with each suitor in turn, under the watchful eye of all, but having a crowd of dancers with her would ease things a little.

The ceilidh began with a lively circle dance. The dancers kicked up their heels and dove in and out, linking arms, and spinning each other around. Presently, Jaimee found herself face-to-face with Duncan Mackay.

The warrior grinned at her. His mood seemed to have improved since being trounced by Gunn at the stone put. Jaimee had heard Connor call his name earlier, which meant the man still believed he had a chance at winning her hand. His stroll with her earlier in the day had emboldened him where she was concerned.

However, a turn around the camp, and a brief conversation, had confirmed what Jaimee already suspected. She wouldn't be taking Duncan as a husband.

"Ye are looking lovely this eve," he greeted Jaimee, as he took hold of her arm and spun her around.

"Thank ye, Duncan," Jaimee replied demurely.

"Yer kirtle matches yer eyes."

They spun apart then, and Jaimee was granted a reprieve as they moved around the circle. However, moments later, they were face-to-face once more.

"I have seen ye grow up, Jaimee," Duncan continued. "Ye were a gawky lass ... but ye have blossomed of late."

Jaimee bit the inside of her cheek to stop a sharp reply. She'd promised herself that she would be pleasant and encouraging to her suitors this evening, and so she swallowed her response.

"My brother is vexed that he didn't get through to the second round of games," Duncan continued, oblivious to her mood. "But although I'm not a chieftain, I can still offer ye a life of comfort. We shall have our own floor at Balnakeil Broch. Does that please ye?"

"I'm sure ye have much to offer a bride," she acknowledged, her tone polite. *But that bride won't be me,* she silently added. She didn't want Duncan *or* Robert Mackay; both men had tried to woo her a year or two earlier, when their families had met to celebrate Beltaine, and she'd rebuffed them. Yet it seemed as if Duncan had forgotten the incident.

Duncan flashed her another grin. "Aye ... and ye'd bear me many strapping sons, I'm sure."

Jaimee looked away, so that he wouldn't see the chagrin in her eyes. Duncan Mackay grated on her nerves even more than he had years earlier. She'd forgotten just how coarse the man could be.

They spun away from each other then before—to Jaimee's relief—the music halted.

She drew to a halt, turned, and dipped her head to Duncan Mackay. *The first dance is done at least.*

10

THE DANCE BEGINS

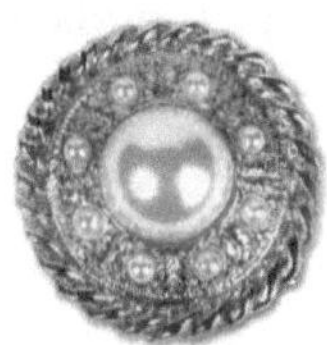

JAIMEE'S RELIEF DEEPENED when she spied Robin Mackay step forward. Offering her a shy smile, the young laird of Melness inclined his head. "Are ye ready for another dance, Lady Jaimee … or would ye like a breather?"

Smiling back, Jaimee extended a hand as the music erupted once more. "No, I'd love to dance. Shall we?"

This one was a slow dance, perhaps a deliberate choice of the musicians to allow the dancers to catch their breaths. And as she moved around the circle, Jaimee studied her suitor. Robin Mackay was attractive, especially when he smiled. He was shorter than most of the warriors here and sturdily built. Robin wore his light-brown hair cut short and had warm hazel eyes.

There was a strength, a gentleness, in him that she appreciated.

"How is it that we've never met before?" she asked as they drew together once more and Robin twirled her around. He wasn't a natural dancer yet was trying his best to keep up with her.

Robin offered her another reserved smile. "I've only recently taken over from my father," he replied, his voice a low baritone. "He was something of a hermit … and hated gatherings ... so we rarely ventured far from our broch."

Jaimee's own smile widened. "Tell me a little of yer home."

They moved around the circle then, arm in arm, weaving in and out of the other dancers.

"Melness is small," Robin replied, a note of apology in his voice. "My lands comprise of a handful of crofters' hamlets west of Tongue Bay." He paused then. "But it is a beautiful spot nonetheless ... especially the wide sandy beaches."

Jaimee's smile turned wistful. There were no beaches near Farr, and she did like to ride along a long beach, listening to the hollow beat of Tor's hooves against hard-packed sand.

Warmth filtered through her then. It was surprising how much she liked Robin. Although they'd just met, he had a manner that immediately put her at ease.

"And are ye an only child?" she asked, intrigued about this man's background.

He shook his head. "I have a younger brother." Did she imagine it, or did his hazel eyes shadow at this admission.

They broke apart then for a spell before the dance brought them together again.

"I'm fond of riding and hunting," Jaimee told him, as she linked her arm through Robin's once more. "Is this something ye would object to in a wife?"

The question was a direct challenge. Jaimee wanted to see how Robin responded to her independent spirit. She couldn't abide a husband who'd forbid her from doing the things she loved.

Their gazes met, and the young laird smiled—widely this time. "Not in the least, Lady Jaimee," he replied. "It so happens that those are two of my favorite pastimes ... and I'd be happy to share them with ye."

Something deep within Jaimee uncoiled at these words. She'd come to this gathering tense and worried that she wouldn't meet anyone she'd consider wedding— but Robin Mackay was a welcome surprise. He was unassuming, endearingly shy, *and* attractive; she could imagine herself growing to like him very much.

The evening passed with surprising speed. Jaimee managed to squeeze in a couple of breaks, although with each warrior keen to take his turn, she soon joined the dancers once more.

During each dance, she was able to form an idea of the characters of the men who sought her hand. Unfortunately, Abel and Fife Munro were both as vain and dim-witted as she'd feared. They spent their dances with her boasting of their prowess in battle—and in bed. Blaine Forbes—easily the most handsome of her suitors—was charming company. Yet his flippant responses to her questions had irked her; she didn't warm to him as she had Robin Mackay.

That left only Fergus Leslie and Alexander Gunn to dance with.

And as Blaine left her with a cocky smile—and more dancers filtered in from the watching crowd—Alexander Gunn stepped forward.

Jaimee's mouth thinned. She'd been so intent on 'interviewing' each suitor that she'd almost forgotten Gunn.

Almost.

Just get this over with, she told herself as she squared her shoulders. *And ye won't have to talk to him for the rest of the night.*

However, it was difficult not to quail as the huge warrior strode toward her, his gaze never leaving her face. Even more disturbing though was the strange heat that rippled through her belly as their gazes locked. She hated how flustered he made her feel, how aware of him she was at a purely primal level.

Gunn halted a couple of feet away and dipped his head. "May I have the next dance, Lady Jaimee?"

Jaimee nodded. Maybe if she remained stubbornly silent this would be easier?

The music began again—another popular dance, where men and women wove in and out of a circle before forming a column.

Jaimee took her place in the circle. She could weather this. She just needed to concentrate on the steps and lose herself in the music. The dance would be over soon enough. Fortunately, they weren't alone, and so Gunn wouldn't dare kiss her as he'd threatened earlier in the day.

But then, he took her hand, and the world shifted.

It was the first time they'd ever touched.

Jaimee wasn't prepared for the shock of his skin against hers, the heat and strength of his big hand as it clasped hers.

Shivers rippled up Jaimee's arm from her wrist to her shoulder. She gasped, and the sound would have been audible to all if the wail of the Highland pipe hadn't obscured it.

His touch made her breathing catch, made fire ignite deep in her belly.

An instant later, his fingers tightened around hers. It was a silent message that sent her pulse wild. Aye, he wouldn't take a kiss, yet this was just as disturbing.

Sweat beaded across her skin. She didn't dare look his way; she couldn't bear to.

The dance began.

It was a relief to move, although when Alexander Gunn released her hand so that she could spin around and link arms with him, a strange sensation of loss filtered through her.

Jaimee bit down on her lower lip. What was the matter with her? When her other suitors had taken her hand—even Robin Mackay—she hadn't reacted so. Yet just the feel of Gunn's fingers curling around hers had set her pulse racing.

The urge to fling herself out of the circle, and sprint from the camp, spiraled up within her.

And yet she fought it.

She fought herself.

As she and Alexander Gunn moved around each other, their arms linked, he spoke once more. "Why do ye avoid my eye, Jaimee? Do I scare ye?"

The challenge in his voice needled her.

"Ye stare at me like a wolf that hasn't eaten in a week," she replied, marveling at just how steady her voice was despite the turmoil raging within. "I don't like it."

"Then I must apologize." His voice rumbled over her like a caress.

She jerked her head up then, her gaze spearing his. Immediately, Jaimee regretted doing so, for the intensity on his face caused her breath to rush from her.

"Alexander Gunn, apologizing?" she queried, forcing herself to hold his eye.

"Aye," he replied, his mouth lifting at the corners. It was hard not to stare at his mouth. His lips were full and shapely—far too beautiful for such a man. "It occurs ... occasionally. It wasn't my intention to frighten ye."

"Really?" They spun apart then, ducking under the arms of another couple before coming together once more. "Just to insult and dishonor me?"

"Those are strong words."

His hand caught hers once more, and he drew her around, before guiding her into a twirl.

As much as she hated to admit it, Alexander Gunn knew how to dance. She would have thought a man of his size would lumber through a circle dance like this, yet he moved with grace and precision.

Of course, the man was lethal on the battlefield. His speed and agility had been honed over the years in a different kind of dance.

They moved into a column with the other dancers then, and Gunn took both her hands, lifting them high to form a roof for the other couples to move under.

The feel of his skin on hers, the strength and warmth of his hands combined with the roughness of the callouses on his palms, caused Jaimee's pulse to race.

For an instant, she wondered what those hands would feel like, caressing her naked skin.

Lord, no. Don't think of such things!

Jaimee tensed as they waited for each couple to pass under their arms—she couldn't allow herself to imagine such wickedness.

She hated Alexander Gunn. She couldn't let herself think about him touching her naked body.

It was their turn then, to link arms and pass under the arms of the others, but instead of linking his arm through hers, Alexander Gunn wrapped a possessive arm around her waist and pulled her against him, hip-to-hip.

Jaimee stifled a gasp. If he had done so in any other circumstances, she'd have turned and slapped him. But they were in the midst of a dance, and he'd made it look like a variation of the moves the others had made.

No one besides Jaimee would have noticed what he'd done.

Trapped in the cage of his arm, she was aware of just how strong and muscular he was. Her own tall stature meant that she rarely felt dwarfed by a man, yet she did now.

As they exited the column, Jaimee tried to twist out of his grasp, yet he didn't budge. It was only when the other dancers formed a circle once more that he released her, spinning Jaimee around, before catching her by the hand.

Jaimee's pulse now hammered in her ears.

She was spinning out of control. This man had her exactly where he wanted her, and she suddenly felt powerless to resist him.

And then the music was dying away, and the surrounding crowd were applauding the dancers.

Alexander Gunn released her and stepped back. His chest was rising and falling fast.

Their gazes met once more, and their surroundings faded. The clamor of voices and laughter all drew back. All that remained was Jaimee and a man who was her sworn enemy.

"I must speak to ye, Jaimee," Gunn said then, shattering the spell he'd cast over her. "Alone."

Incredulity seeped over Jaimee as she stared back at him. The man's lordly arrogance was both breathtaking and vexing. "I already made that mistake," she replied coldly. "I won't do so again."

"So, ye deny this thing between us?" he countered, his gaze searing her.

Jaimee's spine stiffened. The nerve of the man! "There's nothing to deny, Gunn."

"Give me a few moments of yer time ... alone ... and we'll see about that."

"No," she ground out the word. "Not tonight ... not ever!"

Gunn scowled. "I—"

"My turn now. Out of the way, Gunn!"

A hearty male voice boomed across the crowd, interrupting them.

Jaimee turned to see Fergus Leslie bearing down on her. Fergus was a broad-shouldered, stocky warrior with a shock of red hair. Like Robert and Duncan Mackay, he too had shown an interest in Jaimee over the years. And like those brothers, the man was an overbearing boor.

However, Jaimee was delighted to see him this evening. He was her savior. "Finally, Fergus," she greeted the warrior with a bright smile. "Ye have been patient ... waiting so long."

Encouraged by her welcome, Fergus grinned. "Aye, but ye saved the best till last, didn't ye, lass?"

11

I DON'T NEED LUCK

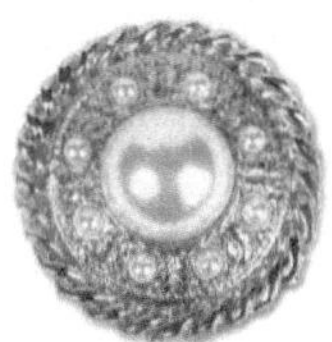

THE ARGUMENT ERUPTED over bannocks.

Dawn had just broken over the strath, the sky glowing pink and gold to the east. Those gathered were enjoying freshly baked bannock—large rounds of oaten cakes had been fried upon iron griddles over the fire—and hot broth as they readied themselves to watch the wrestling.

The Mackays had gathered around their central fire pit, as was their habit, when Robert Mackay made a disparaging comment about the clan-chief's appetite.

"Look at that mountain of bannock before ye, Angus," the younger man jeered. "Leave some for the rest us, won't ye?"

The clan-chief glanced up, from where he'd been slathering butter and honey over a huge wedge of cake, and frowned. "There's plenty to go around."

Robert snorted. The laird of Balnakeil sat just a few yards away and wore a scornful expression this morning. Observing his face from her vantage point across the fire, Jaimee wondered if Duncan had struck the nail upon the head; had being knocked out of the competition the day before put Robert in a sour mood?

It must have been embarrassing to be bested in the strength contests by his younger brother.

However, Robert hadn't glanced her way since she'd joined her kin at the fireside. Instead, his gaze rarely shifted from Angus Mackay.

"Ye are running to fat," Robert continued, his mouth twisting as he dragged his gaze down the clan-chief's portly form. "If ye keep eating like that, yer poor nag won't be able to carry ye."

Silence fell around the fire.

Beside Jaimee, Connor shifted uncomfortably. Glancing his way, Jaimee noted that her brother was watching Robert Mackay, his brow furrowed. Her attention then shifted to two other Mackay chieftains seated nearby. Their reactions were interesting. William Mackay's heavy lips were stretched into a grin, while Hugh Mackay's rawboned face had gone tense.

The fine hair on the back of Jaimee's arms prickled. There had been tension between the Mackays ever since they'd gathered upon the strath two days earlier—yet raw aggression now hung heavily in the morning air.

Hostility had laced every word Robert spoke. He was clearly trying to provoke the clan-chief.

"Is that the best ye can manage?" Angus rumbled after a pause. "A petty comment about my weight." The challenge in the clan-chief's voice rippled across the clearing. He brushed crumbs off his greying beard, his blue eyes hard as he locked gazes with Robert. "If ye have something worth hearing, speak now ... otherwise spare me yer fishwife's tongue."

Robert's expression darkened at these words. Jaimee was secretly impressed. Angus had been taciturn during the gathering so far. He spent most of his time with his nephew and retired early in the evenings. It was easy to think of him as diminished, beaten, since the events in Inverness. Yet watching him now, she was reminded that he wasn't a man to cross.

"All right then," Robert growled. "How about ye give us a real explanation for Inverness? George Gunn made a fool of ye."

The Mackay's gaze narrowed. "He didn't."

"Aye, he did. The man stood before the king and gave a proper speech, while ye ranted and raved, spittle flying from yer mouth like a rabid dog. Ye *shamed* us."

"Robert," Connor cut in, his voice harsh. "Don't speak for the rest of us."

Of course, Jaimee knew that both Connor and Morgan disagreed with their clan-chief's actions at Inverness. But despite their disappointment in Angus Mackay, they would remain loyal to him for the good of the clan.

"Ye know it's true, Connor," Robert countered, his voice rising now. His gaze then traveled around the faces of those amassed around the fire. "This man condemned his only son without blinking an eye."

"Enough," Hugh Mackay growled. "Show some respect when ye speak to yer clan-chief."

"I'm with Robert." William Mackay spoke up then. "These things need to be said."

"And now ye have," Angus replied. His voice was low and hard, his gaze wintry. "But since neither of ye was put in my position, we shall never know if ye would have acted differently."

"They're bickering amongst themselves."

Alexander glanced up from where he'd been sharpening his dirk on a whetstone, to find his brother Will standing before him. He then frowned. "Who?"

"The Mackays." Will grinned. "Ye should have heard them. At each other's throats like dogs. I wandered past on my way to the river for a wash and heard it all."

"Really?" Tavish asked with his mouth full. He'd emerged from his tent later than his brothers and was finishing off the last of the bannock.

"Aye ... Robert Mackay's stirring them all up. Ye should have heard the things he was saying to the clan-chief." Will paused then, shaking his head. "If any of the Gunn chieftains spoke thus to our father, he'd cut off his bollocks and feed them to him."

Alexander huffed a laugh. George Gunn certainly would. However, Angus Mackay was also a man folk usually minded. He wondered then if the Mackay clan-chief was losing his wits after the humiliation at Inverness. Perhaps the full implication of locking away his only heir, possibly for life, was sinking in.

Alexander's mouth thinned. *His* father wouldn't have any such regrets. He had six sons after all. Alexander was the eldest, but that didn't mean his father favored him. In many ways, his sons were his rivals—Alexander especially.

"Bickering is one thing ... but unless it escalates to bloodshed, who cares?" Tavish said then, brushing bannock crumbs off his braies.

"Robert Mackay is a bag of wind," Alexander added. He agreed with Tavish. "I doubt he has the guts to go up against his own clan-chief."

Even so, the news of the discord between the Mackays piqued his interest. "Did the other chieftains speak up?"

Will nodded, even if his expression was now disgruntled. "One of them took Robert's side, but the others didn't. I heard Connor Mackay defend his clan-chief."

Alexander snorted. Of course, Connor Mackay had made it clear where his loyalties lay. The news wasn't surprising.

Nonetheless, their father would be interested to hear about this development. Angus Mackay's isolation amongst his own clan was something the Gunns could exploit.

The news would also hopefully soften George Gunn's temper when they returned home from Halladale. Perhaps if they killed a few Mackays first, he wouldn't fly into a violent rage.

Alexander's mirth faded. Curse it, he really shouldn't care how his father would react to this.

And yet, deep down, he knew he did.

George Gunn's dominance reached him, stole his peace, even here. Silence settled around the smoking fire, and then Will's gaze shifted meaningfully to the dirk Alexander was sharpening. "I thought we were here to cause trouble," he grumbled. "How long are ye going to make us wait?"

"Ye'll get yer fight," Alexander growled. "Just exercise a bit of patience, will ye?"

Of course, Alexander didn't need to sharpen his blade for today's events. There weren't any knife fights scheduled for the games—they were too dangerous. Once he got through to the following day's round, he'd be fighting with a wooden sword. However, with the tensions at play at this gathering, he liked to know his dirk-blade was sharp. One never knew when the occasion for a real fight might arise.

"Just give us the nod when ye are ready," Will replied, surly now.

Tavish smirked. "He's too busy trying to impress Jaimee Mackay to care about killing any of her clansmen."

Alexander ignored the jibe, although Will scowled. "Ye won't find the wrestling as easy to win as the strength contests," Will sniped. "Some of the warriors ye'll be wrestling today are huge brutes. Did ye see the size of those Munro brothers—Abel and Fife?"

Alexander cocked his head. "Aye ... and?"

"Aren't ye a little worried about wrestling them?"

"No."

It was the truth. Alexander didn't let such things concern him. He was supremely confident when it came to pitting his skill and strength against other men.

"Listen to ye," Tavish snorted. "Ye really think ye'll win her hand?"

"Aye." Alexander rose to his full height and stretched out the muscles in his back and shoulders. "All I need is time."

Alexander was still pondering his words when he strode out onto the field shortly after the conversation with his brothers.

Time.

It was running out.

If he was ever to have a chance with Jaimee Mackay, he had to get her alone—yet she made it clear he'd never get the chance to speak with her privately.

Not after what had happened in his tent.

Last night's dance had only given him a frustratingly short spell with Jaimee. He'd spent most of the evening grinding his teeth as he'd watched her dance with the other suitors. Some dances she'd appeared to suffer through—especially those with Duncan Mackay and Fergus Leslie. However, she'd smiled at Robin Mackay and Blaine Forbes.

When Jaimee laughed at something Forbes said, Alexander's fingers had tightened around the wooden cup of ale he'd nursed during the evening. Red-hot jealousy had boiled up within him. When he'd been sharpening his dirk earlier, he'd been imagining gutting the grinning Forbes warrior with it.

Pushing aside the violent thoughts, Alexander joined the other suitors amassing on the edge of the space where the wrestling would take place. They'd erected ropes around the wrestling ring.

"Back for more, shit-eating bastard?" Duncan Mackay greeted Alexander as he went through a series of stretches.

Alexander spat on the ground in response. He was looking forward to grinding Duncan's face into the ground this morning.

Ignoring another insult from Duncan, Alexander glanced around at the other competitors. Nearby Abel Munro—a beast of a man—had already stripped down to the waist and was flexing his muscles while a couple of lasses on the sidelines looked on. The young women's faces were flushed as they giggled and whispered together.

Alexander fought a lip curl. *Show off.*

Heeling off his boots, Alexander removed his lèine, leather belt, and dirk, and carried them over to where his brothers and warriors had taken up position on the edge of the crowd.

"Look after these for me," he told Fynn.

His warrior nodded. "Sealbh math dhuibh!"

Alexander grinned back. The warrior's words were unnecessary. "I don't need luck."

12

HOLD

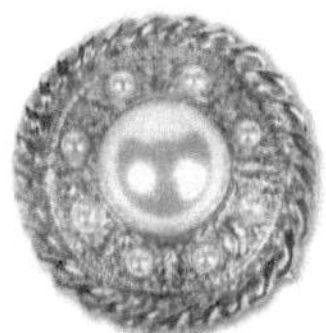

"WRESTLERS, TAKE YER positions." Angus Mackay's voice boomed over the wrestling ring. "Hold!"

Alexander clenched his jaw and locked his opponent in a tight grip. He was facing Blaine Forbes, the grinning warrior from the evening before. Alexander intended to wipe the self-confident smirk off the man's face.

They slammed into each other like rams, gripping their opponent around the waist and back. The aim was to get the other to break his hold or touch the ground with any part of his body save his feet. The warrior to win the best of five rounds would be the victor.

Alexander had already trounced Abel Munro, much to the shock of the watching crowd, and he intended to make even shorter work of Forbes.

Shouting and jeers rang out from the sidelines. Most of the calls were encouraging Forbes to give Gunn a trouncing, although he could hear his brothers shouting to him amongst the din.

A feral smile stretched Alexander's mouth as he shoved hard against Forbes, forcing him backward. The man's bare feet tried to find purchase on the trampled grass, yet Alexander wouldn't let him.

A moment later, Blaine Forbes went down on one knee.

"Bout One goes to Gunn," The Mackay intoned. The clan-chief wore a glower now, his gaze boring into Alexander.

Breathing hard, the two warriors pulled apart.

Forbes wasn't smiling anymore, Alexander noted. By the end of this match, he'd be wearing a very different look upon his face.

Straightening up, Alexander shook out his shoulder muscles before casting the clan-chief a hard smile. Connor Mackay had asked Angus to oversee the wrestling, perhaps not trusting himself to deal directly with Alexander. However, the Mackay clan-chief had arguably even more reason to bear the Gunns ill-will. The man was clearly losing control of his clan, and having Alexander Gunn at this gathering wasn't helping matters.

"Wrestlers ... ready yerself again," the Mackay rumbled, his dark brows crashing together.

Blaine and Alexander did as bid—and once Alexander won the third round in a row, he was pronounced the winner.

Around them, the crowd grumbled, while Blaine Forbes spat on the ground, muttered a curse, and stormed out of the ring with ill grace.

Alexander watched him go before his attention shifted to the sidelines. He'd been so focused on the wrestling that he'd had little time to look elsewhere. It paid to keep one's mind on one's opponent.

However, as he recovered his breath and waited for the next warrior to step up, Alexander's gaze shifted to Jaimee Mackay.

She was watching him. The lass had taken to avoiding his eye—yet not this morning.

Awareness thrilled through his veins, his belly muscles tightening as their gazes locked.

Hers was a bold look, even if it wasn't a particularly friendly one.

Jaimee Mackay had smiles for other men it seemed, but not Alexander Gunn.

Holding her gaze a moment longer, Alexander favored Jaimee with a nod. He was glad she was watching him, glad she saw him thrash each opponent.

Duncan Mackay stepped up then, ready to face him.

Tearing his attention from Jaimee, Alexander smiled, showing Duncan his teeth. Then he sized the man up. Although Duncan stood at a similar height to Alexander, he lacked his breadth and brawn. However, naked to the waist, the warrior's torso was all lean, corded muscle.

I'll have to watch him.

Duncan Mackay had a belligerent look on his face and a gleam in his eye that Alexander knew well. The man was self-assured and had a score to settle.

Alexander's smile widened to a grin. Finally, a worthy opponent.

In response, Duncan snarled an insult.

"Wrestlers," Angus Mackay boomed once more. "Take yer positions!"

Alexander and Duncan did as bid.

"Hold."

The two warriors slammed into each other, and the contest began. Alexander struck fast, using his superior weight and strength to flip his opponent.

A roar of disappointment rose up from the watching crowd, drowning out the Gunn cries of victory.

"Come on, Duncan!" Robert Mackay bellowed, his face flushed an angry red. "Don't let that whoreson show ye up!"

Duncan's expression went feral, and he cast his elder brother a dark look. Fury smoldered in the warrior's eyes as he and Alexander took up their positions once more.

"Hold!"

This time Duncan was ready for him.

The two opponents circled each other, their bare toes digging into the crushed grass. Alexander clenched his jaw; Duncan Mackay was quick and nimble. It was like trying to keep hold of a twisting eel.

An instant later, Duncan's leg hooked around his, and Alexander toppled sideways, hitting the ground.

A roar of victory went up, thundering over the strath. Insults aimed at Duncan's opponent followed.

Keeping his gaze fixed upon his opponent, Alexander climbed to his feet, dusted himself off, and prepared to go again.

The jeering crowd wouldn't distract him. He was out for blood now.

However, Duncan Mackay was the victor in the next round too, managing to throw Alexander off balance once more.

Rage now pulsed in Alexander's ears. And Duncan Mackay's grinning face made him itch to wrap his hands around the warrior's throat.

"Hold!"

They slammed into each other once again, and this time Alexander moved quickly. He stomped on Duncan's foot, crunching it into the earth, before he shoved his opponent sideways.

Duncan toppled.

"Bastard!" Duncan hissed, rolling to his feet. He then winced, for he'd twisted his ankle during that fall.

Alexander held his eye. "Stop whining, Mackay. Let's settle this now."

"Wrestlers ... ready yerselves for the final bout," Angus Mackay commanded, his narrowed gaze flicking from Alexander to Duncan. "This one decides the winner."

Duncan growled another insult.

Alexander ignored him. At least the warrior wasn't grinning at him now.

The last bout began.

Duncan tried to knock Alexander off balance immediately, using his own wrestling style against him, yet Alexander had anticipated the tactic. He kicked hard at Duncan's injured ankle.

The Mackay warrior's hiss of pain echoed across the ring, and then Alexander kicked him again.

Duncan's leg gave way, and he sank down on one knee.

A heartbeat of silence followed.

Breathing hard, Alexander released his opponent and stepped back.

Cheering erupted from the sidelines, although from only one corner. Alexander's brothers and warriors were whistling, hooting, and clapping, huge grins on their faces.

All the other onlookers, Mackays and their allies alike, now wore stony expressions.

"Ye cheated, ye filthy dog!" Duncan gasped out, staggering to his feet.

A beat of silence followed. Alexander's mouth twisted into a sneer. He wasn't about to dignify a poor loser with a response.

Duncan whipped around, fixing his clan-chief with a gimlet stare. "Ye tell him, Angus. The shit-eating Gunn cheated!"

Angus Mackay stared back at him before his heavy brow furrowed. "No, he didn't."

Duncan's face reddened. "Aye. He stomped on my foot and then tried to break my ankle."

The clan-chief wore an uncomfortable expression now. "None of those are illegal moves."

Alexander fought the urge to grin. Indeed. As much as it clearly pained the clan-chief to admit it, for it sounded as if the words were choking him, Alexander had merely employed moves that many wrestlers did.

Duncan's face turned ugly. "So, ye're taking *his* side?"

Angus Mackay folded beefy arms across his broad chest, staring the younger man down. "It's not about sides, *lad*. It's about the rules of the game. Gunn beat ye. Take it like a man."

The men's gazes fused then, and a deep silence settled over the ring. The hairs on the back of Alexander's neck prickled. He knew this sensation. He'd felt it every time he went into battle—the moment both sides faced each other, that indrawn breath before the ringing of sword-blades rent the air.

"My brother's right about ye," Duncan finally snarled. "Ye aren't fit to lead our clan."

An instant later, Duncan Mackay flung himself at the clan-chief and punched him square in the eye.

13

WAR CRY

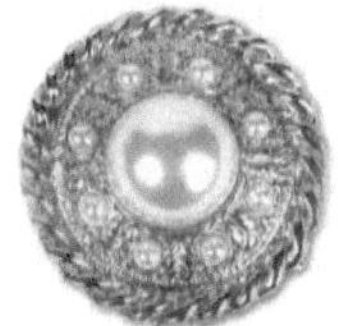

ALL HELL BROKE loose after that.

All the tension, all the hostility that had crackled in the air ever since the Mackays and their allies had gathered here upon the Strath of Halladale, exploded.

It was the excuse Robert Mackay needed.

Unsheathing the dirk at his hip, the laird of Balnakeil lunged forward, bellowing the Mackay war cry.

"Bratach Bhan Chlann Aoidh!"

And just like that, in an instant, that cry unleashed Angus Mackay himself. The big man had reeled after Duncan's blow to the eye, yet he recovered swiftly, drew his dirk, and went after the warrior.

Duncan Mackay was unarmed.

He danced away, twisting to avoid the clan-chief's slashing blade.

Alexander shifted back, narrowly avoiding a collision with Robert Mackay as he rushed toward Duncan and the clan-chief.

Connor Mackay's shout of rage echoed across the strath then, as he followed, weapon drawn. His brother, Morgan, lunged after him. Alexander wasn't surprised to see the brothers move to protect their clan-chief. Both men were doggedly loyal to the Mackay.

An instant later, Mackay warriors filled the wrestling ring. William Mackay had leaped in to intercept Connor, blade slashing. The chieftain of the Mackays of Farr hadn't seen him approaching, for his attention was on the clan-chief and his attackers. Yet Morgan had. He flung himself forward, blocking William's blade.

Gaze still riveted upon the fighting men, Alexander moved back farther. This was a Mackay matter, and he wasn't about to interfere. He glanced then over at the encircling crowd, to see that the Mackay allies had taken the same stance. Not one of them—Leslie, Munro, Ross, and Forbes alike—moved.

John Mackay, the clan-chief's nephew, rushed into the fray. However, he was prevented from reaching Angus Mackay's side by Robert Mackay's warriors. Hugh Mackay lumbered in then; the older chieftain taking the clan-chief's side against Robert and William Mackay and their supporters. Robin Mackay of Melness fought alongside him, cursing as he slashed his way toward Angus Mackay's side.

Alexander moved over to where Jaimee stood next to Connor and Morgan's wives. All three women wore stricken expressions, their faces milk-white.

None were likely in peril at present. Yet if the skirmish went against the clan-chief and those loyal to him, Jaimee and the other women would be in danger from Robert Mackay and those who now followed him.

Alexander gestured to his brothers and warriors to join them. Moments later, they were at his side. Fynn handed him his dirk. Alexander barked a command, and his men fanned out, forming a protective semi-circle around the Mackay women.

Gaze narrowed, Alexander surveyed the fight.

Both sides were evenly matched. All men fought with dirks rather than claidheamh-mòrs. None of them had brought the heavy Scottish broad-swords with them to the gathering, for they were battle weapons. However, a dirk, with its long, wicked dagger, could be just as deadly.

Duncan Mackay fell first, stabbed in the guts and then the throat by Angus Mackay. Alexander watched the clan-chief handle himself, silently impressed by just how strong and fast the man still was. Like Alexander's own father, men underestimated the older warrior at their peril.

Duncan had, and he was now lying dead, his blood draining into the dry earth while the fight raged around him.

"Do something!" A hand closed around Alexander's arms in a vise. Dragging his attention from the pitched battle going on just yards away, Alexander swiveled around to find Jaimee Mackay standing at his shoulder. Her green eyes were huge upon a frightened face as she stared at the fighting.

Connor Mackay had just brought down one of William Mackay's men with a vicious stab under the armpit. Tension vibrated through Jaimee as she looked on; Alexander could feel it where her fingers still clutched his arm.

"Don't just stand there!" She turned her gaze to him then, her eyes glittering. "Stop them!"

Alexander held her eye. "I can't halt this."

"But can't ye help them?"

"Look around ye, lass," he growled. "How many of yer allies have joined the fight?"

He waited while she did as commanded, her attention shifting to where the Munros stood to their right. One or two men had drawn their dirks, as if readying themselves should the fighting move in their direction. Yet not one of them launched himself into the fray.

Jaimee's mouth twisted as she swung around to face Alexander once more. "Cowards ... ye are all milksops!"

Her insult washed off Alexander. "No ... to interfere in this fight ... at this stage would bring dishonor to the Mackays," he replied, ensnaring her gaze with his. "This is their fight ... and one that has been brewing for a while, from the looks of things. We must let them finish it."

"But my brothers—"

"Can hold their own."

And they could. Although he'd managed to slide his dirk under Connor Mackay's guard in battle, Alexander had noted what a worthy opponent the warrior was. He and his brother were something to behold now as they fought back-to-back.

Jaimee didn't reply. Her attention returned to the fighting, although her hand never strayed from his arm, her fingernails biting into his skin.

Alexander welcomed the discomfort, for her touch burned a brand upon his arm.

And in the way of such skirmishes, the fighting, although violent and bloody to begin with, quickly showed a victor.

A short while later, the warriors belonging to Robert and William Mackay, and the two chieftains themselves, lay upon the blood-soaked ground. Robert Mackay had taken a wound to his leg, and his face twisted in loathing as he stared up at Angus Mackay.

The clan-chief towered over him, his face devoid of mercy. A few yards away, William Mackay groaned as he tried to staunch the flow of blood from a wound on his flank.

"Kill me then," Robert hissed, defiant to the last.

"A warrior's death is too good for ye two," The Mackay's voice rumbled over the ring. "Ye and William are coming back to Castle Varrich ... where ye'll hang."

Robert Mackay's face went slack at this. An instant later, he lunged for a discarded dagger that sat a few feet away.

"No, ye don't." Morgan Mackay's booted foot slammed down on the dirk blade, and on Robert's hand.

The crunch of broken bones rent the air before Robert's howl of pain followed.

The gathering had been ruined.

Jaimee should have been relieved about that, yet she wasn't. She'd reconciled herself to her fate, and the last thing she wanted was her own clan turning against each other. Few folk who'd attended this gathering from Balnakeil broch and Dun Ugadale would be returning home.

Robert and William Mackay had been allies in this uprising, yet it had turned against them in the end, for the Mackays of Farr, Hugh Mackay of Loch Stach, and Robin Mackay of Melness had stood by their clan-chief. They'd put aside their own resentments and defended him.

Apart from sporting a black eye and a few minor cuts, Angus Mackay had emerged from the fighting relatively unscathed. His nephew John, who'd managed to slash his way to his side, had a deep wound to his upper arm.

Like their clan-chief, Connor and Morgan had emerged with only minor gashes. However, as they strode from the battlefield, the violence in her brothers' eyes cowed Jaimee.

She'd never witnessed a battle before, not a real one. She'd grown up seeing her brothers spar at sword practice and had watched mock battles during clan gatherings.

But the reality of such violence sickened her.

The bannocks she'd eaten just after dawn churned uneasily in her belly.

As Connor and Morgan approached, Alexander Gunn murmured something to his men, and they stood aside.

Jaimee tensed. The Gunns had formed a shield between the Mackay women and the fighting. It had been a protective gesture, but would her brother take offense at the presumption?

Approaching the group, Connor's gaze went to Jaimee's face before he shifted his attention to Keira and Maggie. And then he glanced Alexander Gunn's way.

The two men stared at each other for an instant before, to Jaimee's surprise, her brother acknowledged him with a barely perceptible nod.

Angus Mackay left for Castle Varrich as soon as his men could ready themselves. They trussed Robert and William Mackay up like Yuletide geese and threw them over the back of two sturdy garrons.

"What do ye wish me to do with the bodies of their men?" Connor asked as the clan-chief swung up onto his heavyset stallion. "Do ye want them returned to their kin at Balnakeil broch and Dun Ugadale?"

The clan-chief scowled. His mood appeared to have darkened even further since the fight ended.

For Mackays to go up against Mackays—especially with Gunns looking on—was humiliating indeed.

Observing the clan-chief's thunderous expression, as she stood with the rest of her kin behind Connor, Jaimee realized that Angus Mackay would brood over this for some time to come. Deep down, he knew he was responsible for this uprising.

"None of those traitorous pieces of shit deserve a proper burial," he growled. "Pile their bodies onto a pyre here, and burn them."

"Aye, chief," Connor murmured. "As ye wish."

Next to the clan-chief, John Mackay swung up onto the saddle. The younger man's face was pale with pain, his right arm in a blood-stained sling.

Angus cut his nephew a look. "Are ye well enough to ride, John?"

"Aye," the warrior grunted.

The clan-chief shifted his attention back to Connor for a moment, before he looked to where Hugh and Robin Mackay stood a few feet away. All three lairds wore inscrutable expressions. Jaimee noted there was little warmth in her brother's eyes as he watched Angus Mackay.

The Mackay perhaps sensed this, for his thunderous expression softened. "I will never forget yer loyalty on this day, lads," he murmured.

14

MUCH TO DISCUSS

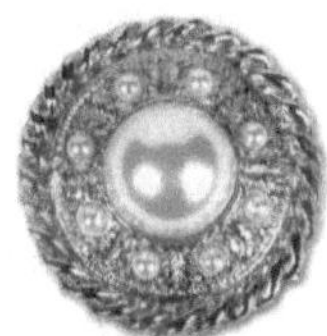

IT WAS STRANGELY quiet that evening.

Of course, the wrestling had ended with Alexander Gunn's bout with Duncan Mackay. The Forbes warriors had left shortly after Angus Mackay, and the other allied clans would depart for their homes the following morning.

The warriors from the various clans—the Gunns included—all kept to their hearths as daylight faded. Conversation was muted.

Wooing Jaimee Mackay didn't seem appropriate now.

As commanded, the men had collected the dead and piled their corpses upon a pyre in the midst of the clearing where the games had taken place. There were a small number of Mackay warriors from Balnakeil broch and Dun Ugadale who'd survived the fight still around, although one of them died from his injuries as dusk settled over the landscape. The others had limped away from the camp to take the news back home.

Jaimee did her best not to look at the inky smoke that drifted into the darkening sky. It was a still evening and so the column rose straight and high into the heavens. The sight reminded her of the year before, when Connor had burned the corpse of their traitorous uncle,

Domhnall. There had been no burial for the man who'd tried to take Connor's place as chieftain.

The pyre had been lit some distance from the tents. Even so, the odor of burning flesh still reached the camp.

Jaimee couldn't bear it.

Swallowing to ease the burning in the back of her throat, she left the Mackay fireside and walked north, to where the wide River Halladale curled its way through brown hills on its way to the sea.

She wore a woolen shawl wrapped around her shoulders this evening, for although the air wasn't cold, it felt as if a chill had drilled deep into her bones.

Today had been a stark reminder of just how fragile the peace was in the Highlands. King James had done his best to settle things down, yet when clansman fought clansman, there was little he could do.

Jaimee's breathing quickened as images of that vicious fight tormented her.

Duncan Mackay had danced with her the night before, and now he was dead, the flames devouring his flesh.

A shiver went through her.

She hadn't liked Duncan much, yet she hadn't wished him dead.

Fool. Why did he do it?

Why had any of them done it? Both Robert and William Mackay would have known they didn't have the other chieftains' support for an uprising. Perhaps, despite the simmering tension of these past two days, things wouldn't have deteriorated further.

If Duncan hadn't lost that wrestling bout with Alexander Gunn.

Jaimee clenched her jaw. Even when he wasn't in the thick of things, Gunn was a troublemaker. His very presence here had been the spark that ignited violence among her own people.

She'd hoped Alexander Gunn would have packed up and departed shortly after Angus Mackay left. But he hadn't. However, he'd had the good sense to keep to his own hearth.

He'll be gone with the dawn, Jaimee reassured herself as she wandered along the riverbank, her gaze traveling to where the gently flowing water reflected the red and gold of the setting sun. *Thank the Lord.*

In the end, she'd understood why he and his men hadn't intervened in the fighting. He was right: even their allies had been reluctant to do so. Nonetheless, she couldn't help but blame him for this whole mess.

Duncan Mackay hadn't been able to stomach being bested by a Gunn.

Jaimee heaved a deep sigh then. She was glad she had left her kin for a short while. Her nerves felt stretched tight, like calf-skin pulled over a Beltaine drum. She wouldn't wander far from the camp, for it was foolish to do so. However, ever since her first encounter with Alexander Gunn, she now wore the dirk her father had gifted her, strapped around her waist.

The weapon gave her confidence.

"Well ... that's it then," she murmured to the croaking frogs. "The gathering is done. I've got a choice to make."

Of course, there was only one warrior among the group of suitors she'd actually consider: Robin Mackay. He was a good, kind man who'd treat her well. His smile exuded warmth. She was drawn to him and wanted to get to know him better.

Jaimee drew her woolen shawl closer to her as she halted on the riverbank and stared down at the lazy river current.

I will go to Connor and tell him I have chosen a husband. Her heart started thumping erratically against her ribs in a blend of nerves and excitement, yet the decision was made.

After this disastrous gathering, she just wanted to get on with her life.

Jaw firming, Jaimee turned back toward the camp.

I will do it now.

However, she'd only gone a couple of steps when the ground beneath her feet trembled. She glanced up to see a huge shape bearing down upon her: the dark outline of a man on horseback.

Jaimee's lips parted, a scream rising within her. It all happened so fast she didn't even have time to reach for her dirk.

The horse was upon her—and Jaimee looked up, straight into Alexander Gunn's face.

Reaching down, he gripped her around the waist and lifted her from the ground as if she were no heavier than a bundle of straw. His arms were iron bands around her chest, cutting off her scream.

The pressure on her ribs eased as he lifted his arm. A large hand then clamped down over her mouth.

Holding the reins with one hand, Gunn shifted back in the saddle, and Jaimee felt the warrior's thighs, pressed against hers, bunch. The huge feather-footed beast he rode responded.

The stallion turned on its haunches, away from the campsite. An instant later, they thundered off into the gloaming.

As soon as they were out of earshot of the camp, Alexander Gunn removed his hand.

"Beast!" Jaimee gasped, struggling in his firm grip. "My brother will cut ye to pieces for this."

Gunn didn't reply.

"He'll slice open yer guts and leave ye to the crows," she snarled.

The devil take him, this man's body felt made of stone. There wasn't the slightest give in him. If only she could get her hand free, she could reach for her dirk. Yet both arms were trapped, pinned against her sides by the cage of his arm.

Panic surged within Jaimee, causing her to struggle wildly, even though it was clearly futile. "What in Hades do ye think ye are doing?"

The brute still didn't reply.

"So, this is what a Gunn does, is it?" She rasped the words. "A woman spurns ye, and ye abduct her?"

Fear gripped her around the throat then. This man didn't want to wed her—he'd made his intentions clear on that first night.

He would ravish her.

The urge to plead with him rose within her, yet she choked the words back. If Gunn was bent on rape, her fear would only likely inflame him. Her heart quailed at what he might to do her, yet she couldn't show how frightened she was. Instead, she had to keep a clear head.

He likely didn't realize she was armed. The gloaming was heavy now, the last glow of daylight fading in the western sky. She hoped he hadn't seen that she carried a dirk at her hip.

The moment we stop, I will use it on him.

A strange calm settled upon Jaimee then, her panic and fear drawing back just a little. She wouldn't let this bully rape her. She'd turn the blade on herself first before that happened.

"I'm not going to force myself on ye, Jaimee." Alexander Gunn spoke then, his voice a low rumble. His breath feathered against her ear, reminding her of their proximity. She sat perched in the saddle before him, their bodies flush.

"Lying dog!" she snarled. He was only trying to get her to lower her guard.

"I'm merely taking ye to a place where we can talk," he replied. "I told ye I wanted to speak to ye *alone*, lass ... and I intend to."

Jaimee's breathing hitched. "This is madness!" She couldn't believe her refusal to give him an audience had resulted in such behavior. "If ye want to talk, we can do that back at camp," she choked out the words. "I demand ye take me back there."

His soft laugh vibrated against her back. "I don't think so."

15

ABDUCTED

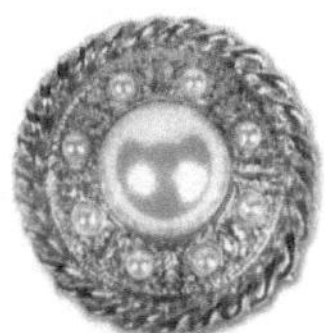

HE TOOK HER NORTH-EAST, toward Gunn lands.

The Strath of Halladale was a wide vale composed of meadows and gently rolling hills, yet Alexander Gunn headed toward the mountains.

And by the time he reached them, starlight lit their way.

"My brothers will track ye down," Jaimee told him. "And when they do, they'll tear ye apart ... and I shall enjoy watching."

Gunn didn't reply to her blood-thirsty threat. He hadn't answered any of the menaces she'd thrown at him over the past hours.

He seemed impervious to insults, to her rage. In the end, she gave up threatening him. Instead, she lapsed into cold, calculating silence.

Gunn wouldn't get away with this.

After a while, he slowed his stallion to a trot, for the terrain became rougher, and the silvery light of the stars illuminated many rocks and tors thrusting up from the earth.

Up and up they rode, into the feet of the mountains that formed a natural barrier between Mackay and Gunn territories. Although pine forest carpeted many of the vales and glens deeper in the mountains, the north-eastern slopes were barren.

Eventually, Alexander Gunn drew up his horse before a large shelf of rock. It formed a natural shelter against the elements, and despite the darkness, for her eyes had adjusted to the starlight a while back, Jaimee spied the remnants of a fire. No doubt this was a popular campsite for hunters.

Gunn swung down from his horse, pulling Jaimee down after him.

And that was when she struck.

Her feet hadn't even touched the ground when she was pulling her dirk free from its sheath. She held it low, as her brothers had taught her, stabbing straight for his groin.

A cry of fury ripped from her throat when his fingers locked around her wrist, holding her fast.

"Easy, Jaimee," he murmured. "Ye don't want to do that."

Gritting her teeth, Jaimee struggled against him. Her wrist was imprisoned, but the rest of her wasn't. Over the years, her father, and her brothers, had shown her techniques for if she was ever cornered by a man intent on raping her.

Her knee came up sharply, aiming once more for his groin.

But he merely stepped in close, so that her knee slammed against the rock-hard muscle of his thigh.

"Ye seem intent on damaging my cods," he said, cool amusement lacing his voice. "I already said I wasn't going to rape ye."

"Liar!" she spat out. "Why else would ye bring me out here … into the middle of nowhere?"

"I said I wanted to—"

"Talk? I'd have to be a lackwit to believe ye. The only words ye have uttered to me, Alexander Gunn, have been rude, disrespectful, and dishonorable. I have no interest in hearing what ye have to say. Take me back to my kin now … before this goes any further … and Connor *may* spare yer life."

She lifted her chin then, meeting his eye for the first time since her abduction.

Starlight gilded the angles of his handsome face and accentuated the hollows of his eyes, his cheeks. He looked like some wrathful god bent on destruction.

A shiver of fear trembled through her, despite her brave words. And when he grinned, his teeth flashing white in the darkness, her knees started to shake. His presence dominated her, the grip on her wrist increasing just slightly in a silent warning.

Long moments passed, and then his grin faded. "I can't help myself where ye are concerned, Jaimee," he said softly. "We lock gazes, and the rest of the world disappears."

Jaimee stared up at him. Fury and fear warred within her. Everything this man said was calculated. She was talking to a serpent.

"From the moment I caught ye staring at me in Inverness, I've not been able to get ye out of my thoughts," he continued. The admission carried a hard edge; his voice was almost accusatory.

Heat rose to Jaimee's cheeks as she recalled how blatantly she'd stared at him that day.

She couldn't deny his words, so she decided to cast an accusation of her own. "Ye *followed* me into the garden that day, didn't ye?"

A slow smile curved his lips once more, and despite that his eyes were largely cast in shadow, she saw them glint. "Aye."

"Why?"

"I imagined ye wished to be followed ... why else does a woman take a walk alone in the rain?"

Jaimee stared at him, disbelieving. When she replied, her voice shook with fury. "Because she wishes to be *alone*, and for no other reason." She started to struggle once more. *Beast!*

He held her easily, his big frame not giving an inch. However, that smirk faded at least.

"I was entranced, Jaimee," he admitted then, his voice lowering once more. "I saw ye leave the keep and knew I had to follow. I had to speak to ye."

"To insult me."

"Ye insulted me too, as I recall."

She had, but then he'd deserved it. The man was a Gunn after all, and he'd nearly gutted her brother in battle. She was hardly going to welcome him with sweet words.

"I thought I'd cast ye from my mind after Inverness." His gaze never left her face as he spoke. "But when I returned home, ye remained." His hold on her remained firm. "Somehow ... I'm in yer thrall."

Jaimee snorted. "Since ye are the one who has abducted me, that's hardly the case."

Ignoring her reply, he pressed on, "When I heard that Connor Mackay was holding games so that his bonny sister might finally choose a husband, I couldn't resist."

Her lip curled. "It wouldn't have mattered if ye had won the games in the end, Gunn. I was never going to accept ye as my husband."

"I knew that," he admitted, his voice roughening. "But I came nonetheless." He paused there, his look searing. "And when I saw ye again, it was worse ... the longing ... the *need*. I've never wanted anything in my life like I want ye, Jaimee Mackay."

Jaimee's heart started to beat wildly at these words, at their rawness and honesty. He wasn't lying. Somehow this brute had developed an obsession with her.

"And so, ye thought ye'd just take what ye wanted," she replied, the quaver in her voice betraying her nervousness.

"I had to get ye on yer own," he answered, stubbornness evident in every word. "And after today, I knew that if I didn't take action, any chance I had would be lost."

A brittle laugh escaped Jaimee. "Any chance?" The man's conceit was astounding. "I've already told ye that I would never take ye as my husband."

"That's just yer prejudice blinding ye," he replied, his tone hardening.

"No, it's fact, Gunn." She lifted her chin then, her gaze narrowing. "As it happens, I've already decided on a husband."

That surprised him. For the first time since he'd abducted her, she felt tension thrum through Alexander Gunn's big body.

"Who?" he asked roughly.

Jaimee continued to glare up at him. "It's nothing to do with ye."

His grip on her wrist tightened a fraction. "I watched ye last night … as ye danced with each of them. Ye don't want any of those men."

Jaimee lapsed into stubborn silence. The arrogance of him. Actually, she liked Robin Mackay. The man was decent and honorable, not like the beast staring down at her.

"Tell me I'm wrong." Gunn's gaze searched her face. "Lash out at me all ye want, but ye feel this too."

Jaimee's breathing hitched. Suddenly, she was all too aware of his hard, muscular body just inches away from hers. The heat of it warmed the cool night air.

A heartbeat passed, and then he spoke once more. "Deny it."

Jaimee flattened her lips into a thin line. She wasn't playing this game.

"Ye feel the pull between us, just as I do," he continued, his voice wrapping around her in a sensual murmur. "Every time our gazes lock … every time we touch. That's why ye are so angry. Ye feel it, even if yer mind rebels." His mouth twisted then. "Do ye think I wanted this either? A *Mackay* woman for pity's sake?"

Jaimee heaved in a deep breath. "It's just lust," she replied, her voice shaky. "It won't last."

His gaze speared her once more. "I disagree."

Jaimee glared up at him, her pulse thundering in her ears. His declarations had angered her, yet the raw need in his voice just then made a treacherous heat rise in a slow pulse in her lower belly.

Aye, it was lust all right. She was a maid and had done nothing more than kiss a man—and even those brief stolen embraces over the years had underwhelmed her—yet she knew what desire was.

She'd seen the way her brothers and cousin looked at their wives, and the way those women held their gazes, an unspoken promise passing between them.

And she'd identified the fire that had quickened within her that day, as she and Gunn had stood in the rain together in that courtyard garden.

Lust. It was a kind of madness. It made her want to lean into him, made her want to inhale the scent of him deep into her lungs.

The need was stronger than anger, stronger than hate—and it scared her.

She wasn't supposed to want a man like him. She'd already made up her mind that she would wed Robin Mackay of Melness—if the warrior was still keen to take her as his wife—and build a new life with him.

"Are ye going to let me go," she eventually managed, her voice catching. "Or are we going to stand here all night?"

"Aye, I'll let ye go," he murmured after a beat. "In a moment, I'm going to release yer wrist, and ye are going to sheath that dirk." He paused then, letting his words sink in. "And then we're going to talk some more."

Jaimee stiffened. "Ye aren't going to take the dagger off me?"

"No, Jaimee. I'm going to trust ye."

Jaimee scowled. What new game was this? "But I just tried to geld ye with my dirk?"

His mouth twisted into a grin. "Aye."

"And what makes ye think I won't try again?"

"Ye won't."

Jaimee ground her teeth. God's teeth, he was conceited. "And after I put my blade away, ye just want to *talk*?"

"Aye."

Jaimee stared up at him, her pulse now fluttering at the base of her throat. "So ... ye won't ravish me?"

He cocked an eyebrow. "I already said I wouldn't."

"I want yer word." What was she doing, asking this man to swear to anything? Wasn't that what had gotten her in this mess?

"And ye have it," he replied smoothly.

Jaimee heaved in a deep breath. "Release me then."

And he did.

Alexander Gunn's grip on her wrist, and on her other arm, released. An instant later, he stepped back.

Their gazes remained fused for an instant, and then Jaimee slowly sheathed the dirk.

What are ye doing? her mind screamed. *Now's yer chance. Kill the bastard!*

But they'd made an agreement.

"Very well." She bit out the words. "Talk."

16

I SEE YE

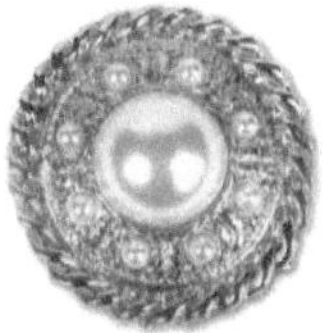

GUNN CROSSED TO the saddle and unstrapped a thick woolen cloak and a sheepskin. "Let's take a seat … under the lee of the rock. We might as well be comfortable."

Jaimee folded her arms across her chest, watching as he loosened his stallion's girth and hobbled the animal so that it could graze yet not wander off. He then spread out the sheepskin against the rock wall. A moment later, he lowered himself down onto it. "Yer throne awaits, My Lady."

Grinding her jaw, Jaimee reluctantly approached. His teasing unbalanced her; it didn't sit with the brutish image she had of him. However, she did as bid, seating herself on the sheepskin as far from Gunn as possible.

"Here." He handed her the cloak. "Put this about yer shoulders. The night will cool off shortly."

Jaimee gave a stiff nod, taking the cloak from him. She'd lost her woolen shawl when he'd grabbed her on the riverbank.

Her chest constricted then, as she thought of her panicked brothers. They would be searching for her now.

They'll also have discovered that Alexander Gunn is missing.

A shiver went through Jaimee as she imagined Connor and Morgan's rage.

"Connor will kill ye for this," she murmured, no anger in her voice now. "Ye do realize that?"

Gunn snorted. "He can try."

Jaimee cast the man a look. Even under the lee of the rock, starlight bathed the cruelly handsome lines of his face. The confidence in his voice, the total lack of fear, awed her.

"So, the rumors about ye are true," she murmured. "Ye aren't like other men."

"And how am I different?" he drawled, clearly amused by the observation.

"It's as if no heart beats in yer chest," she continued. "As if the blood that runs through yer veins is as cold as a loch in winter. Ye fear nothing. Ye are devoid of mercy. Incapable of love."

Silence followed these words. The night was still, save for the occasional snort from Gunn's horse as it moved around nearby. He'd chosen a lonely spot for this talk.

"If that's how others see me, it's for the best," he finally answered. His voice was strange, more subdued than earlier. "A man's reputation is everything ... as yer clan-chief has recently discovered. Any perceived weakness can ruin him."

Jaimee swallowed the urge to snort. Weakness wasn't Alexander Gunn's problem. He was as strong as a mountain and just as hard. Moments passed, while she studied his face. The starlight emphasized the pale scar that slashed down his left cheek.

"That scar," she said finally. "How did ye get it?" As soon as the words were out, Jaimee cursed herself. She hadn't meant to give her curiosity voice, yet the question slipped out unbidden.

"My brother Tavish gave it to me," he replied. "It was years ago now ... during a drunken fight over a lass. I bested him in the end, yet Tav made sure he left me with a reminder of that day." Gunn flashed her a grim smile. "He was aiming for my eye but missed."

Jaimee clutched at the cloak around her shoulders. "What a dreadful family ye have."

"Aye, but the name 'Gunn' strikes fear in our enemies' hearts all the same."

"So, everyone fears ye," she replied with a shake of her head, "but that'll be cold comfort when ye lie on yer deathbed and not one soul sheds a tear."

Silence fell between them. "Ye are probably right, Jaimee," Gunn said eventually. Once again, his voice had altered, softened. "But maybe that's why ye and I are here tonight ... perhaps I want at least one person to grieve for me when I'm gone."

Jaimee stiffened. Mortification built in the center of her chest then, as the full implication of his words sank in. It flooded through her limbs, as if she'd just soaked up to the neck in a hot bath. "Me?"

"Aye. I've never met a woman like ye," he replied, his voice growing strained. "Yer strong will and sharp mind are only equaled by yer beauty." Jaimee stared at him as if he'd just taken leave of his senses, yet Gunn pressed on. "Wed me, and return to Castle Gunn as my wife. Ye would want for nothing, I promise ye."

Jaimee's mouth thinned, her temper quickening. "I have no wish to live in a gilded cage, Gunn," she replied, her tone hardening. "Cease this nonsense."

"Ye think I'd cage ye?" Gunn shifted then and swiveled to face her. "But I wouldn't. Ye are fiery and proud ... yet I'd not tame ye. And I vow I'd never lay a finger on ye. *Never*." Jaimee inhaled sharply, yet heedless to her surprise, he continued, his voice low and forceful. "I see ye, Jaimee Mackay. Ye were never meant to be confined ... but more than freedom it is love that ye seek. I see it in yer eyes. I hear it in yer voice. And I feel it ... right now in the air between us. Do ye deny it?"

Jaimee stopped breathing entirely as she stared back at him. She wanted to fling his words back at him, yet she couldn't. Judas, how had the man managed it? How had he been able to peel back her defenses and see straight into her heart?

His words made an ache rise under her breastbone.

He'd spoken the truth. Love *was* what she wanted. She also wanted fire, passion, and a devotion that would outlive even her own mortal life. Her belly clenched. It was a dangerous desire, one that could result in foolish behavior. Better to grow into love from an initial liking and respect. A man like Robin Mackay would provide a safe haven—but Alexander Gunn, a man who set her blood aflame, would be her ruin.

"Ye realize I can never wed a Gunn, don't ye?" she whispered then. "Some things are impossible."

He shifted closer to her. "We shall make them possible."

Lord, please ... make him stop. The pull between them was almost unbearable; it reeled her in, made sweat bead upon her skin.

"It's wrong," she whispered. She needed him to move away, to let the crisp night air rush in between them. Yet she couldn't move, couldn't speak.

Gunn shifted closer still, so that his knees nearly touched her thighs. Swallowing hard, Jaimee turned to face him.

"We can't," she whispered, despising the tremor in her voice. What the devil had come over her? The man had abducted her for pity's sake. Just a short while ago, she'd tried to geld him, and now the air between them was thick with desire. "Ye need to take me back to my kin, Gunn."

"My name's Alex," he murmured. "Say it."

Jaimee stilled. *Alex.* Not Alexander. Not Gunn. It was too intimate. The name made him seem like a real person, not the ruthless warrior she hated.

"I can't," she gasped.

He took hold of her hand then. It was a gentle grasp, yet it caused shock to ripple up her arm. And then, to her horror, he placed her palm upon his chest. He wore a linen lèine, and the heat of his skin through the material was a brand against her palm. But even more disconcerting was the beat of his heart. It pounded wildly against her hand.

"Say it," he whispered.

Jaimee swallowed once more, before licking her lips. "Alex."

The tempo of his pulse under her palm seemed to quicken further. It bucked like a wild pony.

He leaned in then, his breath caressing her cheek. "Kiss me."

Excitement pulsed in the cradle of her hips, even as she sucked in a shocked breath at his words. She didn't understand him. Their faces were so close, all he had to do was lean in and claim what he wanted.

But Alexander Gunn wanted her to come to him.

She didn't want to, and yet she did. His nearness was overwhelming, and the ragged sound of his breathing made her limbs melt.

She had no idea desire could be like this—utterly consuming. At present, she was struggling to remember who she was, who he was, to recall all the reasons she loathed him.

Long moments passed, and then she swayed toward him.

Her lips brushed his.

Gunn didn't move. He didn't reach for her. He just went still.

His lips were warm and soft, so different to how she'd expected—and aye, she'd imagined what he'd be like to kiss, even if she'd hated herself afterward.

Trembling, Jaimee brushed her lips over his once again. Feather-light—a brush of butterfly wings.

A soft sound issued from his throat, a pained moan. But still, he didn't reach for her.

A thrill rippled through Jaimee. That sound, so primal and yet oddly vulnerable, swept away the last of her reserve.

Her lips touched his once more, this time in a steady pressure.

And then Alexander Gunn kissed her back. His mouth moved over hers, teasing and testing. A moment later, his tongue swept her lips apart.

Jaimee gasped.

His arms went around her, and he pulled her toward him so that she sat astride him upon the sheepskin. With another groan that sounded as if it had been ripped from deep within him, Gunn plundered her mouth.

It was a dominant, hot kiss, unlike anything Jaimee had ever experienced in her brief embraces, and it set her on fire.

He held her by the shoulders in a firm grip. However, not so tight that she couldn't break away if she so wished.

His mouth was wicked.

His tongue slid against hers before it tickled the roof of her mouth. His teeth then grazed her lips, and he gently bit down on her lower one.

An ache pulsed between Jaimee's thighs, a restlessness that made a soft cry rise within her.

And still, Gunn didn't haul her close, didn't press his body against hers. She was perched upon his lap, keenly aware of the hard muscles of his thighs under hers. Slowly, his hands slid up from her shoulders to cup her face.

His mouth feasted on hers, deepening the kiss till she was weak and boneless.

Heart pounding, she kissed him back. She was untutored, yet she let instinct guide her. He tasted delicious, like wood smoke and summer wine, and as she tangled her tongue with his, she heard the rumble of another groan rise within him, felt it upon the palm she still held against his chest.

Her fingertips curled, her nails digging into his flesh through the thin material.

His pulse had quickened further. His heart now thudded hard against her palm.

Jaimee gently bit his lower lip, mimicking the gesture that had made lust spike through her loins.

His groan turned to a growl.

Breathing hard, he drew away from her, his hands sliding back down to her shoulders. He gently pushed her back, his grip tightening.

It was hard not to pant, not to let a moan of need escape her. However, Jaimee managed to restrain herself.

“Come away with me, Jaimee,” he rasped. “Be my wife.”

17

YER FINAL WORD

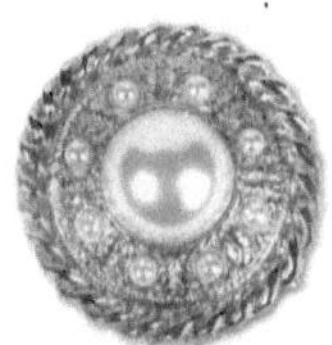

JAIMEE STARED AT Alexander Gunn. His expression was hungry, his gaze gleaming in the starlight.

"No," she whispered.

"So, ye are a Mackay, and I'm a Gunn," he replied, his voice still rough in the aftermath of their kiss. "It matters not."

"Ye aren't thinking straight." Now that he wasn't kissing her, the fog that had completely addled her wits drew back. Suddenly, the reality of what she'd just done hit her like a sack of stones in the face.

What in Hades are ye doing kissing this man?

"Yer father would rather ye wed a rabid dog than a Mackay," she continued, her voice hardening, "and I would never live amongst the Gunns." Resolve settled within her as she said the words. She meant them. "Ever."

His hold on her shoulders slackened, although he didn't drop his hands. "We aren't a pack of two-headed gargoyles, lass. Castle Gunn is a fine holding. Ye would live in comfort." He paused then, his gaze turning steely. "And I would never let any harm befall ye."

Jaimee drew in a deep breath. He wasn't listening. "My father died on a Gunn blade," she reminded him, her voice catching just a little. "I will never forget that …

and I don't want to. It matters not how bonny yer home is—I will never set foot there."

She straightened up and met his eye properly.

His hands still rested upon her shoulders, and she could feel the tension in his heavily muscled thighs, for she remained perched upon his lap. It was too intimate— everything they'd done was far too intimate.

"So, ye will wed another man?" Alexander asked. His voice was low and rough. "Ye'd deny what we have?"

Jaimee's spine stiffened. God's teeth, he was arrogant. "We don't *have* anything," she replied between gritted teeth. Aye, just one touch from this man turned her witless, but that wasn't love. It was madness. "I'm going to do what I should have months ago."

"Yer *duty*?"

She nodded. "It's time."

Silence stretched out between them.

"So, that's yer final word on the matter?" he asked finally, his voice stony now.

"Aye," she whispered back.

Nervousness feathered through her then, and her breathing quickened. *Daft woman, what have ye done?*

She'd just kissed him, and it hadn't been a peck on the cheek but a sensual mating of the mouths that promised so much more.

If he lifted her skirts now and forced himself on her, she would be unable to fight him off. She still wore the dirk at her hip, yet she knew she wouldn't be able to draw it against him.

Not now.

The truth was that she ached for him. Yet letting him take her maidenhead would be her ruin, they both knew it, if she didn't become his wife.

But as the moments drew out, wildness reached out for her, called like a kelpie's song. Jaimee fought it with an iron will she hadn't even realized she possessed.

"As soon as the sun rises, I want ye to take me back to my kin," she said, splintering the tension that simmered between them. "Will ye?"

This was it, the moment of truth.

Would Alexander Gunn heed her wishes, or would he take what he wanted like the brute she believed him to be?

Heartbeats stretched out, and then his hands dropped from her shoulders. "Aye," he replied, his voice flat. "If that is what ye wish."

The dawn was a long time coming. The night stretched out seemingly endless and silent before them. Jaimee leaned against the rock wall, her knees pulled up against her chest, the cloak Gunn had given her wrapped close.

It warded off the chill, yet not the distracting presence of the man seated just a foot away.

Mercifully, Alexander Gunn didn't try to engage her in talk again. They'd had the conversation he'd wanted, only it hadn't gone as he'd hoped.

Even now, she couldn't believe the man wanted to wed her. Clearly, a strange obsession, a compulsion, had settled over him in Inverness, and he'd come to Halladale to claim her as his wife.

It was folly, and yet the things he'd said to her had unleashed something within Jaimee.

I see ye, Jaimee Mackay ... it is love that ye seek.

Powerful words—ones that had stripped away her defenses. Like parched earth after a drought, she'd soaked them up. No wonder she'd kissed him when he'd asked. Even murmuring the familiar form of his first name had done something to her.

Alex.

Jaimee squeezed her eyes shut, trying to block out the memory of that devastating kiss and failing.

The morning couldn't come soon enough.

The night lingered, and Jaimee must have dozed for a while against the wall, for when she opened her eyes, she spied Gunn's broad-shouldered outline move out from under the overhang. He then walked across to his horse.

"The sun is rising," he announced.

Jaimee climbed to her feet, gathered up the sheepskin, and rolled it up, before emerging from the overhang. Glancing to the east, she saw that indeed dawn was breaking. Ribbons of rose and crimson festooned the sky.

Jaimee approached Gunn and handed him the sheepskin. She then began to remove the cloak.

"Keep the mantle," he murmured. "The morning air has a bite to it."

He wasn't lying. Their breaths steamed, and a heavy dew lay around them; they were close to the first frost of autumn.

Jaimee nodded her thanks.

Gunn met her gaze then. His handsome face was aloof, although those purple-grey eyes burned into her. "We'd better go now."

"Ye realize this is going to be ugly," she warned him. "My brothers will be desperate by now ... they'll want blood."

Gunn merely cocked his head, his lips lifting at the corners in that cocky half-smile she'd come to recognize. "I knew what I was doing, Jaimee, when I took ye," he replied. "I understood there would be consequences, but I didn't care. I still don't."

A lump rose in Jaimee's throat as she stared up at him.

"Curse ye, Gunn," she muttered. The bastard was goading her. "Of course ... if I ride away with ye to Castle Gunn, I can prevent this. Ye won't have to fight Connor to the death, and I won't have to watch either of ye die."

He shook his head, his half-smile fading. "Ye think this is blackmail?"

"Aye. Ye are certainly capable of it."

They stared at each other for a heartbeat longer, before he growled, "I could have taken ye last night. I could tie ye up right now and carry ye back to Castle Gunn ... but I have let this be yer decision."

Jaimee took a step closer to him then, so they were nose-to-nose. "That's grand of ye ... since ye gave me no choice in the matter when ye abducted me last night. Ye started this, and now ye are going to punish me for spurning ye."

He stared down at her. The bastard didn't even have the good grace to deny her words.

"What ye did cannot be undone," Jaimee choked out. "My brother will kill ye."

"Does my life matter to ye then, Jaimee?" he asked softly, his gaze glinting in the dawn light.

"No," she spat, too fast. "Devil spawn! I hope he makes ye suffer before he kills ye. I hope he—"

Gunn's mouth crashed down on hers then, cutting her off. This kiss was different to the one the night before. That kiss had been hot yet sensual and languorous. But this embrace was fierce and possessive, with an edge of violence.

Jaimee's hand swung up to strike him across the face, yet he caught it. His fingers tightened, his touch searing her skin.

She gasped, her lips parting under his, and then she was kissing him back. Wildly.

There was no gentleness in this embrace, none at all.

Gunn let go of her wrist, and instead of attempting to strike him again, she reached up with both arms, linking them around his neck. Clinging to him, she let her head fall back.

His mouth left hers, tracing a line of fire down her exposed neck. Jaimee shivered under the sensual touch—a deep, breathy sigh loosing from her chest.

Gasping a curse, Gunn hauled her hard against him, so that their bodies were flush.

The feel of his large frame, all hard, unyielding muscle, made her gasp. An instant later, his mouth claimed hers once more.

Jaimee was falling, and there wasn't anything she could cling to but this man.

Their kisses were bruising now, yet she devoured him just as savagely as he did her. His arms went about her then, and he swung her around, taking her with him up to a tor that rose behind them. With her back pressed against cold rock, she arched toward him.

He slid a thigh between hers, spreading her wide. And then he lifted her against him before letting her core slide down the long hard length of his arousal. Layers of material separated them, yet she felt every inch of him all the same.

Jaimee's breathing caught in her throat.

Lord, how she wanted him.

This was so wrong, and yet she couldn't summon the will to stop him. The feel of his mouth on hers, the dominance in the way he touched her, made her shiver with need, made her feel as if her skin were too tight.

A large hand reached up, kneading her breast through her kirtle and lèine. Jaimee groaned into his mouth. He cupped the breast entirely, the friction of his palm against her aching nipple too much to bear.

She wanted him to rip off her clothes—for him to do all the things he'd whispered to her just three nights earlier. Indeed, she *wanted* him to feast on her nakedness and then sink deep into her flesh. She wanted it so much that her breathing now came in sobbing pants as she bit, licked, and sucked at his mouth.

And then Gunn pulled away.

He too was breathing hard, his broad chest rising and falling sharply. A flush stained his high cheekbones, and his gaze had darkened to deep purple. His lips were swollen from the violence of their kisses.

He stepped back from her then, and Jaimee swallowed a cry of disappointment.

"So, yer final word still stands then, Jaimee?" he asked, his gaze boring into hers. "I would give ye the moon and stars if I could, yet ye still won't come away with me ... won't be my wife?"

Something deep in Jaimee's chest twisted. Leaning back against the tor, her breathing coming in ragged gasps, she stared up at him. This passion between them had turned her witless and foolish. And he knew it too.

He hoped to catch her at a weak moment, yet he wouldn't.

Already the madness was fading, drawing back like winter mist. Swallowing hard, Jaimee shook her head. "Aye, it still stands," she gasped. "I will not wed ye, Gunn. Return me to my family."

18

STAND ASIDE, SISTER

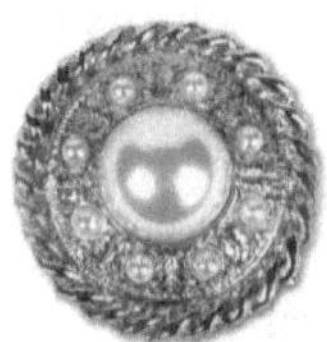

IT WAS A dramatic dawn. The pink and red streaks to the east grew deeper in color until it looked as if the sky were on fire.

It was beautiful, yet Jaimee thought the dawn sky had an ill-favored look. A 'Blood Dawn', such a sunrise was called. She suppressed a shudder at the name. Aye, it soon would be.

She rode before Alexander Gunn on the saddle, jolted against him with each stride his stallion took. He held her close, one arm wrapped around her torso. His grasp was more to prevent her from falling, yet the intimacy of the hold made her grind her teeth.

She could feel his hard body pressing against her back, and the heat of him burned like a coal against her, even through the thick cloak she wore.

Yet, mercifully, he didn't speak.

Enough had been said, and it seemed that whenever they spoke, passion ended up interrupting the conversation.

It was safer to remain silent.

Jaimee's lips still stung from the wildness of their last embrace. The tender skin between her thighs still throbbed from the feel of his arousal. It was as if he'd branded the feel of him on her. She couldn't get the memory out of her head.

They rode south-west, in the direction of the gathering, and as the land smoothed out and they left the rocky tors behind, Gunn urged his stallion into a swift canter. The animal ran easily, its feathered feet throwing out turf behind it. The horse carried the two of them as if they weighed nothing.

The last shadows of darkness had fled from the sky, and the fiery dawn was starting to fade to blue, when she spied horses on the horizon.

Jaimee's heart bucked against her breastbone.

"They've found us," she said, breaking the silence.

"Aye," Gunn murmured. "Sooner than I thought too."

But as the riders neared, Jaimee realized that it wasn't her brothers, or indeed any Mackay warriors, but the Gunns.

Alexander Gunn's brothers rode out front, their dark hair flying behind them. And when they reined their horses in either side of their elder brother, Jaimee observed the grim look on both men's faces.

All the men looked battered. Tavish Gunn sported a rapidly blackening eye, while blood leaked from one of William's nostrils. The youngest of the Gunn brothers held himself gingerly in the saddle as if his ribs were bruised. Behind the brothers, one of the warriors favored a bloodied arm.

"Ye've made us popular," Tavish greeted them. His gaze raked over Alexander and the woman perched before him, taking in the possessive way his brother held Jaimee.

Heat spread over her chest and up her neck. Were her lips still swollen? Was her hair a mess?

The knowing glint in Tavish's gaze told her the answer to both questions was 'aye'.

"Ye've got the Mackays in a right state," William muttered. "We barely escaped the camp with our hides."

Alexander Gunn snorted. "And yet here ye are, brother."

"Ye could have given us some advance warning," William shot back, a nerve flickering under one eye. "Given us time to prepare ourselves."

"It was better this way," Alexander replied, "Best ye knew nothing."

"So we couldn't betray ye?" Tavish growled. "Connor Mackay put his dirk to my throat. I swore that I didn't know where ye'd taken his sister ... but I thought he was going to kill me anyway."

"What stopped him?" Alexander asked.

Tavish's lip curled. "His wife pleaded for mercy on our behalf ... and he heeded her." His gaze shifted back to Jaimee then. "Have ye made her yers? I hope she was worth it."

Jaimee's body stiffened, fury tightening like a clenched fist under her ribcage. Her lips parted as she prepared to give Tavish Gunn the sharp edge of her tongue. However, Alexander Gunn beat her to it.

"No, Tav. I only took her away to talk. I proposed, and the lady refused."

Tavish's gaze narrowed. "*What?*"

"Come on, brother. None of us are fools," William cut in as he wiped at his bloody nose. "Ye have spent the night swiving the woman, and now we're taking her back to Castle Gunn."

"Aye, canny bastard," Tavish added with a harsh smile. "No better way to hit the Mackays of Farr where it hurts the most."

Jaimee ground her teeth as she bit back cutting words.

Tavish glanced back over his shoulder then, his gaze sweeping the southern horizon. "We should move on ... the Mackays let us go once they realized we had nothing to do with the lass's abduction ... but that doesn't mean they won't ride in this direction as well."

"I wasn't japing with ye," Alexander Gunn growled, ignoring his brother's warning. "Jaimee Mackay doesn't wish to wed me, and so I'm taking her back to her kin."

Both brothers stared at him as if he'd lost his wits.

"Connor Mackay wants yer guts, brother," Tavish replied with a scowl. "Ye don't want to face him right now."

Next to Tavish, William's mouth thinned. "I'm not going back there."

Silence fell then, the air between the brothers growing charged. Tavish's face went hard. His hand went to the handle of his dirk, although he didn't draw the weapon. "Enough of this nonsense." His voice roughened. "Let's take the woman home with us. At least her presence should appease father."

Alexander Gunn snorted. Although Jaimee sat before him, and as such she couldn't see his face, she could feel the cold sweep of his gaze as he assessed his brothers. "What's this?" he drawled. "Have yer balls shrunk to the size of walnuts overnight?"

Tavish sneered, his fingers tightening over the hilt of his blade. "If ye want to die, I can save ye the trouble of facing the Mackays."

"I suggest ye keep yer dirk in its sheath, for now, Tav," Alexander replied. "Draw it on me, and ye'll regret it."

Tavish snarled. Next to him, William clenched his jaw, his gaze flicking between his elder brothers.

Jaimee's breathing stilled. From what Alexander had told her of their relationship, she wouldn't be surprised if the brothers drew their dirks on each other. It wouldn't be the first time.

But moments passed, and nothing happened.

Tavish muttered a low curse. "Selfish bastard. Ye're going to get the lot of us killed."

"Enough talk." Alexander urged his stallion on then—and his brothers drew their horses aside to let him pass, as did his warriors. "Come … Chieftain Mackay awaits."

They didn't meet with Connor on the way into the camp. Yet he was waiting for them on the edge of the field where the games had taken place. Morgan and his warriors were with him, as were their lathered horses. They'd clearly just returned from searching for Jaimee.

A group of warriors—Mackays and those allies who hadn't already returned home—had gathered. Keira and Maggie were there too. Keira didn't carry her bairn with her this morning; she would have left Rose with her maid. And just as well, for although the bairn was too small to know what was going on around her, the scene that was about to unfold didn't need to be witnessed by a babe.

The sight of both her sisters-by-marriage standing there—faces ashen, jaws clenched, and hands on hips— made affection rush through Jaimee. Tears blurred her vision then, for the first time since Gunn had swept her away.

Keira and Maggie loved her. They looked ready to tear Alexander Gunn to pieces between them.

However, when her attention shifted to her brothers, a chill swept over Jaimee.

They were worryingly still. Both stood there rigid, the breeze stirring their hair, their gazes boring into her. Their faces were carved from stone. A nerve flickered under Connor's eye, and Morgan's jaw was bunched.

Their hands hung by their sides, in easy reach of their dirks.

No one spoke as Gunn slowed his stallion to a walk and approached the Mackays. Behind them, the Gunn brothers and warriors also slowed their mounts. Jaimee didn't need to glance over her shoulder to take note of the tension, the aggression that rippled off them. She could taste it.

Another pitched battle was about to erupt.

"So, ye brought my sister back," Connor's voice, hoarse with anger, sliced the air then. "After ye raped her."

"I haven't raped her, Mackay," Alexander Gunn replied, his voice a low, arrogant drawl. "Fear not. Her virtue is still intact."

Connor's face twisted at this, and Jaimee's heart started pounding in her throat.

Mother Mary, what was Gunn doing? Did he actually want a dirk in the belly?

"He speaks the truth, Connor," she said then, her voice catching. "Gunn didn't ravish me."

Connor's lip curled, his gaze settling upon her face.

Jaimee tensed. Of course, just like Tavish, he would see her swollen lips and disheveled hair. He would know that Gunn *had* touched her, even if he hadn't taken her maidenhead.

Connor let out a string of growled curses then, each filthier than the last. Jaimee felt herself blanch. She'd never heard her brother say such things before. Even from a few yards distant, she could feel the rage that pulsed off him.

"Get down, Jaimee," he rasped. "Go to Keira and Maggie. Let me deal with this pig."

"Connor," she whispered. "I don't want any bloodshed. This can't—"

"Get down." His order cracked like a whip in the morning air.

Trembling, she held his gaze.

"Do as he says, lass," Gunn murmured. "This is between us now."

"Aye, it is," Connor ground out the words. "This has been brewing for a while, Gunn. I've overlooked too much. But when ye steal my sister ... when ye lay yer filthy hands upon her ... ye go too far."

"He didn't abduct me," Jaimee gasped.

Of course, it was a lie, but she couldn't let this continue. She couldn't let Connor go up against Alexander Gunn. He was too angry. She'd once heard that men often died when they went into a fight driven by rage. It blinded them, made them careless. It was what had claimed Rory Mackay's life at Harpsdale. Morgan had told her afterward, about how their father waded into battle without a thought to his own safety.

Jaimee couldn't let Connor do the same.

She wouldn't.

"I went with Gunn willingly," she continued, holding her brother's eye. It took all her will not to drop her gaze, not to let the lie show on her face. But she fought the urge and brazened the moment out.

Gunn had removed his arm from around her waist, yet she felt his body go rigid all the same, and heard the sharp intake of breath.

Ignoring his reaction, Jaimee plowed on. "He wanted to talk, and I agreed. We rode to a place where we wouldn't be disturbed, and Gunn proposed to me. I refused him, and when dawn rose, we made our way back here." She sucked in a deep breath of her own. "That's what happened."

Connor stared back at her, horror lighting in his eyes. "What?" he croaked.

"Jaimee." Gunn's voice was a warning rumble behind her. "What are ye doing?"

She ignored him, instead replying to her brother, "It's the truth." She pushed back the cloak then, to reveal the dirk at her side. "Look! If he abducted me, why would Gunn let me remain armed?"

All of them stared at the dirk then. Beside Connor, the horror on Morgan's face was almost comical. "Why, Jaimee?" he gasped.

"It matters not." Jaimee threw her leg over the saddle then and slid to the ground. Taking off her cloak, she bundled it up and strapped it behind the saddle, next to the sheepskin they'd sat on overnight.

All the while, she ignored Gunn's gaze as it bored into her. She couldn't look at him, not while she did this.

She then moved forward, halting between Alexander Gunn and her brothers. "The important thing is that I have returned to ye, safe and well."

Connor's face turned feral, his green eyes blazing. "Do ye understand the risk ye put yerself in?" he choked out. "He could have murdered ye."

"Jaimee," Alexander Gunn spoke once more. His voice was rough. She knew she'd shocked him with her false admission, and when she finally glanced over her shoulder at him, she saw he was scowling, his stormy eyes blazing. "Enough. Don't do this."

Shaking her head, Jaimee turned her back on him. She then speared her brother with a hard look. Inside she felt sick. Her belly was in knots, and her heart was pounding so loudly she was sure everyone could hear it. But outwardly she maintained her cool.

No blood will be shed here.

"Let him go, Connor," she said, her voice still holding steady.

The laird of Farr growled another curse and then drew his dirk. "Stand aside, sister."

19

PLEASE, ALEX

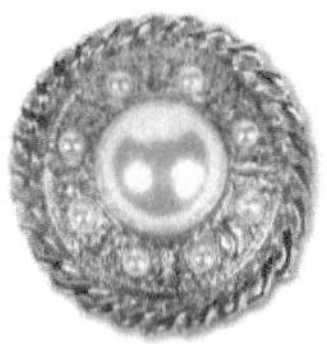

JAIMEE'S HEART LEAPED when she heard Alexander Gunn dismount behind her, the heavy thud of his feet hitting the dusty ground.

No!

She'd upset her kin, had lied to them, to prevent a fight, but it was all for no good.

Connor and Gunn were going to draw dirks against each other nonetheless.

Connor nodded to Morgan then. "Make sure Jaimee stays out of the way."

Morgan nodded and, jaw clenched, moved toward her.

Panic exploded in Jaimee's breast. Things were spiraling out of control. She had to stop it.

Not knowing what else to do, she drew her dirk and stepped in front of Gunn. She then brandished the blade at Morgan.

He stopped short, his green eyes narrowing in disbelief. "What are ye doing?"

"Stopping this before any of ye do something ye regret."

"Put the dagger away."

"No. Ye back off, Morgan." Her gaze swiveled to Connor then. He was staring at her as if she'd just smacked him around the head. "And ye too."

The hand that gripped the dirk-hilt felt sweaty. She'd shown how unskilled she was with Gunn the night before. He'd disarmed her as easily as if she'd been a child. However, maybe she could brazen this out—shock her brothers into leaving this be.

"Please, Jaimee," Keira called out. Her pale face was now stricken. "Ye'll get hurt."

Jaimee ignored her. Instead, she took a step back, halting when she came up hard against a wall of muscle and leather: Alexander Gunn.

"Have ye lost yer wits?" Connor growled, his voice hoarse, his eyes wide. "Why would ye defend this man?"

"Jaimee," Gunn interrupted then, his own voice low and hard. "Ye can't prevent this. Go with Morgan now. Let Connor and I face each other."

It was a command, and she could hear the anger simmering beneath.

She was only trying to help, yet she was dishonoring him.

A warrior like Alexander Gunn didn't need a woman to protect him.

The rasp of steel against leather sounded once more, as Gunn drew his dirk.

"No!" Jaimee whirled on him. "Put yer dirk away, get on yer horse, and go home. I can't let ye do this. I won't let ye!"

He stared down at her, and for the first time in their acquaintance, she saw uncertainty flare in Alexander Gunn's grey eyes. Her behavior unbalanced him, confused him. He'd been ready to face her brothers, and had shown no fear whatsoever, yet her interference had thrown him. She saw it in the way his mouth firmed, the way tension rippled through his bearded jaw.

"I need ye to do this," she whispered, ignoring the stares boring into her back. "For me. If ye have any real feelings for me, any at all, ye will grant me this." She heaved in a deep breath. "Please, Alex."

He gazed at her, stunned. Likewise, the gathered crowd went deathly quiet.

Their eyes locked, and Alexander Gunn's grey gaze darkened to deep purple. Tension now rippled across his face. He then swallowed, his throat bobbing.

"Please," she whispered once more. Pleading had become a habit of late when it came to this man—an irony, for Jaimee Mackay wasn't a woman who begged for anything. She was too proud for that, and yet the situation with Alexander Gunn had brought her to her knees.

He was still her enemy, yet she couldn't bring herself to loathe him. Something had shifted within her. She now saw him as a man, an individual rather than an object of hate.

He'd kissed her, twice, and she'd felt the heat of his body, the hammer of his pulse against her palm.

She didn't understand how or why, but a link had been forged between them the night before.

If Connor killed him, she'd never recover from it.

"Please," she repeated, a tremble in her voice. "I will never ask anything else of ye. Just this one thing."

Alexander Gunn swallowed once more, and then he stepped back from her and sheathed his dagger.

"We're not finished here, Gunn." Connor's voice lashed across the field.

However, the Gunn first-born merely vaulted up onto his stallion's back. He then looked down at Jaimee, his gaze searching her face.

"Are ye listening, man?" Connor shouted. "Stop looking at my sister, and answer me!"

Gunn tore his gaze from Jaimee and shifted his attention behind her. Jaimee didn't turn to look at her brothers; she couldn't bear to do so. She couldn't stand to see the rage on their faces and disappointment in their eyes.

"Yer sister has made a request of me, and I will do as she asks," Gunn replied. His voice was flat, emotionless—at odds with the storm raging in his eyes.

"If ye want blood, ye will have to come after me, Mackay."

And with that, he turned his stallion.

Jaimee jumped back as the huge beast pivoted on its hindquarters. Behind Gunn, his brothers and warriors did likewise, and then the thunder of hooves split the crisp morning air.

Sheathing her dirk, Jaimee looked on as Alexander Gunn rode away.

She remained there, watching the Gunn party go, her body quivering with tension. Any moment now, she'd see her brothers racing past her on their own horses, giving chase.

But it had gone silent behind her. And somehow, although she'd gotten her wish, the hush was so much worse.

Dragging in a steadying breath, and then another, Jaimee squared her shoulders.

And then she turned to face them.

The look on Connor's face was a punch to the gut.

He was staring at her as if she were a stranger.

"*Alex*?" he said, his voice a low rasp. "So that's how it is?" A nerve ticked under one eye.

Jaimee swallowed hard. "I didn't lie with the man," she replied, irritation spiking within her. She shouldn't need to keep repeating this, yet her brother wasn't listening to her this morning. "But there *is* a connection between us."

She shifted her attention to Morgan then. He was still staring at her as if a bean-nighe stood before him. Jaimee wasn't an omen of death from the netherworld, yet she wasn't behaving like the sister he thought he knew either.

Jaimee didn't understand her own behavior either; instinct had driven her.

And yet, as the weight of her actions settled upon her, she didn't feel any shame, any regret.

After spending the night with Alexander Gunn, she felt as if she'd walked through fire. Although the experience hadn't incinerated her, she now bore scorch marks upon her soul.

He'd offered her the thing she longed for above all else, and she'd rejected him.

Straightening her spine, Jaimee stared her brothers down. She wasn't to blame for this mess—Gunn was—yet the night she'd spent with the enemy had changed the way she saw things. The last vestiges of her girlhood had sloughed away, and a strange calmness now settled over her.

Nothing would be the same after this—and that included her relationship with her siblings.

Neither of Alexander's brothers spoke for a long while after they left the Mackays.

He was grateful for their silence. The mood he was in at present, he'd happily slit both their throats.

Please, Alex.

That was all it had taken.

Like a magic charm, the sound of his name upon that woman's lips had turned him into her servant.

At that moment, she could have asked him for anything.

But as the distance grew between him and Jaimee, fury kindled in Alexander's belly—a rage that burned hotter with each passing furlong.

He wasn't even sure where the anger was directed.

At Connor Mackay for thwarting him?

At his brothers for challenging him?

At Jaimee for making him look weak in front of her kin and his?

At himself for doing her bidding like some meek fool?

Fury cramped his belly and caused a red haze to settle over his vision.

Jaimee Mackay had done something to him. In just one word, she'd bent him to her will. She'd done what no other had ever managed—and he almost wished she'd sunk her dirk blade into his belly instead.

Why hadn't she told her brother that he'd abducted her? It had been her chance for revenge, yet she hadn't taken it. Instead, she'd protected him and then pleaded with him.

And she'd done so in front of her brothers and some of her suitors. What would happen to her now?

It was only when they crossed the mountain pass and began their descent into Gunn lands that Tavish finally spoke. He rode his horse up to where Alexander led the column, so that they traveled shoulder-to-shoulder.

"It doesn't look like the Mackays are coming after us," he noted coolly.

Alexander grunted. He was almost disappointed. In truth, he'd itched to lunge at Connor Mackay during that altercation. If Jaimee hadn't been blocking his path, hadn't put herself in harm's way, he would have attacked. Blood-lust still sang in Alexander's veins now, demanding violence.

But then the memory of the look on Jaimee's face, the desperation in those pine-green eyes as she'd stared up at him, knifed Alexander in the guts.

Curse her, she had tormented him, teased him, and then thwarted him, in just the space of a few hours.

He'd been a fool to abduct the woman—had made a grave error in succumbing to his base desires—and now he was paying the price.

20

GOING HOME

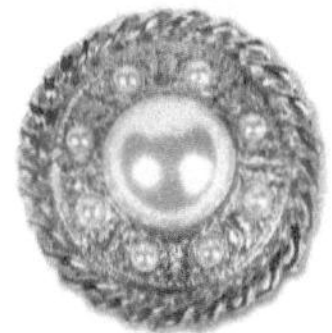

THE GATHERING WAS over. The fighting between the Mackays had been serious enough to stop the games, but the events that had unfolded afterward had firmly put an end to any suitor claiming Jaimee Mackay's hand.

In the past, Jaimee would have been relieved. Yet, as she watched Robin Mackay of Melness ride off with his men, a sense of fatalism settled heavily in her belly.

The warrior, who'd once shown so much interest in her, and whom she'd been about to agree to wed, hadn't been able to look her in the eye this morning.

None of them had.

Robin Mackay had been among the crowd who'd watched the altercation at dawn. He'd seen her defend Alexander Gunn. He'd seen her stand up to Connor.

Nothing more needed to be said.

Drawing her woolen cloak close, Jaimee turned back to where her brother's men had just finished saddling the horses. They were all packed up now; only the trampled grass and the blackened fire pits remained as evidence of their residence here.

The Strath of Halladale would be left empty once more, until the next time the Mackays gathered.

Jaimee drew in a deep breath. The next gathering wouldn't be held in her honor. If one of her former suitors was still interested in wedding her, they could seek her out at Farr Castle.

However, she wondered how many of them would make the effort. She hoped none of them would bother. She wasn't trying to be difficult—for she'd been ready to wed Robin Mackay—but after the night she'd spent in Alexander Gunn's company, she felt different. The brute had created a longing in her that gnawed in her belly like hunger. She'd rejected his offer—she'd had to—but that didn't mean she didn't yearn for him.

It was a bitter irony that the one man who could give her what she craved was someone she could never accept.

Jaimee moved across to her bay gelding, Tor. Her maid, Fern, had already mounted her shaggy garron and was waiting for Jaimee. The lass's eyes were full of questions. Like the rest of the camp, she'd heard what had transpired. Fern now watched Jaimee with a wary expression, as if she feared what she'd do next.

Jaimee didn't blame her. She hardly knew herself these days.

Mounting Tor, Jaimee adjusted her skirts and pulled up the hood of her cloak. It cast her face into shadow and afforded her a little privacy from prying eyes.

At least her brothers were ignoring her for the moment; it gave her space to sort through her own thoughts, to try and understand what had transpired.

She'd expected Connor to rage in the aftermath. But apart from a few cutting words, he hadn't. Likewise, Morgan had turned from her, his back stiff with outrage as he'd stalked away. It was as if neither of her brothers trusted themselves to talk to her.

Jaimee's mouth flattened into a thin line, hurt warring with ire. It didn't matter what she did, she was damned.

She'd tried to do the right thing, but Connor merely saw her as reckless, foolish, and interfering.

No man wanted his sister putting herself between him and his mortal enemy. She'd intervened to prevent blood from being spilled, yet that didn't matter to

Connor. Although she hadn't meant to, Jaimee had dishonored him.

The sight of his home on the horizon made Alexander's chest tighten with pride. Castle Gunn was splendid and strong, a symbol of his clan's might. It didn't matter that he'd grown up here, he never tired of gazing upon it. Every time he approached the fortress, Alexander found himself entranced.

The castle appeared like the lair of some great bird. It had a dramatic setting, here in the heart of Caithness, perched on a peninsula rock looking over the sea. High curtain walls shielded the bailey from the elements, although a three-level stone keep rose high above the walls, its crenelated top outlined against the windy sky.

Gaze still upon the fortress, Alexander's mouth thinned. His father awaited him there—and when he heard about what his eldest son had been up to, he wouldn't be best pleased.

Let him choke on it.

Alexander led the party across a narrow wooden bridge toward the keep. A stone guard tower looked down upon the arrivals. The men there waved, and he raised a lazy hand to acknowledge them.

The horses' hooves clattered against the wooden bridge. Many feet below, waves broke and foamed against the rocks. Seabirds whirled around them, their cries echoing off the cliff-face and the castle walls.

Alexander's mouth softened into a half-smile.

The sound of home. His love for this castle and the land it held dominion over was the only thing that had ever truly moved him.

Until Jaimee Mackay.

His expression turned hard once more. *Stop thinking about her.*

Alexander urged his stallion through the archway and into Castle Gunn's bailey.

Jaimee stole his peace.

It had taken them two days to reach Castle Gunn after leaving the Strath of Halladale. The journey had largely been a silent one, although Alexander had caught both his brothers watching him at times, a speculative look in their eyes.

He didn't like that look.

Aye, Tavish and Will didn't say much, but they didn't need to. They'd just witnessed a woman command their brother—and watched as he did her bidding. Alexander would have to watch his back.

Contemplating this, he drew up Destroyer in the midst of the bailey and swung down. He was about to lead the beast into the stables when a familiar voice hailed him from the steps to the keep.

"Ho, brothers. We were about to send out a search party!"

Roy Gunn descended the steps and swaggered toward him. The third-born of the six Gunn brothers, Roy was one that Alexander had often clashed with over the years. Like Tavish, he begrudged not being their father's heir. However, he was more obvious about his resentment than Tavish.

Big, dark-haired, and battle-scarred, Roy was possibly the broadest and strongest of all of them. However, what he had in brawn, he lacked in intellect. Roy Gunn didn't have the cunning of some of his other brothers.

Roy stopped a few yards back from Alexander and folded beefy arms across his chest. "What kept ye?"

"Sheep rustlers," Tavish called out. "Tricky bastards led us on a merry chase."

Roy cocked a dark eyebrow, while Alexander shot Tavish a questioning look. He'd thought he'd spill the news about their adventures with the Mackays, the moment they arrived. He'd braced himself for it.

Yet both Tavish and Will wore hooded expressions this afternoon. Perhaps they were waiting till they saw their father before dropping Alexander in the shit.

"*Mackay* sheep rustlers?" Roy asked, harshness creeping into his voice.

"Aye, we think so," Will replied, swinging down from his own horse. "Although none were left alive once we were through with them."

Roy's dark brows crashed together. "Where was this then?"

"Just west of Camster," Will answered blithely.

"Aye," Alexander added, realizing that he hadn't yet said a word. "Maddoc Gunn has been losing flocks of late … and we caught the thieves at it."

He then cast another glance at Tavish and Will.

Their faces still gave nothing away.

"Did we miss anything in our absence?" Alexander asked, his attention drifting back to Roy.

"Aye." His brother grinned then, an unpleasant expression with a vindictive edge to it. "Ye have a visit from the north, brother. Ramsay Oliphant is here … and he has brought his daughter."

"I was worried we would miss ye, Alexander," Ramsay Oliphant boomed from the far end of the clan-chief's table. "Robina would have been mightily disappointed." He then nudged the young woman seated next to him with his elbow. "Isn't that right, lass?"

Alexander tensed. Oliphant wasn't wasting time tonight. His arse had barely touched the bench seat when the man pounced.

They'd arrived back in time for supper. Outside the wind had picked up. It now howled against the thick stone walls and clawed at the wooden shutters. But inside the great hall of Castle Gunn, they were sheltered from the elements. Two huge hearths burned at either end of the space, and a fug of smoke hung under the heavy beams crisscrossing overhead. It was loud inside the great hall this evening. His father's warriors and their families lined the long wooden benches, and mead, ale, and wine flowed.

Lowering the tankard he'd been about to take a pull from, Alexander shifted his attention to Robina Oliphant. She was small and slender, as lithe as a willow reed. As usual, Oliphant's daughter's mousy brown hair was pulled back into a severe braid that wrapped around the crown of her head. The style accentuated the elfish shape of her face, her pale skin, and huge, timid hazel eyes.

"Robina?" Oliphant boomed, a crease forming between heavy dark brows.

Throat bobbing, Robina nodded. "Aye, father."

However, the lass didn't look Alexander's way. She rarely did.

Tempering his rising irritation, Alexander dismissed Ramsay Oliphant and his meek daughter with a shrug. Satan's cods, his father's interference was galling. Around him, he was aware of sly looks and sniggers from some of his brothers. All of them were present this evening: Tavish, Roy, Blair, Evan, and William.

Reluctantly, Alexander shifted his focus to his father and met his eye. There was no mistaking the challenge he saw there. Alexander was well past the age when most men took a wife. And as the Gunn first-born, he had a duty to his family.

George Gunn lounged in a huge carven chair. Above him hung a massive iron shield and a banner with the Gunn crest—a hand clutching a dirk—and the Gunn motto: *Aut pax aut bellum*—Either peace or war.

That was how it was for the Gunns. They were one of the Highland's smallest clans, and yet one of the mightiest. His people were said to be descended from Norsemen, and their name meant 'war' in the ancient tongue.

Weariness swept over Alexander as their stare drew out. Despite his growling belly, he wished he could avoid this supper and his father's suffocating presence. He'd enjoyed being free of him for a few days.

"So, the sheep rustlers are dealt with, are they?" George Gunn glanced away, speared a blood sausage with his knife, and dropped it onto the dish before him.

Alexander grunted. He helped himself to some sausage too before tearing off a chunk of bread.

"Ye took yer time," the clan-chief continued.

"They avoided us for a while." Alexander glanced up to find his father watching him once more, this time under hooded lids.

Silence stretched out before George Gunn favored his first-born with a wolfish smile. "I hope chasing Mackays around the hills hasn't tired ye out." He cast Robina an appraising look. "We have a lively cèilidh planned for after supper ... and I know a lass who is keen to dance with ye."

21

FORBIDDEN

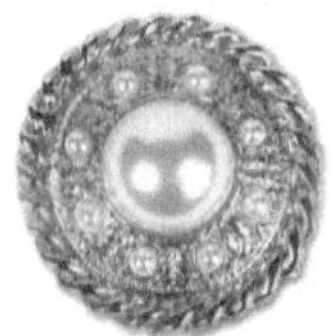

ALEXANDER FOUND HIS brother Tavish dicing with three warriors in the guard tower. Striding into the chamber on the ground floor where the guards took their meals, Alexander pulled up short, his gaze traveling to the silver penny that Tavish had just slammed down before one of his opponents.

A long table dominated the square space; and the air smelled of stale sweat, dogs, and peat smoke. A hearth burned up one end of the room, and two shaggy Highland collies lay curled up before it.

Tavish Gunn wore a disgruntled expression, although it shuttered when he glanced up to see his elder brother standing in the doorway.

Alexander jerked his chin to the three guards who'd also looked up from their game. "Get out," he grunted.

Without a word of complaint, all of them did. They simply rose to their feet, one of them collecting his winnings, and left the brothers alone in the chamber.

"What are ye doing here?" Tavish greeted him with a sour look. "I thought ye'd be dancing with yer wife-to-be for a while yet."

"Fortunately for me, Robina retired early," Alexander replied. "She murmured something about a headache ... much to her father's annoyance."

Tavish snorted. "And yers?"

Folding his arms across his chest, Alexander leaned against the doorframe and fixed his brother with a level stare. He wasn't here to talk about the match his father was determined to make for him.

"What's yer game, Tav?"

Tavish leaned back in his chair and smirked. "What do ye mean?"

"Why didn't ye tell our father about the Mackay gathering?"

Tavish snorted. "I thought it best he didn't know what we've been up to."

Alexander frowned. "Ye have never done me a favor in yer life … and I doubt ye are about to start now."

His brother laughed.

"Out with it then," Alexander growled. "What stopped ye from spilling the whole tale over supper?"

Tavish's expression sobered. He reached for the tankard of ale he'd been drinking during the dicing and took a deep pull. "I've done ye a favor, Alex … so maybe ye will do one for me in return?"

Alexander's frown deepened. "What do ye want then?"

Tavish glanced back at him, his mirth fading. Tension then rippled across his face. "Robina Oliphant."

Alexander cocked an eyebrow. Whatever blackmail he'd been expecting from his sly brother, this wasn't it. He'd never seen Tavish show the slightest interest in Ramsay Oliphant's daughter—not that he'd been paying much attention if he were honest. He thought Tavish would have found her too quiet, too shy.

Apparently, he was mistaken. He could see from the glint in his brother's eye that the man was serious. He really did want Robina Oliphant for himself.

"I want ye to refuse to wed her, no matter how father nags and bullies," Tavish continued. "Find yerself another wife—" his brother's expression turned calculating "—so that I can take Robina for my own."

Alexander held his brother's gaze steadily. "Ye are welcome to her. I never intended to agree to this match anyway."

Of course, Tavish had guessed which woman he'd prefer to wed.

A woman who was forbidden to him.

"Ye might not want to agree to it," Tavish replied with a scowl, "but we both know how forceful the old man can be."

Alexander's mouth twisted. Aye, George Gunn was relentless—but he forgot that his first-born was cast in his mold: hard as granite and just as inflexible.

"And what about silencing the other warriors ... and Will?" Alexander asked after a pause. "The lad has a flapping tongue when he's had a skinful of ale."

"I've already told the others to keep their beaks shut," Tavish replied, his gaze hardening. "Will knows that if he says a word, I'll rip off his balls."

A smile quirked Alexander's mouth. "Aye, well, in that case, we have ourselves an agreement."

"Can ye pass me the bread, Jaimee?"

Jaimee glanced up, from where she'd been pushing the braised cabbage and boiled fowl eggs around her wooden dish. Resisting the urge to purse her lips, she met Morgan's eye and nodded. She then took hold of the basket before her and passed it down to him.

This is getting ridiculous.

Where was her light-hearted, teasing brother? Morgan's tone was off-hand, his manner stiff. Both her brothers were aloof toward her these days.

Mealtimes had become awkward, conversation stilted.

Reaching for the pewter goblet of wine in front of her, Jaimee lifted it to her lips. The noon meal stuck in her throat today, although her appetite had been poor ever since returning to Farr Castle.

It had been a week now, each day longer than the one before it. Restlessness and irritation boiled within her. Her brothers' reserve aside, she'd found it difficult to settle back into her old routine.

"Do ye fancy going for a ride this afternoon, Jaimee?" Seated next to Morgan, Maggie flashed Jaimee a smile. "I plan to take Walnut out."

Nearby, Cait huffed a sigh of disappointment before patting her swollen belly. "I wish I could join ye," she murmured. Kennan cast his wife a sympathetic smile before wrapping an arm about her shoulders.

"Worry not, wife," he said with a squeeze. "We shall take a sedate walk together into Farr village instead."

Swallowing her wine, Jaimee cast Maggie a grateful smile and nodded. Fortunately, only her brothers had been cool with her since Halladale; Keira, Cait, and Maggie treated her the same as they always had. It was as if her sister-by-marriage had read her mind, had sensed her need to escape the castle for a short while. "I'd like that," she replied softly.

"I feel like blowing away the cobwebs too," Keira announced from the head of the table. Connor cut her a quelling look, yet his wife ignored him. "Rose will be fine with Fern and Lara for a few hours ... and Outlaw will forget who I am if I don't take him out for a ride soon."

Indeed. Ever since her pregnancy and giving birth earlier in the year, Keira had ridden upon a wagon with Rose whenever the family had traveled anywhere. Outlaw was a magnificent bay courser, a wedding gift from Connor, and Keira adored him.

"I'll send some men with ye," Connor spoke up then. "Ye shouldn't ride out unescorted."

Keira waved his offer away. "Don't fash yerself, mo chridhe. The three of us can look out for each other."

"We won't go inland," Maggie added, making it clear that they wouldn't be at risk from the Gunns. "I was thinking of taking the coastal road through Swordly and up to Kirtomy Burn."

"We've ridden that way before without an escort," Keira said, reaching out and placing a hand on her husband's arm. "Don't worry, we'll be fine."

They led their horses out of the stables, to the sound of raised voices.

Jaimee glanced over at the forge to see a lanky young man swagger out into the landward bailey, a wooden pail in one hand.

"Cantankerous old shit-bag," Gil muttered as he strode toward the stone trough in the center of the space. "Get yer own water."

However, despite his grumbling, the apprentice did the blacksmith's bidding.

Noting that he had an audience, Gill's gaze swung around to the three women watching him. His lips curled insolently as he met Jaimee's eye. He then raked his gaze over her, a vexing habit he'd developed of late.

"Mind yerself, Gill," she warned him. "Farlan's patience will only last so long."

The lad sneered. "Aye, and so will mine."

Scooping up a bucketful of water, he sloped back to the forge.

Watching him go, Jaimee scowled. She didn't understand why Farlan kept this lout on.

"What an odious worm," Maggie murmured.

"Aye," Jaimee snorted. She turned back to her companions, her mouth curving. "I pity the poor woman who ends up with him."

"Come on," Keira said, swinging up onto Outlaw's back and adjusting her skirts. "Let's go before Connor changes his mind about letting us ride out alone."

Jaimee needed no further encouragement. She was pleased Keira had convinced him not to send a group of warriors with them.

She wasn't in the mood for male company today.

Jaimee was grinning, her face chapped from the wind, when she reined in her horse at the edge of Kirtomy burn. She'd raced her companions to their destination, although Keira had beaten her—not a surprise, for Outlaw was born to run. However, both women had to wait while Maggie caught them up.

Maggie wore a pinched expression as she bounced around on Walnut's broad back. The Highland pony had a short, choppy gait that didn't make for a comfortable ride.

"Well, the outcome of *that* was predictable," Maggie announced as she pulled the puffing garron up. She then leaned forward and stroked the pony's sweaty neck. "Poor Walnut couldn't outrun a pregnant sow."

Jaimee laughed, and for the first time in days, the world lightened just a little.

"Let's take a breather here for a short while," Keira suggested. She swung down from Outlaw's back and loosened the courser's girth a little. Then, she flopped down on the bank of the burn.

Following Keira's lead, her two companions dismounted and let their horses graze while they too sat down. Like the landscape around Farr, this stretch of coast was windswept and treeless. Green hills stretched away in either direction, bisected by a glittering burn that flowed down over grey rocks toward the sea. And just like Farr, emerald hills met sheer cliffs and pounding surf.

Jaimee sucked in a deep breath, inhaling the scent of brine deep in her lungs. The past year had brought great upheaval to the Mackays of Farr, yet the smell of the coast was always the same. It brought her solace.

"I'm glad we came here," Maggie announced. "The atmosphere in the castle has been a little ... tense of late."

Jaimee tore her gaze from the sea to find Maggie watching her. She grimaced. "Aye, Connor and Morgan still haven't recovered from Halladale."

Keira looked up from where she'd just plucked a piece of grass and was rolling it between her fingers. A crease appeared between her brows. "And have ye?"

22

MY PROTECTORS, MY CHAMPIONS

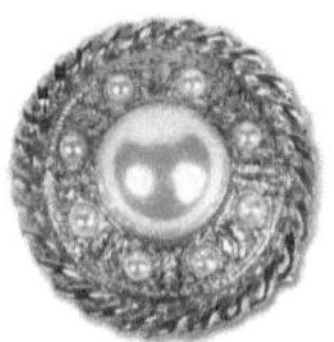

JAIMEE LET OUT a gusty sigh. It was strange, for although Halladale hadn't altered her relationship with Keira and Maggie, they'd avoided talking about the gathering directly since their return to Farr. During conversation, they tended to skirt around the subject. "I haven't recovered … not really," she admitted. "Memories keep coming back to haunt me."

Keira favored her with a rueful smile. "As they do me. I still can't believe ye put yerself between Connor and Alexander Gunn like that. My heart was in my throat watching ye."

"I'm not the only woman here who stands up to her menfolk," Jaimee reminded Keira with a tilt of her head. "Alexander Gunn's brother Tavish said ye prevented Connor from slitting his throat. Is that true?"

Keira's smile faded before she nodded. "I thought I could forget that I was born a Gunn, yet it seems I can't. Tavish Gunn was on his knees and unarmed. I couldn't let Connor kill him." She paused then, her mouth pursing. "However, my intervention was nothing compared to what ye did."

"Aye," Maggie murmured. "Ye have nerves of iron."

Jaimee huffed a bitter laugh. She didn't agree. "I don't think it was courage that made me act that way … more like desperation. I've already lost my father to the Gunns. I didn't want to lose my brother as well."

Maggie's sea-blue gaze narrowed slightly as she studied Jaimee's face. "That's not all it is though, is it?"

"We've both eyes," Keira added. "We saw the way ye and Alexander Gunn looked at each other. A man like that doesn't let a woman tell him what to do."

Maggie snorted. "No … not unless he's smitten by her."

Jaimee's pulse quickened. There was no fooling these two.

She loosed another, ragged, sigh. "I wish I hated him," she whispered. "But I don't."

Silence fell then, while Jaimee's companions took these words in.

"What happened?" Maggie eventually asked.

"It started in Inverness." Jaimee looked away from her sisters-by-marriage and fixed her stare upon the watery horizon to the west. "Do ye recall, Maggie, how ye came across us together in that garden?"

"Aye," Maggie replied with a snort. "How could I forget?"

"What's this?" Keira asked.

"After that awful scene with Angus and Niel in the great hall, I took a walk in the courtyard garden," Jaimee replied, still not looking at the other women. "Alexander Gunn followed me there." She heaved in a deep breath. "We'd exchanged glances a couple of days earlier … and from that moment, he developed an obsession of sorts." She broke off there, her fingers curling into fists on her lap. "That's why he came to the gathering." Jaimee swiveled back to Keira and Maggie, taking in their surprised faces. "I never gave him any encouragement … in fact, I only ever insulted the man … but from the beginning, I felt *it* … a connection between us."

The urge to confide in Keira and Maggie rose within her. She wanted to admit to them that Alexander Gunn had indeed abducted her, had stolen her away with the intention of making her his wife. However, good sense checked her.

These women were her friends, yet they were also loyal to her brothers. She wouldn't put them in the position of having to keep the news from their husbands.

Keira had already nearly destroyed her own life with secrets.

"We spent the night talking," she continued then, dropping her gaze to her lap. "And he did kiss me. He wanted me to return to Castle Gunn with him, to wed him ... but I refused." She raised her chin then, looking at her companions once more. "We all know such a match would be impossible."

How simple her explanation sounded. She'd left out all the important parts—including how he'd seen straight into her heart and revealed her deepest desires. Even now, Jaimee started to sweat at the memory. How it haunted her.

Keira stared back at her. Her midnight-blue eyes shadowed before she nodded.

"And Gunn just accepted yer decision?" Maggie asked then, her voice incredulous. "He didn't try to force himself on ye?"

Jaimee swallowed. "Aye, he respected my wishes."

It seemed preposterous. If she had been Keira and Maggie, she wouldn't have believed her either.

How would they have reacted if they'd known that *he'd* been the one to end both kisses—that if it had been up to her in those wild moments, he could have done whatever he wanted and she wouldn't have resisted him.

Heat flowered across Jaimee's chest, and mortification rose as the blush spread up her neck.

Maggie murmured an oath under her breath. "Who would have thought the man actually had some decency?"

"I couldn't believe it when he sheathed his dirk and rode away from Connor and Morgan," Keira said, shaking her head. "A Gunn never turns his back on a fight."

A pressure built in Jaimee's chest at these words. Suddenly, she felt like weeping. She felt like throwing herself upon the mossy bank and sobbing out the whole sorry story to Keira and Maggie—yet she didn't.

She kept the ache, the treacherous longing for Alexander Gunn, locked deep inside. Her sisters-by-marriage would understand if she poured out her heart to them—but she wasn't sure she was ready to admit the truth of it to herself.

"Well ... it's all over now," she said, forcing briskness into her voice. "I need to move on." She pulled a face. "And hopefully, one day, Connor and Morgan will too." Her jaw tightened then. "I tire of them treating me like a leper."

Keira leaned forward then and reached out, her hand closing around Jaimee's forearm. "Men get bull-headed and overly proud sometimes," she replied with an understanding smile. "Those two could end up sulking till Samhuinn if ye don't clear the air. Go and talk to them."

Talk to them.

It was good advice, sage advice. Yet as Jaimee approached the chieftain's solar, where she knew Connor and Morgan were going over the accounts together, Jaimee felt anger coil in the pit of her belly.

Her gait slowed, and her hands balled into fists at her sides. Aye, Keira was right—the air had to be cleared. Yet right now she didn't want to speak calmly to her brothers, she wanted to rail at them.

Nothing she did of late seemed to please those two. She'd spurned Gunn and had been ready to wed Robin Mackay, yet he'd ridden away from Halladale without a backward glance. She couldn't help but feel as if Connor and Morgan had lain the blame for that at her feet.

Their aloofness both hurt and vexed Jaimee, but she wasn't about to let either of them shame her.

Drawing in a sharp breath, she approached the heavy oaken door to the solar. Then she raised a fist and knocked.

"Enter," Connor called out.

Jaimee pushed the door open and stepped inside.

A warm, masculine space greeted her. She broke her fast each morning at the table in the solar, where her brothers were currently seated. A ledger sat before them, and chits were spread over the oaken surface.

A tapestry, depicting a hunting scene, covered one of the damp stone walls, while a lump of peat glowed in the hearth. The wind had sprung up in the afternoon, gusting in off the sea, and so Connor had closed the shutters. Instead of daylight, the hallowed lights of the cressets upon the walls illuminated the large chamber.

Gritta was curled up before the fire, snoring gently.

Both brothers and the wolfhound glanced up when she entered.

Clenching her jaw, Jaimee deliberately closed the door behind her.

Connor and Morgan looked surprised to see her. However, their pine-green eyes—the same shade as her own—were veiled.

"What is it, Jaimee?" Connor greeted her, his tone wary.

Next to him, Morgan remained silent.

"I need to speak to ye both," she replied firmly.

Connor frowned. "Can it wait? We're busy at present."

"No, it can't wait." Jaimee's voice sharpened, and she took a step toward the table. "Enough of this, Connor. If either of ye have something to say about what happened with Gunn, out with it!"

"Do ye really want to bring it all up again?" Morgan broke his silence then. His dark-blond brows knitted together as he met her eye.

Jaimee folded her arms across her chest. "Not really ... yet it's necessary." Her gaze shifted from Morgan to Connor. "Do ye think I dishonored ye both, is that it?"

Connor stared back at her, a muscle bunching in his jaw. "This isn't just about honor," he growled.

"I think it is. Yer willful sister disobeyed ye, shamed ye, in front of yer kin, yer allies." Jaimee broke off there, her voice catching. "That was never my intention, Connor ... but I couldn't let ye fight Alexander Gunn. I just couldn't."

"Why would ye protect him?" Morgan rasped. Jaimee glanced his way, noting the confusion on his face, the hurt in his eyes. "He's a *Gunn*?"

"Aye, and so was Keira once." Jaimee drew herself up to her full height then and took a deep breath. "Admit it ... ye both think I've ruined myself. What really concerns ye is that no man will want me now."

No one had dared voice the sentiment, yet their allies who'd watched that confrontation would think her a Gunn whore. Connor would have difficulty finding her a 'worthy' match in the aftermath of Halladale. However, at that moment, Jaimee couldn't have cared less if no suitor ever darkened her door again. She'd had enough of trying to please others to her own detriment.

"God's teeth, Jaimee," Connor burst out. "Believe it or not, yer life matters more to me than yer reputation—or my honor. Why did ye go off with him? Anything could have happened to ye." His throat bobbed then. "When we discovered ye missing, I thought the worst, lass. I thought he'd taken ye somewhere to rape and murder ye. I thought we'd never see ye alive again."

Jaimee suppressed a shiver. Aye, when Gunn had abducted her that evening, she'd feared the same thing. It still amazed her how quickly things had changed between captive and captor. Thank the Lord neither of her brothers knew the truth.

The pain on both their faces was so raw that her anger ebbed a little as understanding dawned. They weren't angry that she'd dishonored them or worried about her reputation, as she'd believed, but annoyed at themselves for failing to shield her from harm.

Tears stung the back of Jaimee's eyes, her chest constricting as love for her brothers slammed into her with the force of a blacksmith's hammer. She swallowed hard.

"Ye two are the best men I've ever known," she whispered huskily, her gaze flicking from Connor to Morgan. Both her brothers' eyes were glistening, as if they too were struggling to hold back tears. "Growing up ye were my protectors, my champions." She favored them with a sad smile then. "But ye can't protect me forever. I'm an adult woman now, and I make my own decisions ... ye must let me bear the consequences of them."

23

THAW

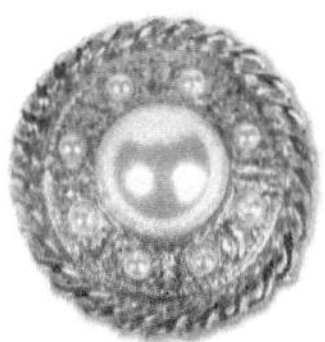

"THOSE BASTARD MACKAYS are stealing from me again." Maddoc Gunn's belligerent voice echoed through the yard outside Camster broch. A chill wind, which brought stinging needles of rain with it, gusted against him, yet the man barely seemed to notice. "An entire flock of my best Shetlands has gone missing over the last week. My men can't find them."

Alexander listened to this, his mouth thinning. He couldn't care less about Maddoc Gunn's bloody sheep. However, it was an irony that Tavish had used Maddoc as an excuse for their lengthy patrol, for just a fortnight later, the man himself sent word to Castle Gunn, asking for assistance.

George Gunn had ordered Alexander to handle the problem—and like an obedient hound, he'd ridden to Camster. Even so, he found it hard to quash his irritation as Maddoc whined on about his prized Shetlands. The quality of the wool from the man's flocks was prized all over Scotland; and as such, they'd had a longstanding problem with sheep rustling from their neighbors.

Alexander heaved in a deep breath, counting to five in an effort not to snarl at the wool merchant. "All right ... we'll deal with them," he eventually growled.

Maddoc nodded, his dark-blue eyes glinting with satisfaction.

Reining Destroyer around, Alexander nodded to his men and his two brothers—Tavish and Roy—who'd accompanied him on this trip. Then, without another word, he led the way out of the broch, under a heavy stone arch and north over the hills. The stallion was full of energy this morning; he raced out in front of the other horses, his feathered hooves flying over dry grass.

Maddoc Gunn's lands stretched to the northern and eastern borders of their territory, an empty landscape of brown hills fit for little more than hardy sheep.

Alexander leaned forward, letting the stinging needles of rain pepper his face. He welcomed the discomfort, welcomed the wind in his hair and the wild sky that stretched overhead.

Satan's cods, this errand grated on him.

In the two weeks that had passed since he'd returned home, the restlessness within him grew stronger. His mood was grim these days; he longed for a fight to ease the tension that coiled within him like an iron trap.

His brothers had taken to avoiding him, and even loyal Fynn, who usually shared an ale with Alexander in the evenings, had let him be.

The Gunn first-born wished to keep his own counsel these days.

As if sensing his son's ill-humor, George Gunn had been even more demanding than usual of late. Alexander's days were not his own. He spent them dealing out justice to his father's men and tenants as required, and leading patrols to their eastern and southern borders.

He'd grown up obeying his father in all things, yet these days every terse command, every growled order, made his hackles rise.

Alexander Gunn had tired of being his father's lackey. He wanted to be his own man.

They rode farther north, passing the Grey Cairns— ancient stone mounds that crested the top of one of the many barren hills. Alexander had visited the cairns a number of times over the years. However, it was a place that many were superstitious about. The fairy folk were said to emerge from the cairns at dusk, and this was certainly not a place one lingered after dark.

Alexander rode by the cairns with barely a glance, while his thoughts shifted, as they often did, to Jaimee Mackay.

How was she faring? Which cursed warrior had caught her eye? Had the other suitors spurned her after he'd returned Jaimee to her kin?

It was likely none of those warriors—all of them Mackays or their allies—would want a woman they presumed sullied by a Gunn. A woman who'd *willingly* gone with a Gunn. She could tell them all that she hadn't lain with him, but few would believe her. Why else would a woman ride off with a man and spend the night with him?

Alexander's jaw bunched. Of course, selfish bastard that he was, he didn't want Jaimee wedding anyone else. Yet he didn't want her shamed or punished for her actions either.

Fury seethed in his blood at the thought of her coming to any harm.

He didn't want to be here, chasing down pox-ridden sheep rustlers. He wanted to be with Jaimee. He'd have given anything to see her again, to hear the husky lilt of her voice once more.

He'd hoped he could return home and forget her, but there was a hole in his life now that no one but Jaimee could fill.

The thunder of the horses' hooves and the whistling of the wind drowned his senses as they rode on. Presently, a ridge of blue-shaded mountains appeared on the north-western horizon. Those peaks formed the natural barrier between the Mackay and Gunn territories. There were a number of villages in the glens and valleys within them—Mackay villages where the sheep rustlers likely hailed from. They would pay them a visit.

However, as they reached the foot of the mountains, Tavish gave a shout. "Look! Up ahead!"

Tavish had the keenest eyesight among them; he often spied things in the distance long before anyone else did.

And it was so today. When Alexander strained his eyes and peered into the distance, he saw sheep running north—a group of men on horseback herding them.

The rustlers—they'd caught them in the act.

Brooding cast aside, Alexander let out a blood-curdling yell and gave Destroyer his head. Feeling Alexander's aggression, the stallion kicked up his heels, flattening into a wild gallop.

His brothers and warriors' whoops behind him told him that they too had all given chase.

The hunt was afoot.

They caught up with the rustlers as they herded the sheep into one of the narrow wooded valleys that carpeted the folds of the mountains. There were six men ahead, their lèines sweat-stained and their hair flying behind them as they urged their shaggy ponies on. However, they were no match for the coursers that Alexander and his men rode.

Letting his brothers and the rest of his men deal with the stragglers, Alexander went after those leading the group. One of them, a big man atop a heavy bay garron, veered left, careening into the pines.

With a roar, Alexander plunged Destroyer into the trees in pursuit. The sharp resinous scent of pine filled his lungs as they crashed through the conifers. The trees were tall and dark, creating a buffer from the biting wind. The ground, a thick carpet of pine needles, was soft and cushiony underfoot.

Alexander barely noticed the trees that sped by; his gaze was fixed on the back of his quarry. Gripping the reins with his left hand, he drew his dirk with his right. He was good with knives and knew he could land his blade straight between the man's shoulder blades if he wished.

But he wanted to look this bastard in the eye as he gutted him.

He wanted a fight.

They thundered deep into the pines, leaving the others behind. The ground grew steeper and rougher, yet the garron didn't slow its pace, and neither did Destroyer.

But the end of the chase came suddenly, as they often did.

A low pine branch plucked the rider off his pony. The man slammed into the ground, while the garron raced on, heedless of its rider, who now lay groaning on his back on the forest floor.

Alexander reined in his stallion, swung down from the saddle, and stalked to the prone figure.

The sheep rustler's eyes went wide with terror at the sight of him. He looked to be about the same age as Alexander, with a similar brawny build. Blood trickled down his temple where the tree branch had caught him, and he had a dazed expression, as if he couldn't believe this was actually happening.

Throat bobbing convulsively, the man fumbled for his dirk, his cry echoing through the trees when Alexander's booted foot came down hard, pinning his fingers to the ground.

"Thieving is dirty work," Alexander growled.

The man stared up at him, his eyes gleaming. They was no anger or belligerence in that stare, only desperation. "Please," he rasped. "I've a wife and three young bairns. We lost our harvest to blight this summer. We're hungry ... we have to eat."

Alexander increased his weight upon the rustler's hand and felt the bones creak. "Then whine to yer clan-chief about it, ye light-fingered piece of shit."

The man's gaze widened, his pulse fluttering in the hollow of his neck. "The Mackay ig—ignored us." He choked out the words, fear and pain nearly rendering him incapable of speech. A damp patch appeared on the front of his braies. The man had just wet himself.

Alexander's lip curled. *Craven.* However, he was aware he must have made a terrifying sight, looming over the man, his blade gleaming in the dull noon light. His fingers clenched around the hilt of his dagger.

There was no point in drawing this out. He'd slit the sheep rustler's throat and be done with it.

"Mercy." The plea was barely above a whisper. "My wife. My b—bairns."

Alexander stilled. He held his dirk aloft, ready to strike.

Mercy.

Jaimee Mackay's words crashed over him.

It's as if no heart beats in yer chest ... as if the blood that runs through yer veins is as cold as a loch in winter. Ye fear nothing. Ye are devoid of mercy. Incapable of love.

The woman he wanted, the only woman he'd ever want, thought him a heartless beast. And that was what he was.

But he could change—for her, he would.

The man before him was a Mackay. If he cut his throat, there would be no going back. If he had any hope of winning Jaimee one day, he couldn't kill him.

He couldn't ever raise arms against a Mackay again.

Heart pounding in his ears, Alexander straightened up.

The urge to strike, to kill and maim, was there—as strong as it had ever been—yet his arm wouldn't answer its call.

Breathing hard, Alexander sheathed his dagger. "Get out of my sight," he said, his voice low and guttural. "Before I come to my senses and end yer sorry life."

The sheep rustler stared up at him, for an instant not daring to believe him. But when Alexander took a step back and released his hand for under his boot, understanding dawned in the man's eyes.

Without a word, he rolled to his feet and scrambled away into the undergrowth.

Alexander watched him go.

A short while later, Alexander stepped out of the pines to find that his brothers, and the warriors that accompanied him, had dealt with the other sheep rustlers. Bodies littered the mossy ground, and their ponies had been caught.

The sheep had been herded back down the valley and now huddled in a frightened, bleating mob.

"Did ye catch the thieving bastard?" Roy greeted him.

"Aye," Alexander grunted. He said nothing else. His brothers would expect the man to be dead, and he wasn't about to disappoint them. He cast a gaze around the valley at the bloodied bodies.

No more.

The certainty settled deep in his gut. Something had shifted in him as he'd stood over that sheep rustler, had been so close to ending his life.

It's as if no heart beats in yer chest.

She was right, none had—until the day they'd locked eyes in the great hall of Inverness months earlier. Until then, his soul had been frozen, like the earth during a long, bitter winter. He hadn't even realized to what extent his life chafed him. Jaimee Mackay was the spring sun; she had melted the ice, had revealed a longing that made his chest ache like an open wound.

There was no going back now, he realized. The only way was forward, which meant things were going to have to change.

And that meant he and his father needed to have words.

"Alex?" Tavish's voice drew him out of his brooding. "Something wrong?"

Clenching his jaw, Alexander met his penetrating gaze. Something had altered between the two of them since the evening of their return to Castle Gunn. Alexander had been taciturn and ill-tempered of late, yet Tavish had stopped baiting him like he usually did.

Alexander still didn't trust Tavish though—he didn't trust any of his brothers. At the slightest sign of weakness, they'd pounce. Tavish's question had made Roy look his way, his gaze gleaming with interest.

“No,” Alexander grunted, scowling.

Tavish nodded, taking the hint. His brother then motioned for the others to move ahead with the flock of sheep. “Come on … let’s get this mob back to Camster.”

24

NO WAY OUT BUT THROUGH

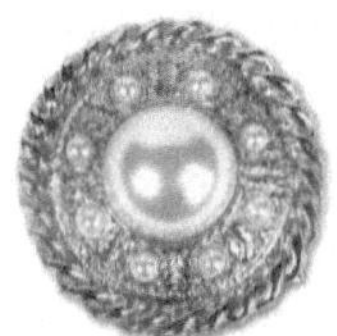

SOME THINGS WERE best not put off.

Alexander could have left the meeting with his father until the following morning, and perhaps he should have. He was exhausted and hungry after a day in the saddle. Yet the restlessness within him was now a writhing beast.

It wouldn't settle.

He couldn't settle.

"Ye look like someone just pissed in yer porridge," Roy commented as they made their way from the stables across the bailey toward the keep. "I would have thought spilling Mackay blood would have sweetened yer mood?"

Alexander snorted.

That was the problem—it didn't.

Once again, he was aware of Tavish swinging a probing glance his way. His brother knew something was up.

It was loud inside the great hall of Castle Gunn. A lad playing a bone whistle was valiantly trying to be heard above the din of drunken voices. They'd arrived at the tail-end of supper.

George Gunn and his men were well into their cups, as were the brothers who hadn't gone to deal with the sheep rustlers. Blair and Evan were playing knucklebones, and judging from the belligerent look on Blair's face, his younger brother was beating him.

"Save some ale for me, ye greedy bastards," Roy boomed, striding across the hall toward the clan-chief's table. "Slitting throats is thirsty work!"

A roar of laughter followed this comment.

"Ye don't need an excuse to drink yerself under the table," Evan jeered.

"So, ye dealt with those thieves?" George Gunn asked. He lounged in his carven chair, a pretty serving lass perched upon his lap. After losing his wife many years earlier, the Gunn clan-chief had never taken another. Instead, a string of comely servants warmed his bed.

"Aye," Tavish replied. "The missing sheep are safely back at Camster." He slid into his place at the table and reached for a jug of ale and an empty tankard.

"Left the Mackays corpses to the crows, we did," Roy added with a grin.

"Good lads," George Gunn replied with a grin of his own. His eyes were slightly glazed as he fondled the serving lass's full breasts through the low-cut kirtle she wore. His gaze then shifted to his first-born.

Alexander had stopped before the table. However, unlike his brothers, he hadn't yet taken a seat. Instead, he watched his father.

Aye, some things couldn't be put off. There would never be a good time to bring this up.

I might as well say it now.

"Take a seat, Alex," he rumbled. "Pour yerself a horn of mead."

"Aye," Evan quipped. "Before Roy drinks it all."

"Later," Alexander replied. "After we talk."

George Gunn's dark eyebrows raised. "Most men can speak and drink at the same time, lad?"

Alexander's brothers guffawed at this. Yet he ignored them all. His gaze remained steady upon his father. "I want us to make peace with the Mackays," he said finally.

The conversation at the clan-chief's table died.

Tavish, who'd been about to take a pull from his tankard of ale, froze, while next to him, Roy gawked stupidly at Alexander.

"Ye heard the king," Alexander continued. Now that he'd brought up the subject, there was no way out but through. "He won't suffer our clans warring any longer. We might have escaped his wrath at Inverness, but next time, yer silver tongue won't save us."

Alexander paused there, letting his words sink in. The whole hall had fallen silent now, and the bone whistle trailed off. Alexander could feel gazes boring into his back, yet he paid none of them any mind.

"I want ye to write Angus Mackay a missive, swearing that ye will hold an official peace. I will carry it to him myself."

Sharp inhales followed this statement. Alexander did shift his gaze from his father's stony face then, noting the varying expressions of shock and disgust on his siblings' faces.

Tavish was the first to recover. "Have ye lost yer wits, Alex?"

Alexander ignored the question. "The feuding will be our ruin. It's time to let it go."

"One signed missive isn't going to do that," Tavish countered. A flush had appeared on his cheekbones. Next to him, Roy had gone the color of turnip.

"A marriage will seal it," Alexander replied brusquely. "I will wed a Mackay to forge the peace between us."

Tavish's mouth twisted, understanding lighting his eyes. "Of course ye will," he murmured.

Farther down the table, Will snorted. "It's *her*, isn't it? Ye handed yer balls to Jaimee Mackay."

Alexander tensed. *Curse ye, Will.* He should have known he'd eventually reveal where they'd been two weeks earlier. Unlike Tavish, he didn't have a good enough reason to keep his mouth shut. The sting of a threat usually wore off fast.

Will's timing was poor—but the truth was always going to come out, sooner or later.

Squaring his shoulders, Alexander awaited his father's wrath.

George Gunn's face had gone still and cold. He removed his hands from the serving lass's breasts and shoved her unceremoniously off his lap. The lass let out a squeal, yet he ignored her. "Jaimee *Mackay*?"

"Aye, we didn't go after sheep rustlers on that patrol a fortnight ago," Will confirmed. "Instead, we rode to the Strath of Halladale … and Alex competed for the woman's hand."

"He'd have won the games too," Tavish added. He was staring at Alexander as if he'd just sprouted horns. "If the Mackays hadn't turned on each other. He's been obsessed with the lass ever since."

"This isn't about her," Alexander replied.

He wasn't lying. Aye, Jaimee plagued his thoughts, every fevered dream—yet this stand was a bid to cut the cord between him and his father. He needed to rid himself of the noose before it strangled him.

"It's time to make peace with the Mackays."

"Enough of this shit-talk," his father snarled. His face had flushed, his dark eyes glittering. "The three of ye lied to me about yer whereabouts. I'll have reckoning for that."

Tavish's mouth thinned at this, while Will paled. Alexander merely stared back at the clan-chief. He could feel his father's temper rising like a spring tide, yet he wouldn't back down.

"I wish to wed Jaimee Mackay," he said finally, his voice echoing across the hall.

His father's jaw bunched. "Clod-head! If ye weren't being led about by yer rod, ye wouldn't even be suggesting this," he spat out the words. "That bitch is making a fool of ye."

Alexander shook his head and took a step closer to the table. "Don't ye tire of the feuding?"

"Never!"

"Ye don't even remember what started it."

"That doesn't matter. Hate is hate."

Alexander was wasting his breath arguing this with his father. He understood only too well that George Gunn lived for the long-running feud with the Mackays. He didn't want to end the fighting. His life would likely lose all purpose if it did.

But stubbornness rose within Alexander all the same. He wasn't going to give up; nothing would stop him from pursuing this. "All this fighting will eventually weaken our clan," he pointed out. "Every year, we lose more good men—men who should be farming our lands, building our brochs, and fathering bairns."

George Gunn stared him down, his dark eyes, which had been slightly unfocused from drink earlier, now predatory and sharp. His gaze raked over Alexander, as if he was taking stock of him for the first time.

When he eventually spoke, his voice was soft yet dripping with scorn. "I was wondering when this day would come … I've always sensed 'weakness' in ye, lad."

Tension rippled down the table.

Alexander cocked an eyebrow. "Weakness?" The question was a challenge. They all knew that he was the most ruthless of all six brothers. Their father had brought him up that way; countless beatings had forged him as hard as iron.

"Aye," George Gunn growled. "Why do ye think I've been harder on ye than the rest. From the day ye were born, I sensed it. I tried to beat it out of ye … tried to make ye into a warrior to be feared … but it was always there, waiting to rise to the surface."

Alexander stared back at him. Long moments passed, and then something deep inside him gave. A cold anger awoke in the pit of his belly.

"All I see in ye, old man, is *fear*." His words fell like ax blows. "Ye have always known this day would come, haven't ye? We won't all obey yer every command forever. One day, yer whelps will rise up. One day, one of them might even *kill* ye."

A heartbeat passed, and then his father moved. With a snarl of rage, George Gunn launched himself over the table toward his first-born. He was a big man, and getting on in years, and yet he vaulted lightly across the surface, scattering tankards, plates, and jugs in his wake.

And as he did, he drew the dirk at his hip.

Alexander was ready for him. The moment he'd uttered those words, he'd known this argument would end in blood.

But he didn't care—he'd ceased caring a while ago.

There was a price to be paid for wanting Jaimee Mackay—and for daring to suggest peace between the two warring clans—one that Alexander would willingly pay.

He was done being his father's henchman, his faithful lackey.

He was his own man now, and freedom tasted as sweet as the first of the summer wine.

Dodging his father's swiping blade—a strike that aimed to gut him—Alexander drew his own dagger.

Warriors and their families scrambled as the clan-chief and his first-born faced each other. The others clustered around the edges of the hall, watching the two men fight with killing precision.

Alexander Gunn was skilled with a blade. His father had taught him well, and when he'd fumbled as a lad, he'd paid the price. So he'd learned not to fumble, to instead second-guess his opponents' moves.

He knew how his father fought—in aggressive and swift lunges—and likewise, George Gunn knew his son's fighting style.

And as such, sweat was soon pouring off both men.

They circled each other, weapons held low, before they attacked, feinted, and parried with mesmerizing speed.

Alexander was vaguely aware of all his brothers rising to their feet at the table. Yet not one of them stepped forward to intervene. Not one dared.

Such a move would earn them a blade to the throat. It was safer to keep one's distance, to let the fight unfold as it should.

This was how it was between the Gunn males. George Gunn had once boasted of how he'd dueled with his own father, how he'd stabbed him in the leg, and how the wound had festered and eventually killed him.

Many looking on perhaps thought this was a challenge for rule—and before he met Jaimee Mackay it might have been—but these days Alexander just wanted to be free of this man's oppressive ways, to choose his own path in life.

But if his father had his way, it would always be forbidden to him.

George Gunn's blade caught Alexander across the forearm, cutting through the leather bracer he wore. It was a shallow cut, yet it stung like the devil. Clenching his teeth, and ignoring the blood that trickled over his hand, Alexander fought on.

It was a clever move, one designed to weaken him, for if the hilt of his dirk became slippery with blood, he wouldn't be able to wield it so effectively—and that would make him easier to beat.

Alexander couldn't let that happen.

He couldn't let this play out any longer.

Driving his father back against the table, he attacked hard. The clan-chief had nowhere to go. Alexander closed in and grabbed his father's wrist as he struck out at him. He then stabbed him in the right shoulder.

George Gunn's roar splintered the air.

The clan-chief sprawled back over the table, his own dirk thudding onto the wooden floor.

Alexander had chosen the location to sink his blade in with care. It wasn't a fatal spot, but it rendered the arm useless.

Standing over his father, Alexander reached down and yanked the blade free. His father's grunt of agony followed.

Father and son's gazes fused. Lying back, splayed against the table, cradling his bleeding shoulder, George Gunn snarled up at his first-born. "End it then." His words lashed across the great hall. "Take yer rightful place."

A heartbeat passed, and then another.

And then, to the shock of everyone looking on, Alexander Gunn didn't stab his father in the throat with his dirk. Instead, he sheathed the weapon.

"I don't want it," he replied, his voice low and cold. "Not anymore."

His father glared up at him, his face turning ashen with fury. "Then ye are dead to me," he rasped. "Leave this castle, and never return."

25

LEAVING

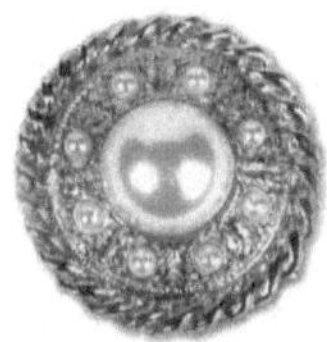

NO ONE UTTERED A word as Alexander left the great hall of Castle Gunn. There was no muttering or whispering. No one stepped forward to bar his way, to challenge him. Nonetheless, he felt the weight of their stares upon his back as he departed. The shock that had settled over the hall had turned the warm, smoky air chill.

Alexander walked out without a backward glance. He didn't go up to his bed-chamber to collect his things. Time was of the essence now. Danger crackled just underneath the weighty silence. If he lingered at the castle, his brothers would likely corner him and do what their father had failed to achieve.

Urgency dogged Alexander's steps as he crossed the windy bailey. The rain, which had come and gone all day, had returned now, sweeping through the darkness and battering the stone walls.

Alexander's mouth thinned. It wasn't a night to go riding, but there was nothing for it. His confrontation with his father made it a necessity.

Entering the stables, he glanced down at his injured forearm. The bleeding had stopped, but it was beginning to throb. The cut would have to be dealt with later though; right now, he needed to get out of Castle Gunn.

He was saddling Destroyer in sharp, deft movements when the scrape of booted feet approaching made him tense.

Had his brothers come for him already?

However, only Tavish appeared in the doorway.

Folding his arms across his chest, his brother eyed him for a few moments before speaking. All the while, Alexander continued to prepare his horse for departure. Destroyer was viewing him with a jaundiced eye this evening; they'd only just returned from a hard day's ride, and the horse didn't appreciate being disturbed again.

"Aren't ye going to bid me farewell?" Tavish drawled eventually.

Alexander snorted. "Don't pretend ye aren't happy to see me go."

Tavish arched an eyebrow. However, confusion shadowed his storm-grey eyes. "I never thought I'd see the day," he admitted. "Yet I find it hard to believe ye are going to give it all up."

Alexander curled his lip, before he turned away and unhitched his stallion from the railing.

"Ye could have rid us all of the old bastard tonight," Tavish said after a pause. "Why didn't ye?"

Alexander flashed his brother a harsh smile. "I'll leave that to ye ... if ye want his seat in the great hall, take it for yerself."

Tavish scowled and stepped aside so Alexander could pass.

They both knew he wouldn't challenge their father for rule. Alexander was the toughest of them all, and yet he hadn't planned on killing his father. Maybe George Gunn had the right of it. Perhaps they were *all* weaker than he was.

Alexander led Destroyer out of the stall and down the aisle toward the stable doors. Outside, icy sheets of rain were now battering the bailey.

Clenching his jaw, Alexander swung onto his horse's back and urged the stallion toward the gates, which had been closed for the night.

"Open up," he called to the guards.

Moments passed before leather-clad men hurried from the warmth of the guardhouse, muttering under their breaths as they fumbled with the iron bar that locked the gates closed.

However, once the gates were drawn open, Alexander had to wait longer still, while the portcullis was raised. The creaking of iron joined the keening wind as the portcullis inched up.

Alexander sat there, staring at the sharp metal teeth. All the while, he was aware of the weight of the stone keep behind him, pressing down upon him. Fighting the urge to glance over his shoulder to look upon it one last time—for this was his home, and he'd never dreamed he'd ever leave it—Alexander tried to ignore the prickling sensation between his shoulder blades.

The sooner he left the better. And yet the portcullis seemed to be taking an age to rise.

"Where will ye go?" Tavish was at his side once more. The rain had sluiced his brother's dark hair back, giving him a hawkish look in the guttering light of the smoking torches that hung on chains from the walls.

Alexander met his brother's eye squarely before he shrugged.

For a few instants, they merely stared at each other—two rivals who'd tried to kill each other on more than one occasion. Alexander was now standing down, and Tavish would be getting what he'd always wanted. He'd expected Tavish to look happier about it, yet his younger brother's eyes were shadowed.

"Watch out for Roy," Alexander murmured. "Now he's second in line, he'll be wanting rid of ye."

Tavish snorted. "I'll handle him."

Alexander's mouth lifted at the corners. "Aye … I'm sure ye will."

Before them, the portcullis finally lifted.

Alexander flashed his younger brother a smile. "Goodbye, Tav … and good luck winning Robina Oliphant's hand."

Tavish favored him with a grin in reply. "Like ye, dear brother … I don't need luck."

Alexander huffed a laugh. And with that, he rode out of Castle Gunn into the bleak night.

"Get out, laggard!"

Jaimee was in the landward bailey, playing tug o' war with Milish, when a fight erupted in the forge.

She'd brought the puppy outdoors in an attempt to distract herself. Although she'd cleared the air with her brothers, she still felt out of sorts. The disquiet within her wouldn't settle. If anything, it had worsened over the past few days. The truth was she couldn't forget Alexander Gunn. And worse still, she didn't *want* to forget him.

Shouting now echoed across the bailey.

Glancing up from where she was pulling a braided length of cloth, while the wolfhound pup did her best to wrest it from her grip, Jaimee frowned.

Seated on a stool next to Jaimee, Cait lowered the lèine she'd been mending and loosed an irritated sigh. "God's teeth, not again?"

Jaimee's gaze settled upon Cait. Her belly was now huge; the bairn was due in less than a month now. Kennan tried to insist that his feisty wife spent her days resting in their bed-chamber or the women's solar, as Keira had during her pregnancy, but Cait refused. She was a blacksmith's daughter after all—a lass brought up never to be idle—and had insisted on bringing her sewing outdoors with her this afternoon.

"Da should really get rid of Gil," Cait muttered. "He's not been himself, ever since he took him on."

Jaimee was about to murmur in agreement—when a roar echoed from the forge.

Both women turned sharply to see a lanky figure clad in a sooty lèine and braies fly out of the stone archway leading into the smith's.

Gil sprawled on the cobbles and barely had time to roll to his feet when a huge man with greying dark hair and bulging biceps burst from the forge and advanced on him.

Farlan gripped Gil by the collar of his shirt and hauled him to his feet, shaking him like a misbehaving dog.

"Da!" Cait heaved herself up off the stool and took a waddling step toward her father.

"Stay back, lass," Farlan warned.

"Farlan," Jaimee picked up the wriggling puppy and also rose to her feet. She then passed Milish to Cait and advanced upon the blacksmith and his apprentice. "What has he done?"

The blacksmith glanced her way. Jaimee had deliberately used a commanding tone, one she'd heard Connor use when his men were brawling. It was a tone that demanded an answer.

"He's bone-idle," Farlan ground out, a vein pulsing in his forehead. "Whines in my ear *all* day … and insults me. I can't take it anymore."

"Gil." Jaimee placed her hands upon her hips, her tone sharpening. "Is this true?"

"Cantankerous old bastard," Gil sneered up at him. "Ye just don't like anyone challenging ye. I don't know how yer fat wife puts up with ye."

"Shit-weasel!" Farlan flung Gil away as if he weighed nothing at all. "I'll not work with ye any longer!" The lad flew across the cobbles, narrowly missing a steaming pile of horse dung as he fell. Maggie had just returned from a ride on Walnut and was unsaddling the garron in the stables; she hadn't yet gone outside to clean up after her pony.

The apprentice scrambled to his feet. His face was red, belligerent. "Ye can't send me away," Gill snarled. "Only the laird of Farr commands me. Not ye—" He shifted his glare to Jaimee, as his mouth twisted "—or this Gunn *whore*."

Jaimee's breathing caught, hot and then cold sweeping over her.

Was that what the men of this keep whispered behind her back?

"Ye *do* take orders from my sister," a cool male voice interjected then. Jaimee's gaze cut left to see Connor standing on the steps to the keep. "And now ye have insulted her, I want ye gone from Farr."

Gil stared at the laird. The youth's face sagged, even if his eyes burned. He then spat on the cobbles. "This isn't fair ... ye should try working for Farlan."

Connor's face went hard, his hand straying to the hilt of his dirk. "I won't repeat myself, lad. Collect yer belongings and leave this castle now, before my patience exhausts itself."

Gil's face twisted. Casting a malevolent look at Farlan, he disappeared into the forge to gather his things.

Moments passed, and then Connor descended the last of the stairs and crossed the bailey. Farlan watched him approach, his expression wary. Connor stopped a few feet from the smith. "Gil had that coming, I believe," he murmured before giving a rueful shake of his head. "Although I think it's time ye reined in that temper of yers, Farlan."

26

DEATH WISH

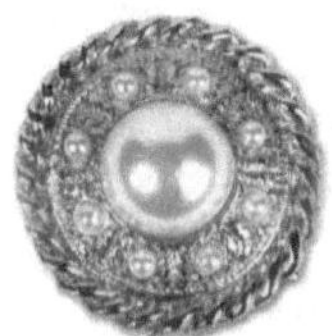

ALEXANDER GUNN slowed his stallion to a walk as he approached Farr Castle. A chill wind gusted off the sea, although the sun warmed his face. Dusk wasn't far off.

What am I doing here?

The night before, he'd ridden out of Castle Gunn, through the biting wind and lashing rain, without any direction in mind. His altercation with his father had driven him from his home, from the only life he'd ever known. A strange numbness that had nothing to do with the foul weather had descended upon him as he galloped into the night. It had come as a surprise the following morning when he found himself upon Mackay lands. He hadn't intentionally traveled in that direction, yet he kept going.

And the end of the next day's journey had brought him to Farr Castle.

Gazing upon the high walls with the churning sea behind them, Alexander was struck by how similar Farr Castle was to Castle Gunn. It didn't have quite the same precarious position, for his father's castle perched on a finger of land that was only accessible via a bridge from the bluff. However, both fortresses crouched upon yawning cliffs, commanding a view over the sea.

Thinking of Castle Gunn reminded Alexander of George Gunn himself, and his mouth thinned. No doubt the old man thought he'd be back one day, groveling on his knees for forgiveness.

That would never happen.

Riding away from his birthright had been hard—and yet he could no longer serve his father.

Let him crush Tavish under his iron fist instead.

Alexander rode through a hamlet on the way to the castle. The villagers were finishing off their last tasks for the day before retreating indoors. Smoke rose from the turf roofs. Curious gazes followed him. However, since he didn't wear a clan sash, none would know who he was.

Alexander was riding toward the landward ramparts and the huge oaken and iron gates that led into the bailey beyond when he spied a thin figure running toward the village. A rat-faced young man, dressed in a stained lèine and leather braies, loped toward him, a leather bag slung over one shoulder.

Reining in Destroyer, Alexander watched him approach. The youth's gaze raked over him, yet he didn't greet the newcomer—and Alexander didn't utter a word.

The man ran past, and Alexander's attention swiveled back to his destination. It had been a long while since a Gunn warrior had set foot in any Mackay stronghold. The fine hair on the back of his neck prickled, yet he ignored the warning.

Ride through those gates, and it'll be the end of ye. The voice of caution, not one that usually dared speak up, niggled then. *Mackay will skewer ye like a boar.*

Alexander grimaced. He probably would. But all the same, he was here. He'd cast off the heavy shackles of being the Gunn heir, and Jaimee Mackay beckoned him, like a siren upon the rocks. He couldn't resist her, even though setting foot inside the bailey of Farr Castle would be his ruin.

He realized then that he didn't care. Jaimee was madness in his blood.

Destroyer snorted then, impatient to keep moving. Even after two days' journey, the stallion was tireless. Alexander urged the horse on and cantered toward the gates.

Jaimee was standing with her brothers and the blacksmith, when a huge black horse thundered into the landward bailey.

Farlan was in the midst of defending his actions to his laird. "*Ye* didn't have to work with him every day," the smith muttered.

Whatever reply Connor was going to make was forestalled by this new arrival. Like his companions, the chieftain of Farr turned toward the gates.

Jaimee's gaze alighted upon the horse and rider, and her breathing stopped.

Surely, her eyes were deceiving her. It couldn't be. *Alexander Gunn.*

For a few moments, they all merely stared, hardly able to believe what they were seeing.

But if it was an apparition, it was a realistic one.

Alexander reined in his beast, his gaze spearing Jaimee with an intensity that made her knees tremble. And then, he swung down from the saddle.

Jaimee's breath rushed out of her. Suddenly, her pulse was thundering in her ears and she felt sick.

What the devil was the man doing here? Did he have a death wish?

Connor murmured a curse, one that was echoed a moment later by Morgan. Her brothers then both drew their dirks.

Jaimee's belly clenched. Was she dreaming? Had her secret yearning for this man drawn him here? Every night she lay abed, staring up at the darkness, and relived those stolen moments with him.

His hot kisses.

The sensual rumble of his voice.

The purple-grey of his stormy eyes.

His touch, which made her blood sing.

The way he'd seen her—as no one ever had.

And now he was here, in the flesh, walking toward her.

Jaimee's gaze raked over him. Alexander wasn't dressed for travel. He wore no cloak, and the dark lèine and leather trews he wore were sweat-stained. His dark hair was unbound and tangled.

Tension rippled through Jaimee then when she spied dark encrusted blood upon his right wrist and hand. Had he been in a fight?

Jaimee's attention traveled behind him, expecting to see an escort. No one appeared. He was alone.

A couple of yards from Connor and Morgan, Alexander halted.

The laird of Farr Castle seemed to have lost his tongue; as such, Morgan spoke first. "Have ye come for that fight, at last, Gunn?"

To Jaimee's surprise, Alexander shook his head. His expression was solemn, his gaze wary. And then to her even greater shock, he unbuckled the dirk about his waist and threw it onto the ground between them.

Surprise rippled through the yard. Jaimee glanced around, realizing they now had an audience. Cait had hurried back inside, as fast as her heavy belly allowed, and called the others down to the landward bailey. Keira, Kennan, Cait, Maggie, and Connor's warriors now formed a crowd behind them.

And all the while, Connor stood still, as if carven from granite.

"I shall never again draw my blade against a Mackay," Alexander announced. His voice was soft, yet it carried in the gloaming. "I swear it on my mother's grave."

Muttering followed this announcement before Morgan replied, "So ye have a mother, do ye? There was I thinking ye'd sprung straight from Satan's loins."

Alexander shifted his attention from Connor's stony face to Morgan, his mouth lifting at the corners. "Some would say I did."

"Why are ye here?" Morgan growled. "I don't recall an invitation being issued."

Alexander's face grew stern. "I have broken with my kin."

Jaimee's breathing hitched once more. Breaking with one's clan wasn't something any Highlander did lightly—especially a Gunn. Their clan was one of the smallest, and as such was incredibly tight-knit.

Morgan's dark-blond brows crashed together. "What?" Beside him, Connor still didn't speak. His silence, and the whiteness of the knuckles that clenched his dirk, made dread twist in Jaimee's gut.

"I suggested a peace agreement between the Gunns and the Mackays," Alexander continued. "My father didn't take kindly to it."

Jaimee's gaze strayed once more to the blood encrusting Alexander's hand. Had George Gunn done that?

"We fought," Alexander continued, confirming her suspicions, "and I bested him."

Morgan's lip curled. "Why aren't ye sitting in Castle Gunn crowing about it?"

"I should have killed him, but I didn't ... so he banished me."

A gasp from behind them followed this comment. Jaimee glanced over at the crowd to see that Keira was wide-eyed; her face had turned the color of milk.

"And ye came here?" Disbelief dripped from Morgan's voice. He shook his head then, as if marveling at the warrior's idiocy.

Alexander nodded before his gaze shifted back to Connor. Tension pulsed across the bailey. "The rancor between us isn't easily overcome, Mackay," Alexander said, his voice roughening. "I tried to kill ye in battle and will admit to rejoicing when yer father fell." Muttering rippled through the surrounding crowd at these words, yet Alexander Gunn pushed on. "Ye should also know that yer sister didn't come with me willingly that night either ... I abducted her."

Jaimee's hand went to her throat, the breath she'd been holding rushing out of her.

No!

Alexander's attention flicked to Jaimee momentarily, an apology in his eyes, before he looked to Connor once more. "Yer sister lied to protect me ... but it's time for the truth. I abducted her ... although I swear I didn't harm her."

A nerve pulsed in Connor's jaw as he stared back at his enemy. He'd gone white around the mouth, and his gaze glittered.

Alexander didn't break his stare. "I see the hate in yer eyes," he murmured. "The same hate that has fueled me since birth. But I choose to end it now. He took a step toward Connor and then sank to one knee. "I pledge loyalty to ye, Mackay. I will follow ye, kill for ye if ye ask it ... all I ask in return is yer sister's hand."

Long moments passed, the longest moments of Jaimee's life.

She was shaking now, like a leaf in the wind. Her belly churned, and her palms were slick with cold sweat. She was horrified: horrified that Alexander would break with his kin, that he'd ride here to Farr—and that he'd dare prostrate himself before her brother and swear loyalty to him.

But the most horrifying of it all was that he'd actually asked her brother for her hand. Connor would slay him for that.

Her chest started to ache; it was hard to draw breath.

Connor moved then. Two stalking strides brought him close to Alexander. He raised his dirk and placed its tip at the hollow of his throat.

"Ye are an arrogant cur, Gunn." Connor's voice was harsh. "Only ye could make such a promise and insult me at the same time. For a long while, I've longed to send ye to hell."

Alexander stared up at him, his gaze unwavering. "Do it then."

27

FIGHT ME, GUNN

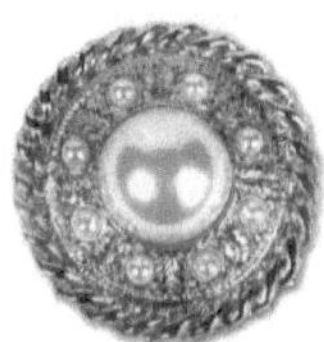

"NO!" THE WORD burst out of Jaimee before she could prevent it.

The cry came from her gut, from a place deep inside that twisted at the sight of Alexander Gunn kneeling there, with her brother's blade at his throat.

Connor would do it too; she knew it from the look on his face. His usually good-humored expression was gone. Violence now burned in his eyes.

Jaimee took an unsteady step forward. Lord, her legs were shaking so badly they felt as if they might give way under her at any moment.

But she couldn't let this go on, couldn't stand by and watch Alexander Gunn die by her brother's hand.

"I love him," she gasped.

And the moment she made the declaration, she knew it to be true. She'd known it for days now but had tried to deny the reality of things. When Alexander had ridden away from Halladale that day, he'd taken a piece of her with him. There was no point in pretending he hadn't.

The look of horror on both her brothers' faces should have warned her from continuing, yet she plowed on. "This connection between us, it's real. Neither of us wanted it, neither of us sought it ... but it won't let us be."

She moved closer, stepping up next to where Alexander still knelt.

He didn't move, although his gaze had tracked her. His grey eyes were wide, and a nerve flickered upon his left cheek, in the thin silver scar that marked it.

Her words had shocked him, even more than they had those looking on.

Connor's gaze flicked to Morgan. "Get Jaimee back from us."

The last time Connor had issued that command, she'd managed to fend Morgan off with a dirk. Yet she carried no weapon now. And perhaps remembering how she'd evaded him previously, Morgan lunged toward her this time. A gasp of outrage escaped Jaimee as Morgan's arms clasped around her chest and abdomen. He then hauled her back to the edge of the watching crowd.

Jaimee struggled. "Let go of me, Morgan!"

He didn't reply, and his iron grip didn't budge an inch.

Meanwhile, Connor stared at Alexander as if they were alone, as if the rest of the world had disappeared and only reckoning remained.

And then, he tossed his dirk aside, reached down, gripped Alexander by the collar, and hauled him to his feet.

An instant later, Connor slammed his clenched fist into Alexander's stomach.

It was a hard blow, and one that would have brought most men to their knees, yet Alexander's sharp exhale was the only sign Connor had winded him.

"Fight me, Gunn!" Connor roared.

Jaimee struggled harder still against Morgan's grip. However, he continued to hold her tight.

Jaimee's heart slammed against her ribs. *Dear Lord, can't someone stop this?*

Alexander's mouth twisted, before he shoved Connor hard, sending him back a pace. "Ye want me to scatter yer teeth all over this yard, Mackay?"

Connor snarled back before he slugged Alexander in the mouth.

An instant later, Alexander's fist slammed into Connor's jaw.

"No!" Jaimee's cry was drowned out by the roar of the watching crowd. Connor's warriors called out to their laird, urging him on as he flung himself at Alexander. Her heart was in her throat now, tears running down her face. But no one noticed, no one cared.

All gazes were on the two men who were pummeling each other in the center of the bailey.

The crowd drew back slightly, to give them space to fight.

"Stop them, Morgan!" Jaimee pleaded, her voice hoarse. "Please do something."

"Ye can't halt this, lass," Morgan replied, his voice hard and flat. "Connor and Gunn need to have it out. Ye can't stop them, and ye shouldn't."

Jaimee shook her head, denying his words. She didn't understand men, and she never would. How would beating each other to death help?

But the fighting continued, and the watching crowd bayed for Alexander Gunn's blood.

Early on, it became obvious that both men were evenly matched. Connor was a big man, although Alexander was possibly even broader in the shoulders. They gouged, punched, and kicked like animals. Jaimee couldn't bear to watch, and yet she couldn't look away.

Cheering reverberated off the walls as Connor punched Alexander in the eye and sent him reeling back. However, when her brother lunged at his opponent to press his advantage, Alexander wrapped his leg about his ankle and tripped him.

Connor slammed into the dusty ground, and the two men ended up grappling there in a parody of a lover's embrace.

Connor managed to get his hands around Alexander's throat, yet a swift knee to the guts loosened his grip enough for his opponent to throw him off.

Panting hard, both men rolled to their feet and then lunged at each other again. They swung punches, the meaty thud of bare knuckles colliding with flesh echoing through the bailey.

The sound sickened Jaimee; she swallowed down bile, yet she still couldn't look away. At this rate, the pair of them would collapse from exhaustion before either gained the advantage.

The fight drew out, and after a while, both men were staggering on their feet. Blood ran down Alexander's face, one eye was purpling, and his bottom lip had started to swell. Likewise, Connor looked a mess. One of his eyes was closed, and grazes marked his forehead and jaw. Blood leaked from his nose.

The end came when Connor made one last lunge at Alexander and head-butted him.

The Gunn warrior lurched back, swaying on his feet before he fell to the ground.

Connor stood over him, waiting for his opponent to rise. Yet Alexander didn't.

Jaimee let out a moan as she struggled against Morgan's hold. Tears now coursed down her face. "Mother Mary, no!"

Connor mumbled a curse through swollen bleeding lips and then his knees crumpled. He collapsed next to the man he'd just felled, insensible.

"Connor!"

Keira's cry rent the air, and then an instant later, she pushed her way through the line of warriors that had formed a barrier between the fighting men and their kin. Her face was ashen, and her midnight-blue eyes glittered. She sank to her knees next to Connor. "Mo ghràdh," she gasped. "Please, wake up."

A long, tense moment passed, and then Connor came to. Rolling onto his back, his eyes flickered open. "Keira," he mumbled. "Ye shouldn't be here ... Gunn—"

"Gunn isn't a danger to ye, me, or anyone else," Keira replied, her tone sharpening. "I wouldn't be surprised if ye killed him."

However, an instant later, a low groan from Alexander intruded. He didn't move, yet his legs twitched.

Connor muttered a foul curse. "No such luck."

"Let me go, Morgan," Jaimee gasped.

She twisted against her brother's grip, and this time, to her surprise, he did let her go. Picking up her skirts, she swept across the bailey to where Alexander lay and knelt beside him.

"Alex," she whispered, taking hold of his hand. The fight had broken the scab on the wound on his forearm, making the injury bleed once more. Sticky blood covered his hand, yet she paid it no mind. Instead, she threaded her fingers through his. "Can ye hear me?"

"Aye, m'eudail," he whispered.

My darling.

It was the first endearment he'd ever used with her, and the sound made her throat ache.

His eyes slowly opened then; their smoky depths were clouded at first as he struggled to remain conscious. But after a moment, they focused upon her. His fingers tightened around hers.

"Jaimee," Connor rasped. "Get back from him."

Her head snapped up, and she speared her brother with a fierce glare. "No."

"Let them be, Connor." Next to her husband, Keira's face had gone taut. Now she was no longer worried that Connor was gravely injured, ire burned in her eyes. "Hasn't this gone on long enough?"

Connor, who still lay on his back and wasn't yet recovered enough to get up, mumbled a curse. "Stay out of this, Keira."

"No. I've held my tongue long enough. Ye wanted to have it out with Alexander Gunn, and now the pair of ye have beaten each other witless. Isn't that enough?"

"No," he said roughly. "Ye don't understand. It will never be enough."

Keira's proud face tightened. "I'm a Gunn too," she reminded him, her voice low and clipped. "And try as ye might, ye can never change that."

"Aye, but ye aren't George Gunn's first-born," he countered. "Ye haven't killed countless Mackays."

"Let it go," Keira replied, her voice hardening. "The man has given up his kin, his future, to come here and swear his fealty to ye. I understand yer need for reckoning ... but how far do ye want to take this?"

Looking on, Jaimee found herself in awe of Keira. She glared down at her husband, not giving an inch.

Connor rolled onto his side and pushed himself up into a sitting position. Concern fluttered through Jaimee when she saw his eyelids flutter. His swollen face paled, and he bowed his head a moment until the spell passed.

Meanwhile, Alexander unwound his fingers from Jaimee's and hauled himself upright. Like Connor, his handsome face was bloodied and battered. Already one eye had swollen shut. On the morrow, his face would be livid with bruises. "My pledge still stands, Mackay," he mumbled through swollen lips. "Our fight changes nothing."

Connor's gaze cut to Alexander. His mouth then twisted, and he wiped at the blood that still trickled down from his swollen nose. "Aye," he muttered. "Ye are right about that." He motioned to the warriors who stood nearby, awaiting his orders. "Take Gunn down to the cave cages."

Jaimee's blood chilled. Alexander would surely freeze to death if he was locked in one of those.

"No, Connor!" She went to launch herself to her feet, yet Alexander's hand shot out, his fingers curling around her wrist to prevent her. Slowly, he drew Jaimee down, so that she knelt next to him. Her eyes misted as she looked into his.

"No, lass," he murmured. "Leave it."

28

THE CAVE CAGE

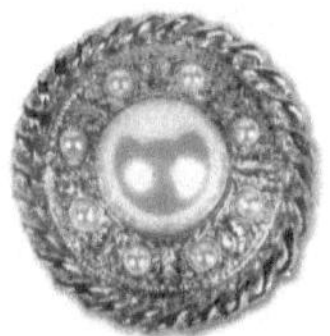

THE CAVE CAGES were aptly named—for that was exactly what they were. Prison cells carved out of the rock under Farr Castle.

There were around a dozen of the cages, and the ones Alexander passed were all empty. A perilously narrow set of stairs led down the cliff face, chiseled out of the rock just as the cages had been.

The sun was setting now, a blaze of burnt gold sliding beyond the glittering sea. An icy wind gusted in, driving through Alexander's blood-and-sweat-drenched lèine. It was going to be a cold night.

Connor's men shoved him into the lowest cage. The space was cramped, just big enough for him to lie down, although when standing, he had to bow his head to prevent cracking his skull on the rough stone ceiling.

A narrow wooden pallet formed a bed, and a bucket in the corner was his privy.

"Enjoy the sunset, Gunn," one of the warriors jeered before slamming the iron gate shut. The man then padlocked it, cast Alexander a wide grin, and departed with the two others who'd escorted him down here.

They left Alexander alone—alone with the biting wind, the magnificent dusk sky, and the shags that nested on the cliff-face next to him.

Stifling a groan, Alexander lowered himself onto the pallet. There were no covers, not even a scratchy blanket to ward off the chill.

Mackay clearly wants me to freeze to death tonight, he thought wryly.

Alexander clenched his jaw before letting out a hiss of pain. The bastard had nearly dislocated it during their fight.

Connor Mackay was impressive with his fists. Few men had ever bested Alexander Gunn in a bare-knuckle fight, yet the laird of Farr Castle had. Not that Alexander hadn't left Connor's once pretty face battered. By dawn, Connor would look as hideous as he himself would.

And yet, Connor had won that fight and had deserved to.

But despite the rancor that burned in his green eyes, Mackay hadn't killed him. Alexander was still breathing, and that had to count for something.

I love him. Jaimee Mackay's declaration still echoed in his ears. Those words wrapped around him then, warding off the chill.

With a sigh, Alexander leaned back on the rough stone and tried to ignore the fact that there wasn't a part of his body that didn't hurt.

Deep inside his chest, he felt something tug and twist. Was it guilt?

He didn't deserve Jaimee's love, not after everything he'd done—but that wouldn't stop him from accepting it, from clinging to it. He breathed her declaration in, and it warmed him from the inside out.

She had spoken true: this wasn't something either of them had actively sought. He'd been vexed that day in Inverness after their meeting in the courtyard garden. The woman had insulted him, enchanted him.

He'd known then, deep down, that he wouldn't be able to free himself of her.

And that obsession had driven him to her door.

He should have been dead now; he certainly hadn't expected to survive another meeting with Connor

Mackay, especially in the man's own castle. The fact that he wasn't dead gave him hope that all was not lost.

Jaimee loved him, and he wished he'd told her he felt the same. However, everything had happened so fast. He hadn't been able to let his guard down in front of the Mackay brothers. His warrior's pride be cursed, he wished he had.

Jaimee Mackay deserved nothing less.

The following morning, Connor's face looked even worse than Jaimee had imagined it would. One eye was swollen shut, his mouth and nose were swollen and crusted in scabs, and livid purple bruises stretched across his cheekbones and jaw.

The sight made Jaimee feel queasy. She looked down at the congealing bowl of porridge before her and realized that she wouldn't be able to eat it.

And her brother's battered face wasn't the only reason.

If Connor looked this bad, after his wife's best efforts to clean him up, how would Alexander's face be? The man had spent the night in one of the cave cages, the outdoor dungeon that had been built during her grandfather's rule of Farr. She'd lain awake all night listening to the howling wind, and the rain beating against the shutters, and had feared the worst.

Coldness seeped deep into her bones. Would he even be still alive?

A tense silence filled the solar this morning. Eventually, Jaimee shattered it. "What will ye do with him, Connor?" she asked, reaching for a cup of milk.

Her brother looked up from where he was buttering a piece of bannock. All her kin were attendance this morning. Even wee Rose, who suckled at her mother's breast while Keira did her best to eat without dropping crumbs on the bairn.

"He can rot in the cage for all I care," Connor mumbled. His swollen lips made talking difficult, yet Jaimee pushed aside her empathy for the pain her brother was clearly in.

"He'll die of cold first, as ye well know. Is that what ye want?"

Connor sighed. He cut Keira a look then, and judging from the way the woman's full lips thinned, Jaimee realized the two had already spoken of this.

A rush of affection for her sister-by-marriage warmed Jaimee's breast. She'd appreciated how Keira had spoken up the day before. If there was one person her brother would listen to, it was his wife.

"I told Keira, and I'll tell ye," he muttered. "It's no less than the bastard deserves." He scowled then. "He abducted ye, Jaimee ... and ye lied for him."

The words were bald, yet Jaimee caught the hurt in them.

Connor was a complex man. Far more so than she'd once believed. He'd always been her brave, dependable older brother—the serious one, the level-headed one. Yet, the past months had shown her that her brothers weren't actually who she thought they were. Connor, in fact, merely swallowed his anger, his resentments, even when they risked damaging him. Meanwhile, Morgan let his burn like a Samhuinn fire but was able to move on from things much quicker.

Morgan was also watching his elder brother closely this morning, a speculative look in his eyes.

"Gunn truly did a job on yer face," he commented. "I think he might have broken yer nose."

"He didn't," Connor replied with a scowl. "Cullodina checked it last night."

"All the same, his right hook is impressive."

"As is my left," Connor growled back. "Don't tell me ye are softening toward the bastard too, Morgan?"

Morgan shrugged, before taking the wedge of bannock that Maggie had just smeared with butter and heather honey and passed to him. He flashed his wife a smile in thanks. "I wouldn't go that far ... although ye have to admit it was brave of him to kneel before ye as he did."

Connor snorted. "Brave or unhinged. His obsession for our sister drove him like some cow-eyed idiot to our door, nothing else."

"Excuse me," Jaimee interjected stiffly. "Don't talk as if I'm not even here." Her fingers tightened around her cup of milk as her temper quickened. "It's more than an obsession, Connor ... for us both. I told ye, I *love* him."

"Satan's cods, Jaimee, please stop saying that. He isn't fit to kiss yer boots."

"He's given up everything for me." Jaimee leaned across the table toward him, aware that all gazes were now upon her. "I've always wanted the kind of love Ma and Pa had," she admitted then. "But I never thought I'd find it ... not until Alexander."

Dismay shadowed her brother's eyes at this declaration. "Do ye realize what ye are saying?" he rasped.

Stubbornness reared within her. "Would ye give up everything for Keira, if it came to that?"

A nerve flickered in Connor's bruised cheek.

"Would ye?" she pressed.

"Aye," he said roughly. "I would."

"So, ye understand how we both feel."

Connor muttered another curse. "But he's *Alexander Gunn,* lass. Ye could have given yer heart to anyone else ... to a decent man who'd treat ye well. Why him?"

"He *will* treat me well," she replied, her throat thickening. "I want to wed him. Please free Alexander ... let us live together at Farr."

"Ye aren't wedding that bastard."

"Well then, we'll live in sin."

"No, ye won't!"

Silence fell in the solar. Outdoors the wind still howled. The shutters were closed against an overcast sky and churning sea. Jaimee and Connor glared at each other, brother and sister not budging.

"I won't have him living in my keep," Connor eventually ground out.

"Then we will live outside, in the village."

"No, I won't let ye live beyond the safety of these walls."

Jaimee drew in a deep breath, fighting the anger that boiled in her belly. How tired she was of Connor ordering her around. She knew he was only trying to protect her, but it was getting too much.

Cait cleared her throat then, intruding on the siblings' rapidly escalating argument. She sat, hands upon her swollen belly, watching Connor and Jaimee with a veiled expression. "There is a solution," she said softly. "One that would ensure Jaimee remained at the castle yet didn't reside with Gunn inside the keep itself." Cait paused there as all eyes turned toward her. "My father needs an apprentice, and Gunn has a blacksmith's brawn. There's a storeroom annex next to my father's lodgings behind the forge. If it was cleared out, they could live there."

Jaimee stared at Cait, her breath catching. Hope flickered in her breast, yet she suppressed the urge to jump up, rush to Cait, and hug her.

Cait's suggestion was a good one, yet there would be no celebration if Connor didn't agree to it.

She shifted her attention back to Connor, as did everyone else at the table. Everything hinged on his next words.

"It makes sense, Connor," Cait pressed on, filling the tense silence. "Think about it. This way, Gunn isn't one of yer warriors, yet he would still reside here, *and* be of use."

At the far end of the table, Connor loosed a deep sigh. He then reached up and pinched the skin between his eyes—one of the few places on his face that wasn't bruised and scabbed.

"I can't believe I'm saying this but ... very well," he muttered. "If yer father agrees, Cait, Gunn can work the forge with him. However—" Connor paused there, his gaze swiveling to Jaimee and pinning her to her seat "—

ye *aren't* wedding him, sister ... in fact, ye aren't to have anything to do with him." Connor's expression hardened. "And that is my *final* word on the subject."

29

FARLAN'S NEW APPRENTICE

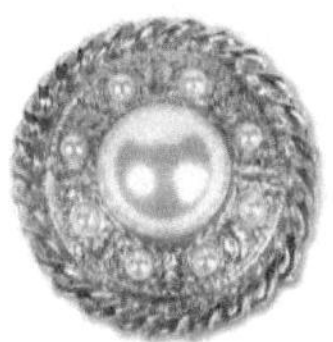

THE BLACKSMITH CAST a jaundiced eye over the warrior before him.

Alexander Gunn had bathed and been given fresh clothing. Nonetheless, his face was a swollen mess, and his body still ached from the beating he'd taken.

"Is this Connor's idea of a joke?" he muttered. When Alexander didn't reply, the smith frowned. "He's punishing me, I know it."

Still, Alexander said nothing. He didn't understand what the man was talking about.

Farlan finished his scrutiny before giving a non-committal grunt. "I suppose ye'll do … ye've got the strength in yer shoulders and arms at least." He scowled then. "Ye have never worked iron, have ye?"

Alexander shook his head. A clan-chief's son didn't work alongside the castle smith. "No," he mumbled through swollen lips, "but I'm a quick study."

Farlan muttered something under his breath that Alexander didn't quite catch. "Ye'd better be." He motioned to a broom leaning against the far wall of the forge. It was mid-morning, and the two men stood alone in the space. "Sweep the floor."

Alexander moved toward the broom without hesitation. He'd happily sweep the floor of the forge all day if it meant he didn't have to stay in that hellish cage. He'd spent a sleepless night shivering in a corner of his cell, willing for dawn to break.

And shortly afterward, Connor Mackay himself had appeared before his cage.

"I'm giving ye one chance, Gunn," he'd growled. "Don't mess it up."

The laird of Farr had then unlocked the cage and opened the door, before leaving.

And Alexander had no intention of squandering the opportunity.

He hadn't seen Jaimee, although he didn't expect to. Mackay most likely had her locked up in her bedchamber, for fear she'd seek him out.

However, the situation with Jaimee could be worked out later. For the moment, he had his freedom and a role inside Farr Castle.

Mackay had shown him a surprising amount of mercy.

Mercy that wouldn't have been returned if he'd been in the same situation at Castle Gunn. The realization made Alexander uneasy. He kept waiting for the sting, the knife between the shoulder blades, but it was yet to come. These people were vastly different to his own, something that would take him a while to get used to.

He swept out the forge before getting started on the other menial tasks Farlan gave him. He cleared the cold ashes away and then cleaned the blacksmith's tools: hammers, chisels, tongs, punches, and fullers.

"I've a set of knives to make this week," Farlan informed him as he finished polishing the last of the tools. "So I could do with an extra pair of hands."

"What happened to yer last apprentice?" Alexander asked. They were the first words he'd spoken since their introduction.

Farlan's greying brows knitted together at the question. "He talked too much."

Taking the point, Alexander turned back to his task. If the smith wanted to work in silence, it suited him just fine.

Farlan worked him hard, even if he wasn't allowed to touch any of the objects the blacksmith was working on. Alexander had a brief break at noon, when he ate a meal of bread, cheese, and braised kale. He sat in the forge, a wooden dish balanced on his knees, while Farlan joined his wife, Maeve, next door in their lodgings.

Outdoors, through the open door of the forge, he could see dust devils dancing across the deserted bailey. The wind hadn't let up all day; just like Castle Gunn, Farr Castle's exposed position meant that harsh weather often plagued it, especially during spring and autumn.

Alexander ate hungrily, glad that the smith's wife had brought him a decent-sized meal. He'd barely eaten since leaving Castle Gunn and was light-headed with hunger. He hadn't seen anyone save Farlan and his wife since beginning work. If anyone usually visited the forge, they didn't today.

Most likely, folk had heard of the demon that now worked there and decided to give it a wide berth.

Alexander welcomed the isolation, as he had the silence. Nonetheless, all of this felt strange to him.

In just a few days, he'd gone from a position of relative authority and power to the role of skivvy. Surprisingly though, his fall from grace didn't bother him nearly as much as he'd anticipated.

Relief had settled over him during the morning as he did the blacksmith's bidding. Some would say he'd just exchanged one tyrant for another, yet Farlan was a lamb compared to his father—and the smith didn't require anything of him except his physical service.

George Gunn had demanded his soul.

Taking a bite of coarse bread, Alexander wondered how Jaimee was faring. Fortunately for her, Connor Mackay wasn't a harsh man; Alexander doubted he'd make her suffer. Even so, the longing to see her burned in his gut like the coals glowing in the forge behind him.

She was so close to him now, physically—yet he felt as if she was slipping away from him.

Perhaps he'd been wrong about Connor Mackay not being cruel; maybe this was his ultimate punishment. The man knew Alexander wanted his sister, yet he would deny him Jaimee while dangling her within arm's reach.

He didn't have long to dwell on Jaimee though, for Farlan reappeared in the forge then and barked at him to hurry up and finish his meal.

Shortly after, they began their afternoon chores. More sweeping ensued, interspersed with bumping bellows to keep the coals hot, and hauling in charcoal, heavy lumps of iron, and water for the slack-tub. As the afternoon wore on, a fine dusting of black dust coated both men.

Retrieving yet another bucket of water from the trough in the landward bailey, Alexander reflected that an apprentice's life was indeed one of drudgery. Farlan was likely to have him beating out blades eventually, but only when he was good and ready. First, he'd enjoy showing his new apprentice who was master.

The hard work didn't bother Alexander though; if anything, he welcomed it.

"Alex." A woman's soft voice drew Alexander from his thoughts. Straightening up, his gaze settled upon Jaimee Mackay.

Dressed in a sky-blue kirtle, her red-gold hair tangling in the wind, she was a welcome sight indeed.

An ache rose in his chest at the sight of her.

For a few moments, they merely stared at each other, and then she moved closer, skirting around the edge of the water trough. Alexander swiveled to face her. She stopped before him; they were only a hand-span apart, and he inhaled the scent of lavender blended with the sweet musk of her skin.

Hunger writhed in his belly, yet he fought the urge to reach for her. Curse him, why did he have no self-control where this woman was concerned?

Jaimee raised her chin, so that she continued to hold his gaze, and then to his surprise, she reached up, her fingertips tracing the ravaged lines of his jaw and cheeks. "God's bones ... yer face."

Alexander grimaced. "I saw yer brother first thing this morning ... he doesn't look any better than me."

"No, he doesn't." She paused then, her green eyes shadowing. "I thought ye were going to kill each other."

His mouth quirked. "It was a good fight."

"Ye enjoyed it?" Her tone was incredulous.

"Aye ... there's nothing I like more than pitting myself against a worthy opponent."

Jaimee shook her head. "Is that why ye came here then ... to get a thrashing from my brother?"

He gave a long, hot look. "Ye know why I came here, Jaimee."

They stared at each other, and a blush rose to her cheeks.

"Connor forbids our marriage," she said huskily. "I don't know if he will ever change his mind."

Reaching up, Alexander caught her hand as it started to lower. "I'll wait," he replied. He heard the desperate rasp of his own voice. They shouldn't be standing out here in the bailey like this. Anyone could see them. And yet their surroundings faded into the mist when Jaimee Mackay locked gazes with him. The feel of her hand in his made his breathing quicken, his pulse race. "No matter how long it takes ... I'll wait."

Her lips parted, and Alexander's pulse sped up. How he wanted to haul her into his arms and feast on that sweet mouth. The taste of her had tortured him ever since Halladale.

And yet he didn't. His own mouth was scabbed and swollen, and he was keenly aware of how visible they were.

He didn't care about incurring anyone's wrath if it were for himself, but he didn't want Jaimee punished. He'd already put her through too much.

"Have things ... been difficult for ye here?" he asked then. "Since Halladale?"

She favored him with a soft smile, although her eyes shadowed. "Not really." Her mouth lifted at the corners. "Although my actions chased away my suitors."

Relief rushed through Alexander at this admission. "Ye weren't punished?"

She shook her head.

Alexander swallowed. "Ye lied for me, Jaimee. I couldn't let ye do that."

She swallowed. "I can't believe ye told Connor ye abducted me … as if he needed *another* reason to kill ye." Her fingers curled around his, the blush on her cheeks deepening. "This thing between us … it's madness."

"Aye," he agreed huskily. "But I can't resist it anymore. I don't know if yer brother will let me stay on in Farr long-term, but I swear I'm not leaving here without ye, m'eudail."

She stared up at him, her green eyes glistening.

"Gunn!" A rough voice intruded. Alexander stepped away from Jaimee and glanced back to the forge. Farlan filled the doorway, hands on hips. "How long does it take to fill a bucket of water?"

Alexander nodded to him. "I'm on my way." He then heaved the bucket from the trough and headed back toward the forge. However, as he went, Alexander glanced over his shoulder and flashed Jaimee a smile.

It had been a stolen moment, but it lightened his heart. The brief encounter gave him hope that one day Jaimee Mackay would be his.

"Wipe that smug look off yer face," Farlan growled as Alexander walked past him into the forge. "Wulvers will rain down from the sky before Mackay lets ye wed his sister."

Alexander walked to the slack-tub—a large wooden container where the smith quenched hot metal—and poured in the contents of his bucket. However, his smile remained. He knew that, yet he was prepared to wait.

Dusk was settling over Farr Castle in a grey cloak when Farlan showed Alexander to his new lodgings. "My former apprentice used to bed down with the stable lads … but it's best ye keep to yerself for a while," the smith grumbled. "Maeve has cleaned out the lean-to for ye." He heaved open the wooden door. "It's cramped, but it'll do."

Alexander's gaze swept over the tidy interior. The musty smell of grains, for that was what the space had been used for storing, greeted him, mingling with the acrid tang of peat-smoke. The lean-to had a sloping roof and rough wooden walls. However, it was clean and dry, and there was a bed in one corner and a hearth with a lump of glowing peat in the other. They'd even brought in a narrow table, where a candle burned next to a platter of food. From the looks of things, Maeve had left him a freshly baked pork pie and a wedge of cheese.

A tired smile curved Alexander's mouth, and an odd sense of well-being filtered over him. His body ached, and his face throbbed from his fight, yet he felt strangely light of heart. He'd expected to be bitter over leaving Castle Gunn. His birthright, his land, was now lost to him. But at this moment, he couldn't have cared less.

"Aye," he said softly. "It'll do."

30

BREATHLESS

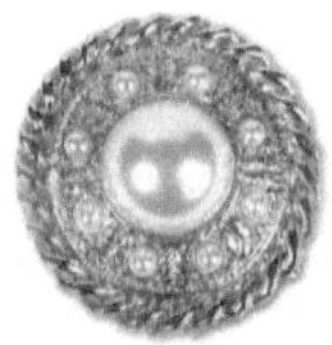

"IT'S A LAD." Kennan's face was creased into a proud smile as he strode into the solar. "A healthy bairn with a lusty cry."

"We all know that," Morgan replied from beside the hearth. "There isn't a soul in the keep who didn't hear its wailing." He rose to his feet then, grinning, and stepped forward to embrace his cousin. "Congratulations, Ken."

"What will ye name him?" Maggie asked, moving in for a hug once Morgan had released Kennan.

"Blake," Kennan replied, "after my Da."

"A fine name." Connor slapped Kennan on the shoulder before pulling him into a bear-hug.

"How is Cait faring?" Jaimee asked. She too had been waiting in the solar while Cullodina helped Cait give birth. It had taken much longer than when Keira had birthed Rose, and they'd all begun to worry.

"She's tired, but Cullodina says she did well."

"Can we see her?" Keira asked, her eyes gleaming with joy. "And the bairn?"

Kennan grinned. "Of course, ye don't need to ask."

Clutching Rose at her side, Keira hurried off, with Maggie and Jaimee following close behind. They found Cait in her bed-chamber, propped up on a mound of pillows, a swaddled bairn in her arms. Cait's usually pert face was slack with exhaustion, yet she was smiling. Cullodina, Farr's healer, sat at her side.

"How is wee Blake?" Keira rushed over to the bed and perched next to Cait.

"He's a big lad," Cait replied with a grimace. "I never thought I'd manage it."

"But ye did," Maggie murmured with a wistful smile.

Something in Maggie's voice made Jaimee's gaze settle upon her. She knew of Maggie's history, of the fact that she'd lost a babe when she'd been wed to her first husband, Campbell Munro. The birth had been difficult, and the healer had pronounced her barren afterward. Usually, Maggie acted as if her inability to have children didn't bother her. But there were glimmers, like now, when Jaimee realized that her sister-by-marriage carried a little sadness in her heart.

As if sensing the same, Cait reached out and clasped Maggie's hand. "Come closer ... do ye want to hold him, Maggie?"

Maggie's smile grew tremulous. "Can I?"

Cait handed the bairn to her, and Maggie's eyes widened. "Hades, ye were right. He's a big lad ... and he's got his Da's red hair."

Cait laughed. "It seems so."

Watching the tender tableau before her—Cait the proud mother, surrounded by a group of women who were as close as sisters to her—Jaimee's throat thickened. How she loved these women. Cait had been in her life a while now, yet Keira and Maggie were relative newcomers to Farr. How glad she was that her brothers had wed them.

But even so, a shadow lay over her, even at this happy time. Frustration boiled within her—and it grew with each passing day.

Three weeks had passed since Alexander Gunn had started work as Farlan's apprentice—and apart from that stolen moment at the water trough, she hadn't spoken to him. She'd glimpsed him once or twice from a distance, yet there had been no opportunity to talk.

Connor watched her like a hawk these days. He'd even taken to posting guards on the landing outside her bed-chamber, so she couldn't sneak out at night and visit Alexander.

It was humiliating and vexing.

Jaimee's jaw tightened as she dwelled on her brother's heavy-handed behavior. She wasn't sure how much longer she could weather it. She tired of being the obedient sister.

Need for Alexander tied her belly in knots and clawed at her breast. Every night, she went to her bed aching for him. She couldn't bear months of this, of being kept apart from him.

She ground her teeth together so tightly then that pain lanced through her ears.

"Do ye want to hold Blake, Jaimee?" Cait asked, intruding on Jaimee's brooding.

"Aye, of course." Jaimee stepped up and took the babe from Maggie. She gazed down at the bairn's crumpled red face and shock of dark-red hair. The bairn stared back at her with those sightless eyes that newborns possessed. Gazing upon him, Jaimee's breathing slowed.

She'd never felt the maternal instinct before, yet at that moment, something stirred within her. As she stared down at Blake Mackay's face, she realized that she wanted this for herself.

Wanted it with a yearning so fierce that it left her breathless.

Connor held a feast that evening to celebrate the birth of Blake Mackay. Kennan only stayed a short while, before he returned to his wife's side, but that didn't stop Connor and Morgan from downing horns of mead once the meal had ended. Raucous, off-tune singing soon echoed high into the rafters.

Listening to her brothers singing bawdy drinking songs, Jaimee exchanged an arch look with both Keira and Maggie. It was rare to see Connor let go like this; he usually left the drunken singing to his younger brother. It seemed that after the tension of the past weeks, the laird of Farr Castle wanted some release.

Maggie leaned in then and cast Jaimee a conspirator's smile. "The men will be in their cups this eve," she murmured. "*All* of them."

Jaimee stared back at Maggie a moment before realization dawned. Likewise, Keira was smiling. She then cast a pointed look in the direction of the long tables beneath the dais where the Mackay warriors were playing drinking games.

Excitement curled in Jaimee's belly, swiftly followed by a flutter of nervousness. Both women were alluding to the fact that the men guarding the landing might not be as vigilant as usual.

A slow smile stretched Jaimee's lips before she nodded. Nothing more needed to be said.

The Mackays went to their beds late that night, Jaimee included. But unlike most of her kin, she had drunk little. She had been too on edge. Instead, she nursed her pewter goblet of wine and chatted with Keira and Maggie until the great hall started to empty out.

Bidding goodnight to her drunken brothers, who were now indulging in an aggressive game of Ard-ri, Jaimee rose to her feet. Ard-ri was a board game in which the Scots defended themselves against Viking marauders. Connor was trying to protect his king, yet Morgan closed in and took away his defenders, piece by piece.

As Jaimee left the chieftain's table, she heard Connor mutter an insult. It sounded as if Morgan was getting too close to his king.

Leaving the hall, Jaimee went upstairs. Nerves and excitement knotted in her belly, yet her shoulders were set in determination.

Enough of being a prisoner in her own home. She'd started to resent Connor of late. He didn't trust her to make her own decisions. His need to protect her was bordering on tyranny.

Jaimee's mouth thinned. She wouldn't put up with this treatment any longer—nor would she be kept from the man she loved.

Entering her bed-chamber, she found Fern waiting for her. "Good eve, Lady Jaimee," she greeted her with a smile. "Ready for bed?"

Jaimee favored the maid with a smile. "Aye," she replied. "Could ye brush some rose-water through my hair tonight?"

A short while later, Jaimee found herself alone in her bed-chamber, dressed in a thin night-rail, her hair falling over her shoulders in heavy waves. It was warm in the chamber, and rose scented the air. Impatience thrummed through her, and she suppressed the urge to start pacing.

How long should I wait?

At least until her brothers had gone to their beds—and Lord knew when that would be, as once they started at Ard-ri, they usually played a few games before one of them got tired of losing.

She couldn't go yet; it was too soon.

Jaimee gave into her restlessness then and paced barefoot around her chamber, before she sat down in front of the hearth and picked up the sewing that she'd been working on for the past weeks—a tiny smock for Cait's newborn. She frowned as she examined it; her needlework had never been the tidiest, and she wondered if it was already too small for Blake.

With a huff of frustration, she tossed the garment down and resumed her pacing. This evening seemed endless. She could still hear the rumble of men's voices from the great hall below.

But of course, all evenings came to an end eventually, and finally, the keep settled and grew silent.

Waiting as long as she could bear, Jaimee opened the door to her bed-chamber, peeking out into the landing beyond. There were usually two guards out there, and two shifts overnight. It was now halfway through the first shift.

Tonight there was only one guard, and he was sitting on the floor, back against the wall, snoring.

Jaimee's gaze narrowed. She wasn't sure where the second guard was—perhaps he'd gone to the privy—but this was her chance. She had to go now or the opportunity would be lost. She just hoped the other guard wasn't lurking somewhere.

Ye are risking Alexander's neck by doing this. The warning niggled at her as she reached for her cloak, pulling it on over her night-rail. Jaimee stilled a moment, considering the position she was about to put Alexander in.

Aye, it was dangerous—but she just had to see him.

Surely, Alexander longed to see her too.

Heart beating loudly in her ears, Jaimee stepped into a pair of slippers and let herself out onto the landing. The cressets burned low, casting long shadows across the rough stone. She crept across the landing toward the stairs, all the while her gaze riveted upon the snoring guard. She'd gone a few paces when he snorted and shifted position against the wall, his eyelids flickering.

Jaimee froze, her pulse thundering in her ears. *Mother Mary, no!*

Someone above heard her prayer, for the guard resumed his steady snoring once more. Palms sweating now, Jaimee inched past him before diving down the stairs. Noiseless in her soft slippers, she raced down three flights of narrow stone steps and reached the entrance hall below. Doors led off to the great hall and kitchens, yet Jaimee headed for the door leading outdoors.

Pushing it open, she stepped out into the night.

The cold air stung her cheeks, and she glanced around, anxious that there might be more guards out here. However, she remembered that it was rare for Connor to post sentries at the doors. There would be guards on the walls and the rampart gates, but not here.

Drawing her cloak tightly around her, she descended the steps and then cut right toward the forge. It was a still night; the wind that had been howling for weeks had died away, giving the night a watchful, slightly eerie feel. A waxing moon hung overhead. They were just three days away from Samhuinn now.

It was shadowy in the landward bailey, with few torches to light her way. However, Jaimee knew every inch of this fortress like the back of her hand. As such, she made her way to the lean-to where she knew Alexander was lodging, without knocking into anything or running up against any walls.

Halting before his door, she drew in a deep, steadying breath.

This is it. After tonight, there would be no going back.

They would face Connor's wrath tomorrow, yet right now, nothing would prevent her from going to the man she loved.

Jaimee raised a hand to the door and gently knocked.

31

A KNOCK AT THE DOOR

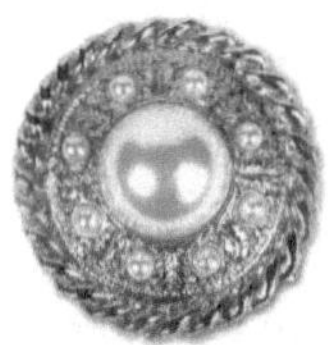

IT SEEMED AN age before anyone answered the door. It likely wasn't that long, it was just that standing outdoors, Jaimee started to feel exposed. She didn't want one of the men on the walls to glance down and see her there.

A sigh of relief gusted out of her when she heard the scrape of the wooden bar being lifted.

An instant later, the door opened and Alexander stood there. Clad in nothing but loose braies, which sat low on his hips, he wore a sleepy expression. His long dark hair was unbound and mussed. The faint glow of a nearby hearth outlined the sculpted planes of his chest and arms. He'd been big and muscular before, yet the weeks working with Farlan had made him even stronger.

She'd roused him from a deep sleep; she could see that. Alexander worked from dawn till dusk in the forge. He probably fell into bed exhausted each night.

However, the moment his gaze settled upon her, Alexander's eyes widened, his body tensing.

"Jaimee," he whispered her name, as if he couldn't believe she was standing there. He then stepped forward, his gaze snapping left and right.

"It's all right ... no one knows I'm here," Jaimee murmured. "The guards outside my door were distracted tonight, so I managed to slip away."

Reaching out, he took her hand and drew her inside the lean-to, closing and bolting the door firmly behind them.

It was a small space, yet a warm and comfortable one. A narrow, straw-stuffed mattress covered in rumpled blankets sat against the wall, below a sloping ceiling. Straw covered the dirt floor.

And yet Jaimee's attention didn't remain for long on her surroundings. Instead, she tilted her chin up, her gaze devouring the handsome lines of Alexander Gunn's face. Aye, like Connor he looked himself again. His bruised and battered features had healed. His eyes were dark pools as he stared down at her.

"Was it wise to come here, lass?" he murmured.

Surprise stilled Jaimee's breath. She'd expected him to haul her into his arms, to rip her cloak and night-rail from her body and take her roughly on the straw-strewn floor. She hadn't anticipated this reaction.

"Don't ye want to see me?" she asked huskily. Her chest tightened as misgiving washed over her. Perhaps his feelings had changed in the past three weeks? Maybe he no longer wanted her?

"Of course I do," he rumbled, his gaze never leaving hers. "But I've gotten ye into enough trouble of late … and yer brother—"

"Connor has interfered enough," she cut him off. Her pulse raced as her fingers tightened around his. He hadn't released her hand after drawing her inside. She swallowed then, as doubt surfaced. "But my presence here does put *ye* at risk … do ye want me to leave?"

"No," he said softly. "I don't care about myself … it's ye I want to protect."

Long moments passed, and then Jaimee wet her lips. "Do ye remember what ye said to me in yer tent at Halladale?"

His mouth curved. "I will never forget it." The heat in his voice made a shiver pass through her. "Afterward ye struck me across the face in reply … punishment I well deserved."

Swallowing, Jaimee held his gaze. "Aye, but our circumstances have changed now, Alex … I want ye to do those things to me."

His gaze grew hot at these words, burning into her.

Jaimee released his hand and stepped back from him. Then, before her courage failed her, she shrugged off her cloak. It fluttered to the ground, revealing the filmy night-rail she wore underneath. She heard the rasp of Alexander's sharp intake of breath.

His reaction thrilled her. His reticence wasn't because he didn't want her, but because he worried about what might happen to her as a result of their coupling. But she didn't need protecting. She was tired of men trying to shield her. Connor meant well, yet he was suffocating her.

When she was with Alexander Gunn, she felt free.

Without another word, she reached down, gripped the hem of her night-rail, and hauled it over her head.

An instant later, she stood before him naked.

Alexander's gaze devoured her from head to foot. Glancing down, Jaimee saw that her breasts jutted out to greet him. She'd always thought her breasts too small—especially when she compared herself to Keira, who had a magnificent bosom—yet they grew tight and achy under the weight of his stare, her nipples drawing into hard peaks.

He stepped toward her then, his hands fastening on her naked shoulders, and pulled her close. Alexander's mouth slanted over hers, claiming her mouth in a wild kiss. His tongue slid between her lips. A low growl rose from deep in his chest as he tasted her.

That sound was her undoing. With a moan of surrender, she melted into his arms. His body was so warm, so strong. She inhaled the musky smell of his skin, blended with the faint scent of lye soap.

How long had she dreamed of this, relived those kisses from the night he'd stolen her away? She could hardly believe this was finally happening, and yet it was. Alexander Gunn no longer haunted her dreams. He was here in flesh, bone, and blood, before her.

The fantasies about true love she'd once cherished seemed silly and girlish compared to what she'd found instead: yearning that sucked the air from her lungs, and passion that burned like a fever in her veins.

Her hands slid down his chest, her nails digging into the firm skin. He groaned, and she realized he liked the rough touch. Encouraged, she gently bit his lower lip. In response, he wound his fingers through her hair, pulled her head back, and let his teeth graze the line of her jaw, the column of her neck.

He then lowered himself before her, his hungry mouth fastening on her breasts.

The feel of his hot mouth, as he drew each nipple in and suckled hard, made her release a soft mewing cry.

"Alex!" she cried out once more as his teeth grazed the swollen nipple before nipping it. Her legs were trembling under her. She wasn't sure how much longer she'd be able to remain standing. He didn't relent, and soon she was writhing in his arms, her head falling back as his wicked mouth continued its assault.

He picked her up then and carried her across to the bed, laying her down upon the rumpled blankets. They were scratchy against her skin, yet Jaimee barely noticed. Instead, her gaze was fixed upon the man standing before her, as he unlaced his braies and pushed them down.

Her gaze slid over the magnificence of his body, which gleamed in the lambent firelight. He was even more beautiful naked than she could have possibly imagined. However, when her attention slid to his groin, her breathing hitched.

Jaimee's lips parted, heat suddenly pulsing between her thighs.

He was huge.

If she was honest, she'd spent too much time over the past weeks thinking about Alexander Gunn's manhood. She'd never seen an aroused man naked before, although one couldn't grow up in a crowded castle without ever seeing a man's rod.

She had no idea they could be so big when excited.

Nervousness flickered to life in the pit of her belly, blending with a pounding excitement. Could that massive, curved shaft that thrust proudly up from a nest of dark hair against his flat stomach actually fit inside her?

Jaimee's breathing quickened. Shortly, she would find out.

Alexander lowered himself onto the narrow mattress, parted Jaimee's thighs, and knelt between them.

Staring up at him, Jaimee's breathing started to come in short, excited pants. She couldn't believe this was finally happening. Hades, how she wanted him.

He loomed over her then, his mouth claiming hers once more.

It was a savage, hungry kiss—one that she answered with equal passion. Her fingernails raked his shoulders, his back, as he moved down her body, feasting on her sensitive breasts once more.

Breathing hard, he drew back then, spreading her legs wider still. His fingers brushed over the downy red-gold hair there, and then he gently slid a finger inside her.

Jaimee bit down hard on her lower lip, to prevent the cry of want that clawed at her throat. She didn't think it was possible to ache for someone like this.

"Ye are so wet," he breathed as he gazed at where he touched her. "So tight."

And with that, he inserted a second finger, sliding up to the knuckles into her.

Jaimee arched against him, swallowing another cry. He was touching her deep inside, curling his fingers up to stroke a place that turned her lower belly molten. She shivered against him, while he continued to plunge his fingers into her. Her limbs trembled, and she would have collapsed against the mattress if his free hand hadn't wrapped under her backside, holding her up as he pleasured her.

Finally, he released her. Breathing hard, Jaimee gazed up at Alexander through hooded lids. There was so much she wanted to say to him, yet her lips wouldn't move. Her body felt weak and boneless.

Alexander gave her a slow, sensual smile and sat back on his heels. He then took himself in hand and gave his rod a long, hard stroke. His hiss of pleasure filled the small room.

Heart pounding, Jaimee curled up into a sitting position. She loved to see him touch himself like this. However, it made her hungry to do the same, and she reached for his shaft.

Watching her, Alexander released his grasp on himself, allowing her to pleasure him instead. He was so big, her fingers barely met when she took him in hand.

And when Alexander let out a strangled moan, a thrill arched up inside her.

"Grip harder," he grunted. He wrapped his hand about hers and showed her how to work him. He grew harder and hotter still when she did. The swollen head of his rod gleamed wetly, and without even questioning her behavior, just following her instinct, Jaimee leaned down and tasted him.

Alexander groaned a curse, but Jaimee hardly noticed. He was delicious. She drew him deep into her mouth, dragging her tongue over the tip of him while her hand continued its slide up and down.

Alexander gasped. His fingers dug into her hair, holding her fast as she sucked him, as she took her own pleasure on him. Her core ached now, restlessness writhing in the cradle of her hips. She loved his dominance, loved his taste—loved everything about this.

However, Alexander was the one to end her ministrations. Breathing hard, he pulled her off him and pushed her back onto the mattress, nudging her trembling thighs wide with his knee.

"I will try to make this good for ye," he said, his voice tight with need. "But a lass's first time can be painful."

Jaimee didn't care about pain. She'd heard rumors of what it was like for a woman's first bedding, from servants in the keep. Some had said it hurt terribly. However, Cait had assured her that it was often little more than a few moments of discomfort. Unlike Keira, who tended to blush pink at such talk, Cait wasn't so easily embarrassed.

Jaimee had squirmed at the time, yet she was relieved that Cait had spoken so frankly now.

She wasn't afraid.

On the contrary, she felt as if she'd die if he didn't bury himself to the hilt inside her this instant.

32

FOR NOW, AND FOREVER

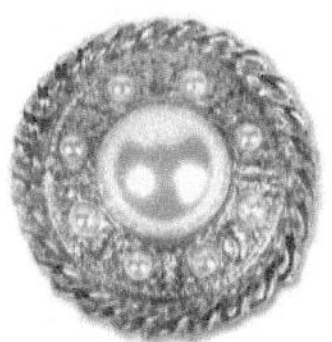

"I TRUST YE, Alex," she whispered, her voice a husky rasp.

And she did. This was what she wanted—to give herself completely to a man she trusted.

A muscle bunched in his jaw as he spread her legs farther apart and placed the tip of his shaft at her entrance, slowly inching in. Jaimee arched her hips up to meet him, wrapping her legs around his hips to pull him closer. Yet he resisted her, moving in just a few inches at a time before withdrawing.

"I'll hurt ye," he managed between gritted teeth. "This needs to be slow at first."

Jaimee nodded, even if frustration bubbled up inside her. This was exquisite torture.

Inch by inch, he slid into her, stretching her with each penetration. Eventually, he reached the barrier of her maiden-head, and when he slowly pushed through it, a sharp twinge made Jaimee tense.

Their gazes locked as he withdrew and slid a little farther still inside her.

Sweat gleamed off Alexander's torso now as he held himself back.

And then, with one final, long, slow slide, he buried himself completely.

Gazes fused, they paused there a moment.

The aching fullness of him inside her was almost too much at first, although as she adjusted to him, Jaimee was glad he'd gone slowly. Instinctively, she knew there wouldn't be any more pain.

Jaimee groaned, lifting her hips to him. "I'm ready, Alex," she whispered.

Whispering her name, he began to move inside her in deep, determined thrusts. And each time he sank into her, an aching pleasure built in Jaimee's lower belly.

He filled her, stretched her, and completed her. And all the while, his gaze held hers prisoner. It was intimate, almost unbearably so; it felt as if he could see into her soul. As if every secret she'd ever held was being stripped bare.

There could be nothing better than this. Nothing.

And yet the pleasure that coiled tight, that made her arch hard against him, made her dig her heels into his buttocks as she urged him on, only grew in intensity. Alexander rode her relentlessly, not letting up till pleasure exploded deep within her, in rolling, rippling waves.

She bit down on the heel of his hand as she shattered, for if she hadn't, her scream would have echoed through the night. And an instant later, he arched back, his face contorting as he too reached his peak.

Bodies shuddering, they collapsed together on the tangled blankets, their skin slick with sweat and their hearts thundering.

It was a while before either of them could speak.

Jaimee pressed her face to his neck, breathing him in. Her senses reeled. She'd never felt so vulnerable yet so protected. It was a new, wondrous, sensation.

Alexander pushed himself up off Jaimee, for he'd collapsed on top of her, and although she liked the feel of his body on hers, it was getting difficult to breathe. Withdrawing from her, he rolled onto his side.

Jaimee twisted to face him, and once more their gazes fused.

Reaching out, he pushed sweat-damp hair off her face. Alexander then traced her lower lip with the pad of his thumb. "Ye are mine, Jaimee Mackay," he said, his voice rough. "For now, and forever."

"Satan's stinking cods," Connor growled. "Please tell me ye didn't lie with him."

"I can't tell ye such … because I have." Jaimee held her brother's gaze, her jaw firming. Her hand tightened around Alexander's. "We wish to wed this morning. Please give us yer blessing."

Standing in the chieftain's solar, hand-in-hand with Alexander, she noted that both her brothers looked a bit worse for wear. Their faces were pale, their eyes bloodshot, and lines bracketed their mouths.

Clearly, they'd both overdone it on the mead the night before.

It was early. As soon as the sun cleared the eastern walls, Jaimee and Alexander had gone to see Connor. Everyone except Cait and Kennan was present at the table. Cait wouldn't leave her bed so soon after giving birth, and Kennan would be breaking his fast with his wife.

Jaimee's stare with Connor drew out, and nerves clenched under her ribcage. She wasn't sure whether it was wise to have this conversation with Connor when he was in such a state. Yet, it was too late. They were standing before him now, and it was clear to everyone seated at the table what had transpired.

She'd wanted this—and that meant she had to stand up to her brother.

Next to Connor, Keira's eyes went as wide as moons, while Maggie halted in the midst of buttering a wedge of bannock. Both women looked shocked at her appearance. They'd been complicit in all of this, yet hadn't expected Jaimee to take such a bold move.

And yet, wasn't it Keira who'd once said that life trampled the meek?

If Jaimee wanted a chance at a life with Alexander, she needed to face Connor.

Tension pulsed through the solar. Morgan mumbled an oath and rubbed his temples. "It feels as if a mob of sheep just ran across my head," he muttered. "Can't this wait?"

"No," she replied, the word carrying across the solar. "It can't."

"I love yer sister, Mackay," Alexander spoke then, his attention fixed upon Connor. "And I promise to protect her ... with my body and my life."

Connor's mouth thinned, his attention shifting to the man at his sister's side. "And what do ye have to offer her, Gunn? Ye gave up everything to come here."

"Only myself," he replied quietly. "With Jaimee's blessing, it will have to be enough."

Alexander's words sent a ripple of disbelief through the solar, and Connor's lip curled.

"He *is* enough," Jaimee whispered. "He's all I want." Tears pricked the back of her eyelids as she spoke. Despite their passionate night together, Alexander hadn't yet told her he loved her. Instead, he'd waited until he stood before her brothers to say the words.

She wanted to turn to him, to throw her arms around his neck and kiss him wildly, heedless of who looked on. However, she checked the urge.

She needed to focus on her brother at present. "Ye can't stop this, Connor," she said firmly. "Not without losing me forever—" her gaze hardened then "—for that is what will happen, if ye prevent Alex and me from wedding—if ye harm the man I love."

As she watched him, Connor leaned back in his chair and raked his hands through his unbound blond hair. He then muttered a curse, one of the saltiest Jaimee had ever heard him use.

Jaimee didn't flinch. "Will ye keep me prisoner forever, in an attempt to save me from myself?" she demanded. "Ye have done a fine job as laird since Da died … he'd be proud of ye … but is this what he would have wanted?"

"He wouldn't have wanted ye to wed a *Gunn*," Connor growled back.

"And what about Ma?" she demanded, refusing to back down. "She'd turn in her cairn to see us at war like this."

Connor stared back at her, a muscle ticking in his jaw. "Jaimee," he began, a warning edge to his voice. "I—"

"I've tried to be the sister ye wanted," she cut him off. "I know I was willful, and I tried to change that. I cast aside my dreams of love and attempted to do what was expected of me … to do my duty … but events conspired against us all." She swallowed, cursing the sudden huskiness of her voice. "Alex and I love each other. Can't ye just be happy for us?"

She left it there, blinking back tears.

Long moments passed, and she watched the conflicting emotions that warred in Connor's eyes. Eventually, a weary sigh gusted out of him. "Fighting ye on this is like trying to hold back the tide," he rasped. "I can see it's a battle I will eventually lose." His eyes shadowed then. "I don't want to destroy our relationship over yer choice of lover, lass."

Jaimee held his gaze, her own never wavering. "Then give me yer blessing."

Connor's throat bobbed. "Very well." His voice was barely above a whisper. "If this is what ye truly want … then I give ye my blessing."

Relief crashed over Jaimee, the sensation so violent that her knees nearly buckled. Instead, she clung to Alexander's hand, for only he could anchor her. He squeezed back in a wordless answer.

Connor's attention then flicked back to Alexander, and his brows drew together. In an instant, the vulnerability he'd shown his sister vanished. "Ye had

better look after her, Gunn," he growled. "I'll be
watching ye."

The two men stared at each other, and then, to
Jaimee's surprise, Alexander smiled. "I'd expect nothing
less, Mackay."

They wed in the doorway of the chapel in Farr Castle's
seaward bailey mid-morning. Father Lachlan conducted
a brief ceremony while Connor, Keira, Morgan, and
Maggie bore witness to their vows.

Jaimee wore her favorite jade-green kirtle and a soft
shawl of lambs-wool, pinned around her shoulders with
her cherished mother-of-pearl brooch. Fern had brushed
out her hair before drawing half of it up into a braid that
wrapped around the crown. Alexander wore a clean pair
of peat-brown braies and a dove-colored lèine. His dark
hair was unbound, stirring in the brine-scented breeze
that feathered across the bailey, and he'd trimmed his
beard close to his jaw so that it was barely more than
stubble.

Jaimee couldn't take her gaze off him, and likewise,
Alexander held her eye throughout the entire ceremony.
At the end of it, he leaned down and kissed her. It was
gentle, tender—different from the heated kisses he'd
given her the night before. However, the softness of it
made Jaimee's breathing hitch.

He didn't need to say a word; the tenderness of that
lingering kiss told her that he loved her.

They turned from the priest, their hands still clasped,
their attention settling upon the four witnesses who
looked on from the bottom of the steps. Both Keira and
Maggie were weeping, although they smiled through
their tears.

Jaimee wasn't sure what she expected to see on
Connor and Morgan's faces—anger and sadness perhaps.

But instead, a half-smile curved Morgan's lips, a look of quiet resignation in his eyes. Connor's expression was softer than she'd expected, although his green eyes were veiled. Meeting her gaze, his mouth lifted at the corners.

"Don't think ye are getting the day off," Farlan greeted Alexander as he appeared in the doorway to the forge, hand-in-hand with his wife.

"I wouldn't dream of it," Alexander replied, his mouth quirking. Farlan's gruff manner didn't bother him. In the weeks since he'd started work in the forge, he'd realized the blacksmith's bark was worse than his bite. He'd come to respect the man and enjoyed learning from him.

Farlan huffed, crossing beefy arms across his chest. His gaze then flicked from Alexander to Jaimee. "I suppose I should congratulate ye both."

"Only if ye wish to, Farlan," Jaimee replied blithely.

"Aye, well, 'congratulations' then," the blacksmith grumbled.

"Thank ye." Alexander favored Farlan with a smile before he glanced over at Jaimee. "Go on, lass. Get settled in the lean-to. I'll see ye later on."

Jaimee nodded before raising her chin to kiss him. She then favored him with a sultry look that promised much, turned, and left. Alexander watched her go, the smile still lingering upon his lips. When he turned back to the smith, he found Farlan frowning at him.

"Come on then," the older man grumbled. "Grab yerself a hammer and help me with this blade." He motioned to the glowing length of iron he'd just pulled from the embers with a pair of pincers. "It won't forge itself."

33

CAN'T BE UNDONE

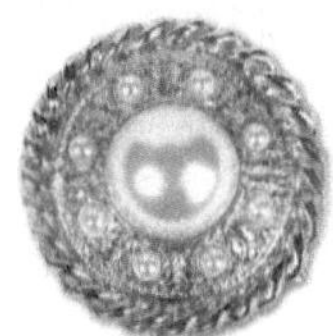

JAIMEE BRUSHED HER hair away from her sweaty face and stepped back, her gaze sweeping over the interior of the lean-to.

Her new abode was half the size of her bed-chamber in the keep, and yet it had taken a while to make it feel like home. Surveying her work, she thought she'd never seen anywhere cozier. Earlier, she'd gone up to her chamber, and with Fern's help, had chosen a small selection of her clothing to bring downstairs. Two warriors had carried in a leather trunk, which held her most cherished items, although a few of her best kirtles now hung on the rough wooden walls. She'd brought fresh linen down too and made up the bed, removing the coarse blankets. Sprays of heather now hung from the ceiling, and lavender sprigs lay amongst the straw on the floor, scenting the air. A mutton stew—a recipe Farr's head cook, Elsa, had taught her—was simmering over the hearth. It had been cooking since late morning, awaiting her husband's arrival.

Husband. A smile stole over Jaimee's face. It hardly seemed real, and yet it was.

She and Alexander were wed.

This was their home now. No longer would they have to sleep apart or hide their relationship from others.

They'd passed through fire to reach this point, and it had forged an unbreakable link between them.

The past weeks had opened Jaimee's eyes. She'd learned that love was different for everyone. For years, she'd modeled her expectations on her parents' relationship, and then on those of her brothers and cousin. But what she had with Alexander was different. It was special.

Her man had rough edges. He'd grown up in a harsh world, and it had given him a carapace of iron. Yet she wouldn't change him.

Fern had wept earlier as she helped Jaimee pack. Now that her mistress was married to the blacksmith's apprentice, she'd no longer serve her. Instead, Fern would take up a role as second maid to Keira, and when Rose got old enough, she would serve her. Fern wouldn't lose her position, yet the lass had cried all the same.

Although Fern would never admit it, Jaimee knew she couldn't believe Lady Mackay would give up all her comfort and finery for Alexander Gunn.

Jaimee's smile turned rueful. It was likely most folk within the walls of Farr Castle, and in the village beyond, thought she'd lost her wits.

Yet she hadn't. She'd never been saner, or happier, than this moment.

The door to the lean-to opened then, and Alexander stepped inside.

A smile creased his face when he looked around him. "I hardly recognize this place," he murmured, his smile widening. "It certainly takes a woman's touch to turn four walls into a home."

Jaimee grinned back, ridiculously pleased by his comment. "I've made stew," she replied, suddenly overcome with shyness. All of this was new territory. She wasn't sure exactly how to be a wife. "I hope it's good."

He glanced over at where their supper simmered over glowing embers. "It smells delicious."

Reaching up, he massaged a muscle in his shoulder. He then glanced down at his sooty, sweat-stained clothing. "I should bathe and change before eating though."

"I've warmed some water for ye," Jaimee replied motioning to the wash-bowl, lye, and drying cloth that sat on the table under the tiny shuttered window.

Alexander stepped close to her, his gaze settling upon her face. "Thank ye, wife," he murmured. He then leaned down and brushed his lips over hers.

It was a graze, a sensual promise, and a shiver of desire trembled through Jaimee. It wasn't that long since they'd lain together, yet despite that she'd kept busy all day, each hour apart from him had felt like an eternity.

Stepping away from her, Alexander pulled off his soiled lèine and stripped off his braies. Then, naked as the day he was born, he stepped up to the washbowl and started to bathe.

He was completely at ease naked, as most men seemed to be. Jaimee couldn't take her eyes off him. She marveled at the long, sculpted muscles of his back, his narrow waist and hips, tight buttocks, and heavily muscled legs. Even the cross-hatching of silver scars on his back couldn't dim his beauty.

The man was delicious to gaze upon. She'd never tire of it.

Jaimee waited until he'd nearly finished bathing before she stepped up next to him. She then reached for the washcloth and block of soap. "Here," she murmured, her voice thick with desire. "Let me help."

Mouth quirking, he stood back, allowing her to soap up the cloth and slide it down his belly. His shaft was already hard, as if he'd felt her gaze upon him while he'd been bathing.

She washed his groin boldly, thrilling as his rod grew engorged and hot in her hands.

"Ye seem to be paying a lot of attention to just one part of me, Jaimee," he rumbled, a smile in his voice. "I'm dirty *all over* ye know."

She laughed, the soft sound filling the room. "Aye, can ye blame me?" Jaimee raised her chin then, meeting his eye once more.

Their stare drew out, and the teasing smile upon his lips faded. "Is this real?" His voice turned husky, sensual. "I feel as if I'm about to wake up from the best dream of my life."

"Ye aren't imagining this," she whispered, her fingers clasping his shaft. She tightened her grip, just as she knew he liked it, thrilling as a low groan escaped him. "Nor this." She slid her hand to the root of his rod and then back up again in a powerful sweep.

She then leaned in, and raised her chin, her mouth grazing his.

Alexander muttered a curse and hauled her hard against him. This kiss was hungry, possessive. An instant later, his hands were ripping at her clothing, tearing off the plain woolen kirtle and lèine she'd donned for cleaning out the lean-to and preparing the supper. It would take her days to repair them, if the garments could be salvaged at all.

Jaimee didn't care about her ruined clothing. She just wanted his mouth, his hands, on her naked skin. She wanted to drown in him.

Alexander hadn't planned on taking Jaimee quite so soon after entering the lean-to. He was weary after an afternoon hammering out blades in the forge. He was a fast learner, and Farlan was now letting him do more interesting work, in addition to the menial chores that kept the forge running. As such, the muscles in his back, upper arms, and shoulders ached, and his belly demanded its supper.

However, the moment he stripped off his clothing and began to bathe, the moment he felt his wife's gaze tracking his every movement, his exhaustion vanished, as did his rumbling stomach.

Suddenly, there was only one thing he was hungry for—and it wasn't mutton stew.

He stripped the clothes from her, his blood heating at her shocked gasp. Then, as soon as she was naked, he fell upon her lithe body. She was lovely, all coltish, long limbs and creamy skin. Lowering himself before her, he focused his attention upon her breasts: those delicious pert tits that begged to be sucked.

The mewing, gasping sounds she made as he suckled her, the way she pulled at his hair, urging him on, nearly drove him insane with lust. This woman was every torrid dream he'd ever had come to life.

He had to be inside her. Now.

Scooping Jaimee up into his arms, he crossed to the bed. It looked far different to the nest of coarse blankets they'd risen from that morning. Alexander laid her down upon a soft coverlet. He realized then that the air smelt faintly of lavender, a welcome change from the pervasive odor of peat smoke.

However, his attention didn't linger on the changes to the room for longer than an instant. Instead, he fell upon his wife's body once more, working his way from her lips to her breasts, and then down to her belly. As he delved between her trembling thighs, her cries and whimpers nearly drove him over the edge.

He'd spent all day imagining this moment. Cupping his hands under her buttocks, he pulled her up to meet his questing lips and tongue, holding her while she squirmed under him.

And when he finally released her, Jaimee gazed up at him, her cheeks flushed, her green eyes glassy. Her lips were parted, her breathing coming in sharp, needy pants. Jaimee's red-gold hair rippled around her on the pillow like a halo.

Shifting back, Alexander raised Jaimee's long, shapely legs and hooked them over his shoulders. Gripping her hips, he lifted her up to meet him once more, as he slid into her in one deep thrust.

Jaimee's cry of pleasure echoed through the lean-to. No doubt anyone nearby, especially the blacksmith and his wife, who lived next door, could hear. Yet neither Jaimee nor Alexander paid them any mind. They were wed now. The whole world could listen in. Alexander didn't care.

"How do ye want this, mo leannan?" he rasped, as he
slowly withdrew, readying himself for the next stroke.
"Gentle or hard?"

My lover. His chest tightened. This woman was so
much more than that.

Her green eyes gleamed, her breathing quickening
further still. He loved how her fierce passion matched
his. "Hard," she whispered.

A growl rumbled through his chest. Satan strike him
down, she had no idea what she did to him. Her throaty
answer nearly undid him entirely, nearly made him spill
his seed within her then and there.

He did as she bid, thrusting into her in deep, hard
strokes that had her gasping his name and pleading for
more. She raised her hips to meet each thrust, as if she
couldn't get enough of him. The wetness, heat, and
tightness of her stretched his self-control to the limit.
Each time he buried himself in her, it unraveled
something deep inside him.

"I need more, Alex," Jaimee gasped then, clawing at
him. "Please."

Cursing, for her words nearly made him forget
himself entirely, Alexander withdrew from Jaimee,
flipped her over, and raised her up on all fours. He took
her like that, driving into her like a man possessed while
she sobbed with pleasure.

Reaching forward with one hand, Alexander tangled
his fingers in her hair and pulled her head back so that
her back arched. Then, with the other, he reached
between her slick thighs and stroked her while he plowed
her harder still.

Jaimee's hoarse cries filled the room, and her body
shuddered against his. He felt her shatter around him. If
he hadn't been holding her up, she'd have collapsed.

Alexander gave a ragged groan and let himself go.
He'd never given himself up to a woman like this. Never.
He'd always held something in reserve, even the night
before when he'd taken Jaimee for the first time.

But not tonight. Wildness consumed him. A need he
never realized he was even capable of drove him. He was

caught up in a torrent and couldn't free himself. He plunged into her till his own climax barreled into him. The force of it made him let go of Jaimee, his spine snapping back. His cry echoed through their bower.

Panting, Alexander collapsed against Jaimee and slammed a hand down on the mattress under them both to stop himself from flattening her. His heart was galloping so fast, it felt as if it would burst free of his chest. For a few long moments, he couldn't move, couldn't speak.

Breathing hard, Jaimee hung there, arms and legs trembling. She would have collapsed if he hadn't been holding her up—one arm wrapped around her waist. Her throat was raw from the sobs of pleasure that he'd torn from her. She thought the night before couldn't have been bettered. Yet the way he'd just taken her, the way they'd both let go, had utterly ruined her.

Her vision misted, and she heaved in a shaky breath. However, it was impossible to stem her emotions.

Alexander pulled out of her then, in a long, sensual slide that left her feeling empty, bereft. She didn't want him to leave. She ached for him still. She would always ache for him.

Wordlessly, he lowered them both onto the mattress. And then he reached out, gently grasping Jaimee by the shoulder, and rolled her over to face him.

"Ye are weeping," he rasped, a groove forming between his eyebrows. "Did I hurt ye, love?"

Jaimee's throat constricted. She was aware the tears were trickling down her cheeks, yet she couldn't stop them. "No," she whispered. "That was ... wonderful ... I just don't think I'll ever recover from it."

Alexander stared at her, his purple-grey eyes glistening. He swallowed convulsively then, and she realized that he too was fighting the storm their coupling had unleashed. "Neither will I," he replied, the rough edge to his voice giving him away. He reached out then, brushing away the tears on her cheeks. "I'll never recover from *ye*, Jaimee."

She held his gaze; her heart was too full for her to answer.

Moments passed, and then Alexander's throat bobbed once more. "So much has happened lately. I'm lost in the woods, lass ... I don't know who I am anymore."

Watching the tension that rippled across his face, Jaimee's throat tightened. "Ye are still Alex Gunn," she murmured, catching his hand with hers and squeezing. "This is merely a fresh start."

Alexander drew in a deep breath. "But the past can't be undone. Violence is all I've ever known. I'm the eldest son. I'd scarcely been weaned from my mother's tit when my father taught me how to wield a dirk. I've been fighting ever since."

Jaimee searched his face, wondering at what kind of childhood this man had suffered. "Those scars on yer back," she said finally. "Did yer father give them to ye?"

He nodded. "I clashed with him over something trivial when I was around sixteen. He whipped me unconscious and left me in a pool of blood ... made sure my other brothers looked on, so they'd think twice before ever standing up to him."

Bile stung the back of Jaimee's throat. It shouldn't have surprised her that George Gunn would do that to his own son—but it did.

"And yer mother," she whispered. "Ye swore on her grave ... on the day ye arrived here. What happened to her?"

Alexander's gaze shadowed. "She died when I was a lad. Not long after my youngest brother, Will, was born. She broke her leg, and it never healed." He halted, before clearing his throat. "When she died, the healer let me in to see her. Afterward, I was sitting outside her sick room, bawling my eyes out. Father found me there, hauled me to my feet, and smacked me around the head until I saw stars." He pulled a face. "I learned to keep my *weakness* hidden after that."

"Grief isn't weakness," Jaimee corrected him, horrified. "Yer father beat any gentleness out of ye. He taught ye to deny that part of yerself ... but he was wrong. Ye do see it now, don't ye?"

Alexander stared back at her, and the pain in his eyes made her throat ache. She'd had no idea of the battle this man waged with himself.

Moments passed, and then he pulled her into his arms, wrapping his own tightly around her. "I do ... thanks to ye," he said huskily. "I love ye, Jaimee Mackay."

34

AN OUTSTRETCHED HAND

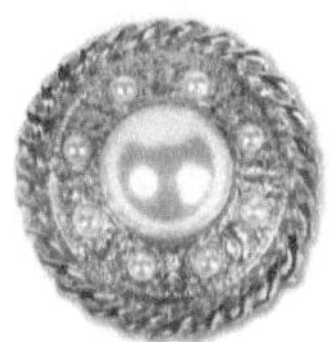

ALEXANDER HAD JUST started work for the day, and was retrieving a bucket of water from the trough in the landward bailey, when Connor, Morgan, and Kennan led their horses out of the stables.

Straightening up, Alexander raised a hand in greeting.

Nearly a moon had passed since his marriage to Jaimee. The weeks had flown by. The fire festival of Samhuinn had gone by, and the days were now short and cold, heavy frosts often freezing the ground. It hadn't frozen this morning though, for a wind whipped across the hills, ruffling the manes and tails of the three horses, and stirring the hair of their riders as they made a few final adjustments before riding out.

Connor held Alexander's eye for a moment before lifting his hand to acknowledge him. An instant later, he favored him with a wary smile.

"Out for a hunt?" Alexander asked. He'd noted the longbows slung over the three men's backs.

"Aye, I'd like to have venison on the table at Yuletide," Connor answered. He paused then before glancing across at Morgan. A look passed between the brothers, and Connor shifted his attention back to Alexander.

"Do ye want to join us, Gunn?"

Alexander tensed, surprise rippling through him at the offer. Ever since he'd wed Jaimee and she'd moved into the lean-to with him, they'd seen little of the laird. Connor had deliberately kept away, and Alexander knew it had nothing to do with giving the newlyweds their space.

Connor Mackay was avoiding him.

Alexander didn't mind much, yet he knew Jaimee had been hurt by her brother's aloofness. She wanted Connor to accept her husband into the Mackay family, even if Alexander had reassured her that such a change would take time.

But, perhaps, Connor's offer this morning was an outstretched hand. The chieftain was ready to move on.

"Hunting?" A gruff voice intruded then. Farlan appeared in the doorway to the forge, his heavy brow furrowed. "Are ye about to rob me of the best apprentice I've ever had, Connor?"

A kernel of warmth ignited under Alexander's ribcage at these words. The blacksmith wasn't usually lavish with his praise.

Connor's smile widened. "Just one day's hunting. We'll be back tomorrow. Can ye spare him?"

The blacksmith huffed before folding his arms across his chest. "I suppose so," he grumbled.

"Good," Connor replied, gesturing to the stables. "Go on, Gunn. Saddle up that hell-beast of yers."

Alexander cocked an eyebrow. "Destroyer?"

Connor snorted. "Aye. He won't let anyone but ye ride him it seems."

Alexander smiled, the warmth within him spreading. Over the past weeks, he'd gotten used to living at Farr Castle. It was a simple life: he spent his days assisting the blacksmith and his nights in Jaimee's arms. He was happier than he'd ever been, and yet the laird's invitation made him realize he'd missed the male camaraderie of his old life. There was nothing he liked more than a stag hunt.

Alexander carried the bucket to the smith, setting it down at his feet. He then winked at Farlan. "I'll see ye tomorrow then?"

The blacksmith pursed his lips. "Aye. Don't worry, ye can sweep out the forge on yer return."

Still smiling, Alexander turned toward the stables.

"If there's a hunt, I'm coming." An irritated female voice carried across the bailey then. Jaimee had appeared and stood there now, hands on hips. "Tor needs some exercise, and it's been too long since I went out hunting."

Morgan grinned across at her. "Ye are a wedded woman now, Jaimee," he teased. "Shouldn't ye be taking a paddle to yer husband's dirty clothes instead of going hunting?"

"I'll take a paddle to *yer* arse, brother, if ye continue," she countered, her green eyes narrowing. She then strode toward the stables. "And since I'm the sharpest archer in this keep, I'd say ye need me."

Alexander's smile stretched into a grin as well as he watched his wife march by.

Jaimee never failed to surprise him. Just when he thought he was getting to know her, she came out with something new. She'd told him she used to hunt, but he hadn't realized she was skilled with a longbow.

Connor huffed a long-suffering sigh. "Very well ... hurry up and saddle yer horses. We have a long ride before us."

They rode east, toward the blue-hued silhouette of mountains that grew gradually clearer as the morning wore on. Watching the horizon, Alexander felt uneasiness steal upon him. They were still on Mackay lands and wouldn't cross the ridge of mountains that formed a natural border between the two territories—yet the sight of the mountains reminded Alexander of everything he'd left behind.

He missed none of it, but he still found himself wondering how his brothers were faring, and if his leaving had caused any further upheavals within Castle Gunn.

Had Tavish managed to secure the hand of Robina Oliphant as he'd wanted?

Dismissing thoughts of his kin, Alexander cast a glance over at where his wife rode next to him. Jaimee's cheeks were flushed from the cold, her eyes bright. Her bay gelding danced, eager to run. Like his stallion, the beast had been cooped up for too long. He could feel the leashed energy within Destroyer this morning. The stallion chafed at the bit, infuriated that three other horses rode ahead of him.

The yapping of the pack of hounds they'd brought with them filtered through the crisp air. Morgan Mackay's wolfhound, a brindled grey bitch that followed him faithfully everywhere, loped at his horse's side, while the others ran ahead.

Feeling his gaze upon her, Jaimee glanced Alexander's way. She then flashed him a wide grin. She'd donned leggings under her skirts so that she could ride comfortably astride and cast a woolen cloak over her shoulders. Like her brothers, she carried a longbow and quiver of arrows on her back.

Alexander didn't carry a bow. Instead, he wore a hunting knife at his hip.

An unexpected gift from Farlan earlier.

It appeared the blacksmith was full of surprises this morning. He'd intercepted Alexander as he'd led Destroyer from the stables and handed him the sheathed knife, hilt first. "Here," he'd said gruffly. "Ye won't be much good out hunting without one of these."

Smiling at the blacksmith's taciturn expression and the way he'd stomped back into the forge afterward, Alexander reflected that this wasn't a bad life at all.

Aye, he'd lost everything—his rank, title, family, and inheritance—but he'd gained much more. These days, he woke every morning with a smile curving his lips, with the woman he loved curled up in his arms.

And being out on a hunt, the cold wind rushing through his hair, the thunder of hooves shaking the ground, he felt as if his life was finally complete.

They rode deep into the western pockets of the mountains, into the shadowy vales between the craggy peaks, where herds of red deer roamed. The landscape here was vastly different from the windswept and barren coastline. Dense woods surrounded them, and the air was heavy with the scent of pine and moss.

All conversation ceased as they journeyed farther east. Even the hounds quietened as they followed the scent of the deer that lived in this valley.

After a while, the pines drew back, and they rode onto a steep meadow.

Up ahead, Connor drew up his horse and pointed.

Alexander's gaze swept the vale, before it alighted upon a magnificent stag, flanked by two hinds. The three of them were trotting along the bottom of the vale, oblivious to the danger that stalked behind them.

Connor raised his hunting horn to his lips then. Its wail cut through the silence, and the hunt was on.

The stillness shattered, and they were off in pursuit, hooves flying and dogs baying.

The thrill of the stag hunt caught fire in Alexander's veins. These animals symbolized the Highlands: they were fast, sure of foot, and difficult to catch, which made them all the more sought after.

However, these hunters and their dogs were experienced, Alexander noted. Two of the dogs raced after the stag itself, seeking to separate him from his hinds. The stag cut right then, bolting away from the female deer, and then the rest of the pack gave chase.

Alexander leaned forward, squeezing hard with his thighs as he felt Destroyer try to lunge from under him. The stallion's urge to outrun all the others was so strong he could almost taste it. However, he managed to hold the horse in check.

Now that they'd singled out the stag, the hounds closed in. A long chase ensued, down the grassy side of the valley, through a bog, and into the trees. And with each furlong, the horses and hounds drew closer.

Eventually, the stag would tire and stop, and stand at bay—face down the baying hounds. The dogs had been trained to hold the stag there rather than attack. For as soon as the hunters neared, one of them would loose an arrow to bring the beast down.

Alexander glanced across at his wife, checking that she was still with him. Jaimee rode like the wind, her hair streaming behind her. She hadn't yet unslung her bow; she would wait till the stag tired before she did.

The hunters thundered up the hill after the fleeing beast, weaving between trees.

Not long now. Alexander let Destroyer lengthen his stride as he leaned low over his neck. It looked like Mackay would have venison on his table at Yuletide after all.

But then the unmistakable 'twang' of a releasing bowstring cut through the thunder of their horses' hooves.

Alexander was about to glance back at his wife, surprised that she'd fired so soon, when a fletched arrow embedded into the trunk of a tree just in front of him. It had flown so close to his face that he'd felt the whisper of the arrow's fletching against his skin.

A shout from Morgan followed as another arrow sped by, narrowly missing Alexander once more.

Alexander reined in his stallion, swinging down from the saddle. They were under attack and vulnerable if they remained on their horses' backs. His companions all did the same, sliding off their horses and crouching low amongst the bracken while arrows flew around them.

The stag raced on, heedless of what was happening behind it, as did the caterwauling hounds.

One of the horses squealed as an arrow found its mark. Alexander saw Kennan's beast go down, nearly crushing Kennan, who'd been sheltering behind it.

"Jaimee!" Alexander reached for his wife, hauling her close so that he could protect her body with his.

"Who is it?" she gasped, her green eyes huge on her pale face.

"I don't know," he muttered, drawing the hunting knife at his side. His gaze swept the trees, and then he stilled, his blood chilling.

There were a few of them, advancing toward the Mackay hunting party. They wore clan sashes: a dull green threaded with red cross-hatching. It was a plaid that Alexander would know anywhere, for he'd donned it often enough over the years.

The Gunns had them surrounded.

35

FOR YE

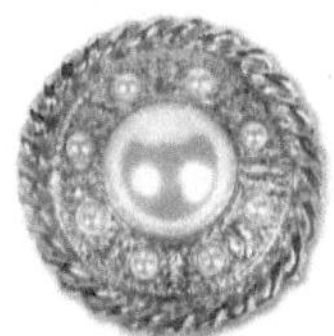

IT SEEMED THAT Connor realized who their attackers were at the same time as Alexander, for he muttered a low, filthy oath.

The laird then unslung his longbow from his back and nocked an arrow.

Shifting away from Alexander, Jaimee did the same.

The twang of arrows releasing filled the forest once more. Alexander didn't like to see his wife so exposed, for she had to move clear of their horses to fire her weapon, yet after the first arrow, he realized she hadn't been exaggerating about her ability.

Her aim was true. Her first arrow hit a Gunn warrior in the thigh, sending him crashing into the bracken, while her second sliced one straight through the throat.

The Mackay retaliation was swift and efficient, yet it wasn't enough to stop the attack. Warriors crashed through the undergrowth toward them now, dirk-blades glinting. Once they got close, arrows would be useless.

"Draw yer dirk, but stay back," Alexander warned Jaimee. "Remain with the horses."

His wife met his gaze for an instant before she nodded. They both knew what would happen if one of those warriors reached her. Jaimee's face was taut, yet he admired her calmness. She kept control of her fear.

Around them, Connor, Morgan, and Kennan had now all abandoned their longbows in favor of their dirks.

Coldness settled over Alexander then, a sensation that he recognized as an old friend. He'd always called it his 'battle chill'. Many men said their blood caught fire when they went into battle, but for Alexander, it was the opposite.

His pulse slowed, his vision sharpened, and he moved with a hunter's stealth. It was this that made him so dangerous in battle—this was why he was so feared.

Ahead of Alexander, Connor lunged at the first Gunn warrior to reach them, his dirk flashing in the murky forest light.

Alexander followed him. Unlike the long, thin daggers that the others wielded, his hunting knife had a wider blade; however, the weapon was just as lethal. Farlan had sharpened it that morning.

Surprise widened the eyes of the Gunn warrior he faced first. His name was Dougall, a man he'd grown up with and fought alongside. However, that relationship had been severed the evening Alexander had ridden from Castle Gunn.

Contempt swiftly followed shock, and Dougall's mouth twisted. The man he'd once followed was now his enemy. Dougall cursed, angling his dirk toward his opponent's belly.

Alexander's blade sliced into Dougall's neck, and the warrior collapsed against him, his own weapon slipping from suddenly limp fingers. Dropping him, Alexander whirled, narrowly missing a swiping blade from his next attacker.

He took down two more. He'd half-expected to see Fynn—the only man at Castle Gunn he could have counted as a friend—among the attackers, yet was relieved to see he was not present. He was aware of the fight around them continuing. Connor, Morgan, and Kennan Mackay were holding their own, slowly turning the fight in their favor.

Alexander had just dealt with a warrior who'd tried to gut him, when a hulking figure barreled into him.

The impact sent both men tumbling through the undergrowth. Caught underneath the stocky figure, Alexander looked up into yet another familiar face.

Roy.

He should have known he'd be here. His brother had led this war party into Mackay territory intent on finding prey. He likely couldn't believe his luck at discovering the chieftain of the Mackays of Farr himself out stag hunting.

However, his luck was about to change.

Alexander had fought Roy many times—in the training yard at Castle Gunn, and a few times in earnest when Roy had drunk too much ale. Drink tended to turn him belligerent.

Roy's blade ripped through the sleeve of Alexander's lèine, drawing blood, yet Alexander barely noticed. He dropped his own blade and smashed his fist into Roy's nose, feeling bone and sinew crunch.

Roy roared, stabbing blindly at Alexander through his rage.

Alexander grabbed his wrist, preventing him from slicing the blade into his neck, and punched his brother once more, this time in the throat.

Roy made a choking sound and fell off him.

Alexander rolled to his feet and retrieved his hunting knife. He didn't want to kill his own blood if he could help it, yet if Roy refused to stand down, he would.

It appeared though that the blow to the throat had felled his brother. Roy lay wheezing and coughing as he clutched at his windpipe. However, his eyes blazed up at Alexander with hate.

Around them, the fight was drawing to a close.

Alexander's companions had dealt with the remaining Gunn warriors.

Only Roy remained alive.

Breathing hard, Connor wiped his blade clean on some moss at his feet before sheathing his dirk. He then rose to his feet, his gaze sweeping over the bodies strewn around them. "Swine," he growled. "I should have known this day would come again."

"I'd say they were tracking us," Morgan replied. His blood-splattered face was all taut angles as he glared down at the last man he'd killed. "Just as we were hunting the stag."

Alexander's mouth thinned. Morgan was right. They'd been so focused on the hunt, none of them had realized the Gunns had been stalking them. He tensed then, as both brothers' gazes settled upon him.

The chill in his blood was thawing, and as it did, his mood shadowed.

Would they think he'd somehow had a hand in this?

It was ridiculous to think such a thing, yet the relationship he'd forged with these people was still new and fragile.

However, there was no rancor or suspicion in either man's eyes.

Instead, Connor nodded to him before gesturing to the groaning man lying in front of him. "One of yer brothers?"

"Aye," Alexander replied. He reached down then, hauling Roy to his feet. "Meet Roy, the third-born son."

"We should kill him too," Kennan growled. The auburn-haired warrior was splattered in blood, although none of it looked like his own.

"Tempting as that is, I ask ye to let him live," Alexander replied. He cast Roy a long, hard look. "I'd like someone to tell the clan-chief what happened here ... as a warning."

Roy managed a croaked curse then and lunged for his elder brother, punching him in the chin.

Alexander bit down on his tongue and tasted blood. Recovering, he kicked Roy in the shins and sent him reeling. Then he hauled his brother to his feet once more. "On second thoughts, he's all yers, Kennan."

"No ... ye are right," Connor spoke then. "Let him live. Let George Gunn eat crow."

Alexander nodded, before he shoved his brother in the direction of the trees. "Go on, Roy. Run like a hunted hare. Before Mackay changes his mind."

His brother needed no further urging. However, he didn't intend to go quietly. Wheezing curses, Roy Gunn staggered off, stumbling over the bodies of the fallen.

Alexander watched him depart, his gaze lingering on the shadows between the tall pines where his brother had disappeared. He'd thought to one day face his brothers as enemies, yet he hadn't imagined it would happen so soon.

They had likely been wondering what had become of him after his departure from Castle Gunn.

Now they knew.

A slender hand clasped his then, and Alexander tore his gaze from the trees to find Jaimee standing next to him. Her face was still pale, yet her expression was as fierce as her brothers'. "How dare they attack us?" she ground out, her gaze sweeping over the bloodied bodies scattered around them. "On our own land."

"It wouldn't be the first time," Connor replied, his mouth twisting. "Nor will be the last."

"How did it feel?" Morgan's voice cut through the snap and crackle of burning wood. "To draw a blade against yer own kin?"

Jaimee tensed. She cut her brother a hard look across the fire, yet he ignored her. There was no missing the challenge in Morgan's voice as he met Alexander's gaze.

"I didn't give it much thought at the time," Alexander replied before cocking his head. Firelight caressed the handsome lines of his face. A bruise was coming up on his jaw where his brother had slugged him. "I was too busy staying alive."

Next to Morgan, Connor snorted a laugh, as did some of the other warriors seated nearby. Jaimee relaxed a little then.

The Mackays huddled around a roaring fire. Dusk settled over the mountains, bringing winter's chill with it. They'd made camp near the banks of one of the many creeks that flowed through the mountain passes, throwing branches of pine on the fire and watching as the flames licked high into the night, chasing away the cold and damp.

Jaimee stretched out her chilled hands, holding them as close as she dared to the dancing flames. However, the slight tremor in her hands wasn't just due to the cold, but as a result of that violent skirmish. Everything had happened so fast, yet she'd found herself trembling like a reed in the wind in the aftermath.

"Still," Morgan continued, clearly not ready to let the subject drop. "Ye killed men ye would have grown up with."

"I did," Alexander admitted, "and I would do so again ... if they threatened my wife." He paused then, his gaze shifting to Connor. "I pledged loyalty to ye, Mackay ... and I intend to keep my word."

Silence fell around the campfire, and all gazes rested upon Alexander Gunn's proud face. An ache rose in Jaimee's chest as she watched her husband. After today, how could anyone doubt him?

Across the fire, Morgan's expression had softened, while Connor watched his brother-by-marriage keenly. Alexander stared back, unflinching. The look drew out, and then Connor's mouth quirked. "I'm glad to hear it."

The hunters ate a supper of bread, cheese, and cured sausage as the darkness around them deepened. A waxing moon crested the heavens, frosting the world in silver. Conversation around the fire was muted, although Connor and Morgan spoke to each other quietly, heads bowed close. Their voices were too low for Jaimee to catch their words.

Turning her attention to Alexander, she saw that he was staring into the flames, his handsome face set into grim lines.

"Alex?" she ventured softly. "What is it?"

Blinking, Alexander emerged from his reverie and glanced her way. His gaze was veiled, his expression guarded. "I want nothing more than to make a new life for myself with ye, lass," he said after a pause. "But I don't think I'll ever be able to leave my past behind. Once my father learns that I have taken up with the Mackays of Farr, his hate for yer clan will burn all the brighter." He paused then, his gaze guttering. "I have brought trouble upon ye all."

Jaimee snorted, even if unease rippled through her at these words. "Let him do his worst," she replied, raising her chin. "He will only fail."

Alexander stared back at her a moment before giving a wry shake of his head. His mouth then curved. "Ye were brave today," he murmured, "and yer aim true. Ye truly are an exceptional woman, Jaimee ... in every way."

Jaimee swallowed. "Only, I've never killed men before," she reminded him huskily.

His expression sobered. "Aye, it changes ye."

They both lapsed into silence then, and Jaimee found herself reliving that brutal clash. She'd witnessed her husband, brothers, and cousin deal with their attackers ruthlessly. Her own involvement, the way she'd fired at those Gunns without a moment's hesitation, made her stomach roil.

She'd once lamented being born a woman, yet she didn't feel that way any longer. Now that she'd been part of a violent skirmish, she never wanted to see another. Despite her brave face, her husband's earlier words concerned her.

"Do ye really think yer father will launch a campaign against us?" she asked finally, worry creeping into her voice.

Alexander gazed deep into her eyes. "He may ... but I will fight again if necessary, for yer brother ... and for ye." He reached out then and traced her cheek with his fingertips. "And for our bairns, when they come."

36

WORTH THE PAIN

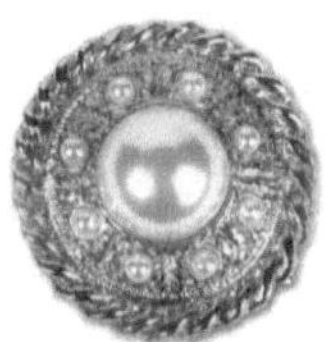

THE MACKAY HUNTING party returned to Farr Castle the following afternoon—a mighty stag slung across the back of one of their horses.

On the way in, Jaimee left Alexander riding alongside Morgan. She urged Tor into a canter to join Connor. Her brother had deliberately ridden on ahead for most of the afternoon, almost as if he preferred to keep his own counsel. However, Jaimee wished to talk to him before they returned home.

"Is anything amiss, brother?" she greeted him, reining Tor in next to him.

Connor glanced her way, blinking as if she'd just caught him deep in thought.

His mouth curved. "No ... just ruminating."

"On what, exactly?"

He laughed. "On how I came to have such a head-strong sister."

"No, ye weren't," Jaimee huffed.

He arched an eyebrow. "I was thinking about what the past year and a half has brought us. So much has changed for our family ... for our clan."

Jaimee nodded. Indeed, in that time, they'd lost their parents, Connor had taken over as laird, both he and Morgan had wed, Connor was now a father, as was

Kennan—and Jaimee had lost her heart to Alexander Gunn.

"If someone had told me what would come to pass, I'd have thought them cracked," she admitted. "The parliament in Inverness ... and the rift within our clan hasn't helped things though."

Connor's brow furrowed. "Aye, but the bad seeds have been dealt with. Robert and William Mackay will no longer stir up trouble." His mouth pursed then. "Our clan-chief will never regain the trust he lost though ... I stood by him at Halladale, but I can't see him in the same way."

Jaimee didn't blame him—neither could she. Angus Mackay had stepped over the line the day he'd sacrificed his son. "And what of Niel?"

Connor's frown deepened to a scowl. "That poor bastard will remain on Bass Rock until the king decides otherwise. Morgan did his best to free him, but he had to let it go ... we all did. All of us must look to the future now."

Jaimee considered her brother's words. He'd spoken wisely. She didn't want to dwell on the turmoil of the past months. In many ways, she felt as if her life was just beginning. She had so many things to look forward to.

Connor gave her a searching look then, his expression softening. "Are ye happy, lass ... does Gunn treat ye well?"

A soft smile curved Jaimee's lips. She appreciated her brother's concern, yet it was misplaced. "I've never been happier ... and yes, Alex treats me like his queen."

Connor snorted and gave a rueful shake of his head. "I don't want to like the bastard, yet I do believe he's growing on me."

Jaimee's smile widened. She leaned toward her brother then and gave him a playful punch on the arm. "He's not that bad," she assured him.

The stone bulk of Farr Castle appeared on the western horizon then, outlined against a dusky sky. Nightfall wasn't far off.

Letting their conversation lapse, brother and sister urged their horses on, closing the distance quickly. Fires burned on the walls, and the heavy odor of peat smoke mingled with the salt tang of the sea, welcoming them home.

The party clattered into the landward bailey to find a crowd awaiting them.

"Finally!" Keira greeted Connor as he swung down from his stallion. The laird's wife had Rose perched on a hip, a woolen shawl wrapped around them both to ward off the chill. "I was beginning to worry."

"Aye, well, we had a spot of trouble with the Gunns yesterday," Connor replied, stepping close and stooping to kiss both his wife and daughter. "But we dealt with them."

Keira's gaze widened before she glanced over at where Alexander reined in his horse behind Connor's.

Seeing the direction of her stare, Connor shook his head. "It seems my brother-by-marriage is a man of his word."

Brother-by-marriage.

Warmth suffused Jaimee's chest at this declaration. Connor had no idea just how much it meant to her. This was her home, and she wanted Alexander to belong here as much as she did.

Cait moved forward, wee Blake swaddled close. A few yards away, Kennan slid off the back of another warrior's horse—after losing his mount, he'd ridden double home—and the couple embraced. "Thank the Lord ye weren't harmed," Cait breathed, cupping Kennan's face tenderly as she stared up at him.

The warrior favored her with a cocky smile. "I can look after myself in a scrap." Kennan then gestured to the huge stag that hung over the back of the horse behind him. "And look what will grace our Yuletide table."

Cait snorted. "Aye, fresh venison is appreciated, yet I'd prefer my husband returned home in one piece."

Jaimee shared a smile with Alexander at this. She then moved toward her husband, leaning into the circle of his arm.

Meanwhile, Morgan had dismounted, and was glancing around him, his brow furrowed. "Where's Maggie?"

Cait drew away from Kennan, her gaze meeting Morgan's. "She went to see Cullodina earlier."

Jaimee didn't think anything strange in the comment, for Maggie had become good friends with Farr's healer of late, and often visited her cottage in the village to assist her with preparing salves and tinctures.

However, something in Cait's expression made Jaimee still. Her face was unusually tense. "What is it?" Jaimee asked, her pulse quickening.

Cait glanced her way, yet her answering smile was strained. "Probably nothing ... she hasn't been feeling well of late."

Morgan frowned. "Maggie didn't say anything to me." He passed the reins of his horse to Kennan. "I'll go find her."

"There's no need, Morgan ... I'm back."

A woman's voice intruded, and a moment later, a cloaked figure emerged from the shadowed gateway.

Maggie drew close, pushing back her hood.

Jaimee's breathing caught when she saw her sister-by-marriage's heart-shaped face was pale, her cheeks tear-streaked.

"Mo ghràdh." Morgan stepped toward her, his voice roughening. "What is it?"

Maggie halted, her throat bobbing and her eyes glittering as she stared back at her husband. "I'm with bairn."

Morgan stopped sharply, his lips parting. "What?"

Maggie raised trembling hands to her face. "I don't understand it ... the healer at Contullich Castle said I couldn't."

"What did Cullodina say?" Morgan asked.

"She says whatever damage the last birth did to me, I'm healed from it," Maggie rasped. "The bairn will be born in April." Tears started to trickle down her cheeks once more. "Sorry … it's come as a shock. I can't quite believe it." Her gaze fused with Morgan's, and suddenly it was as if everyone surrounding them faded into shadow. Just the two of them remained. "I so wanted to bear ye a bairn, my love, but I was sure I couldn't."

Jaimee's throat thickened. Maggie had been stalwart over Keira and Cait's births. She'd never shown any disappointment or bitterness, yet sometimes Jaimee had seen sadness shadow her sea-blue eyes. She knew how much she'd longed to have a family with Morgan; she'd just buried the longing deep and gotten on with her life.

"My heart." Morgan closed the distance between them in two strides and hauled his wife hard against him. Tears wet his cheeks as he wrapped his arms around Maggie. "This is wonderful news."

Jaimee led Tor into the stables, wiping away tears of her own. Tying up the gelding in his narrow stall, she set about unsaddling him. Sniffing, she blinked in an effort to clear her vision.

Silly goose, she chided herself. She never used to be this sentimental. However, she knew how much this would mean to Maggie. Indeed, this pregnancy was a miracle—one that Maggie and Morgan would cherish.

She sniffed again, trying to stem the tears—yet they now streamed down her face.

A moment later, Jaimee realized she wasn't alone.

Turning, she faced her husband. He'd left Destroyer in the stall next door and ducked around the partition. "Is everything all right?" he asked softly, concern clouding his face

"Aye." She favored him with a watery smile. "Just the events of the past two days catching up with me, I suppose."

He reached up, gently brushing away her tears with his knuckles. "I thought they might … eventually."

Their gazes fused then, and an ache rose in Jaimee's throat. "I don't think I could bear it if I lost ye, Alex," she admitted huskily, fresh tears trickling down her cheeks. "It would tear my heart asunder."

A shadow moved in the stormy depths of Alexander's eyes. "None of us can control such things, mo chridhe."

She swallowed hard. "I saw the fear on Morgan's face when he thought Maggie was ill," she whispered. "It's the same dread that twists my guts when I think of ye falling on a Gunn blade."

Alexander snorted. "Well then, I will try not to." He stepped closer and leaned in, his hands cupping her face. "Any fool can go stumbling into battle with a blade in his hand … but letting another soul into yer heart requires far more courage." He paused there, his gaze searing. "Loving makes ye vulnerable to the agony of loss … but the joy is worth the pain."

EPILOGUE

BLESSED

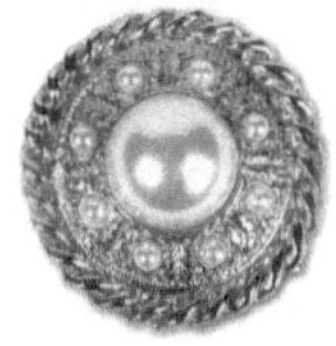

Five years later ...

"MA, CAN I have some apple cake?"

"Soon, my love. Ye shall have to wait till the noon meal."

The little girl's face fell, her lower lip trembling. Jaimee watched her daughter, wondering if a tantrum was brewing.

Their daughter was a sweet child, yet she possessed a strong will—much like her parents.

Jaimee and Anice stood together in one of their dwelling's two living spaces. The lean-to they'd moved into together after their marriage had expanded. The nearby granary had been moved to the other side of the landward bailey, and they now had a main living area, where they could cook, eat, and rest in the evening. Anice had a sleeping area at the back of the living space, separated by a heavy hanging. The other room was Alexander and Jaimee's sanctuary—the place they retreated to together at the end of the day.

A cooling apple cake sat on the table by the window, its sweet scent filling the home.

Jaimee smiled. It was tempting; she couldn't blame Anice for wanting some. Yet they would both have to wait. Jaimee had been feeling a bit peaky earlier in the morning, yet the queasiness had passed now, a ravenous hunger taking its place.

Taking a bowl from the table, Jaimee carried it over to the fire and lowered herself down onto one of the stools there. "Here ... help me shell these walnuts." She beckoned to her daughter. "Ye can have one or two if ye like?"

Anice's face brightened. Needing no further encouragement, the lass joined her mother at the fireside, taking each nut that Jaimee cracked, and peeling off the hard shell with her chubby fingers.

Watching her work, Jaimee's breathing constricted. She hadn't thought it possible to love someone as much as she did Alexander—but when Anice was born, she realized she could.

Anice had brought so much joy into their lives. Jaimee would never forget the tears in Alexander's eyes as he'd held his newborn daughter in his hands and the look of wonder upon his face.

Fatherhood suited him. Being parents suited them both.

Breathing a contented sigh, Jaimee helped herself to a piece of walnut before handing one to Anice. Life was good, and she didn't take one moment of it for granted.

Once the walnuts were shelled, Jaimee threw the empty husks on the fire and rose to her feet. Glancing out of the tiny window, for she'd opened the shutters earlier to let in the morning sun, she smiled.

"It's almost noon," Jaimee said, looking back over her shoulder at Anice. "Shall we go and fetch Da?"

"Aye!" Anice exclaimed, her face lighting up. The lass worshipped her father.

"Come on, lassie." She took hold of her daughter's small hand. Anice was four now and growing taller with each passing day. "Let's go."

Mother and daughter stepped outside into a bright early winter's day. The cold weather had been slow arriving this year, and the sun's friendly face warmed the landward bailey.

Laughter rang against stone, drifting across from the western edge of the keep. Keira and Maggie were at work in the small walled garden inside the nearby seaward bailey. Often Jaimee and Anice joined them, but not today.

Another smile curved Jaimee's lips at the sound of mirth. One of the laughs, low and throaty, was definitely Maggie's. No doubt she would have her daughter, Tara, with her. The lass was only a few months older than Anice and just as strong-willed.

A brood of offspring lived within the walls of Farr Castle these days. Connor and Keira now had two sons—Rory and Quinn—in addition to their daughter, Rose; and Kennan and Cait had another son, Logan.

The landward bailey was busy at this hour. Connor was overseeing the farrier as he inspected the hooves of one of the horses that had foundered over the summer, while Morgan led a group of warriors through drills with wooden swords on the northern edge of the bailey. Male grunts and curses lifted high into the crisp winter air.

Jaimee paused a moment, still grasping her daughter's hand, as she watched her brothers.

Life had been blissfully quiet of late, yet Connor and Morgan worked hard to keep Farr strong. They saw little of their clan-chief these days; over the years, the Mackay had become increasingly reclusive. He'd lost his wife to illness a few years earlier, and his son, Niel, was still incarcerated in the prison of Bass Rock. King James had refused all further appeals for his release.

However, despite that the clan-chief's family had been diminished, harmony had been restored within the clan itself. The new lairds of Balnakeil broch and Dun Ugadale weren't the trouble-makers Robert and William Mackay had been.

Things had even gone quiet with the Gunns recently too. The reckoning that Alexander and Jaimee had both feared would come upon the Mackays of Farr never eventuated. George Gunn had died suddenly three years earlier, and Tavish Gunn was now clan-chief. It appeared that he wasn't the warmonger his father had been.

Glancing up from speaking to the farrier, Connor spied his sister. He flashed her a smile and raised a hand in greeting.

Jaimee grinned and waved back before she turned right toward the forge.

Milish lay outside the workshop, gnawing upon a sheep's shin bone. The bitch had taken to following Alexander around and liked to guard the forge while her master worked. Spying Jaimee and Anice, Milish gave a whine of greeting, her heavy tail thumping against the cobbles.

Murmuring an endearment to the hound, Jaimee paused in the archway and let her gaze feast upon the man she'd wed.

Even five years on, the sight of Alexander Gunn made excitement flutter low in her belly.

Alexander hadn't seen them. He was bent over a blade, which he held over an anvil as he hammered it out, the clang of iron vibrating across the forge. Farlan wasn't present. Of late, the blacksmith let Alexander take on a lot of his work, for the older man struggled with back pains.

No longer an apprentice—Alexander had shown a real flair for working iron and steel.

He wore a thin, sleeveless lèine this morning, the sweat gleaming off his bulging biceps. His long dark hair was tied back at the nape, and his face was creased in concentration.

"Alex."

She said his name softly, yet he heard her nonetheless. Straightening up, Alexander wiped his sweating brow with the back of his forearm before favoring his wife and daughter with a smile. "Is it noon already?"

Jaimee's mouth curved. "Almost. I've made an apple cake, and Anice is impatient to try some."

His smile widened to a grin. "Apple cake, eh ... is it a special occasion?"

"Not really ... just a windfall that needs using up."

"Ready, Da?" Anice chimed in.

Setting the blade down on the anvil, Alexander reached for a cloth and wiped the sweat off his face, neck, and arms with it. "Aye, lass."

Casting aside the cloth, he approached Jaimee and Anice, before placing his hand upon his wife's belly. It had just started to swell, although the skirt of her kirtle hid the curve for the moment. She was around five and a half months on now. Her next child would be a spring bairn, as Morgan and Maggie's daughter had been.

Jaimee's gaze fused with Alexander's. The heat of his hand burned into her belly through her clothing, the same heat that smoldered in his eyes. Jaimee's breathing grew shallow. The desire between them hadn't dimmed. If anything, it burned hotter than ever, and just like when she'd been carrying Anice, her need for him seemed even keener.

Once they put Anice down for a nap after the noon meal, they would retreat to their room together. Her skin prickled at the thought of what they'd do once they were alone.

As if reading her thoughts, Alexander gave her a slow smile. "Let's be off and try some of that apple cake then," he murmured.

"We've got boiled mutton first," Anice announced, pulling at her mother's skirt and her father's braies to get their attention. "Ma says we can't have any cake unless we eat our meat and vegetables."

Alexander laughed, a deep rumble in his chest. He then bent down and scooped his daughter into his arms. Watching Anice wrap her arms around his neck, Jaimee marveled at how alike they looked. Anice shared her father's bone structure and raven-dark hair. However, she'd inherited the Mackay pine-green eyes from her mother.

"Yer mother is a sage woman indeed," he replied with a grin, kissing his daughter on the cheek. "We should listen to her."

Jaimee snorted. "I shall remind ye *both* of that in future."

Alexander laughed again. Moving forward, he slid his arm through Jaimee's. "I always listen to ye, my love. I'd be a fool not to."

Jaimee smiled up at him, warmth spreading through her chest. Aye, she had everything she wanted in life: this man, this child—and the one she carried in her womb—and their humble home. She was indeed blessed.

"Aye ... come inside then," she murmured before whistling to Milish to follow at their heel. "Let's not let the food get cold."

And with that, they went in for their noon meal.

The End

FROM THE AUTHOR

What an adventure! Alexander Gunn fascinated me from page one, and I hope you enjoyed watching his character develop. I needed him to have a dramatic character arc yet didn't want him to lose his 'edge'. Alex and Jaimee were such a great match. I loved Jaimee's strong will and fierce independence, and the way she stands up for herself. This romance is one that starts out as an obsession and develops into something so much deeper. Sigh. It was the perfect way to end this series.

Well, dear reader, that brings us to the conclusion of STOLEN HIGHLAND HEARTS. However, this isn't really the end. This series has become a reader favorite, so I will definitely be continuing with more novellas and novels in this world. Tavish Gunn and Robina Oliphant's romance is coming up at the end of 2021, and Niel Mackay's story (you didn't think I'd forgotten about him, did you?) will be Book One of a new series in early 2022!

Jayne x

HISTORICAL NOTES

This is a highly character-driven series. Even so, as with all my novels, I've based the Stolen Highland Hearts series around real historical figures and events.

The feud between the Mackays and the Gunns was a real one. HIGHLANDER FORBIDDEN begins in 1427 in the aftermath of the Battle of Harpsdale (an actual battle between the Mackays and the Gunns) and the parliament in Inverness (a real council in which King James I dealt out punishment to the warring Highland clans).

Angus-Dow Mackay and his son, Niel (who was imprisoned in the previous book), were real historical figures (full character glossary on the next page), as was George Gunn, the Gunn clan-chief. However, I made up the names and identities of his six sons.

Although I made up the characters of Robert Mackay of Balnakeil, Hugh Mackay of Loch Stach, Robin Mackay of Melness, and William Mackay of Dun Ugadale, there was indeed an uprising against Angus Mackay during these years. While Niel was held prisoner at Bass Rock, his father's cousins, Neil Neilson Mackay and Morgan Neilson Mackay (you can see why I had to change the names .... too confusing otherwise!), attempted to take over the Mackay lands of Strathnaver with the support of the Murrays of Aberscross and the Clan Sutherland. However, they were defeated by Angus's forces, who were led by his second son, John Mackay I of Aberach at the Battle of Drumnacoub in 1433. Angus was killed during the battle.

John Mackay of Aberach appears in HIGHLANDER FORBIDDEN as well, although I have altered his relationship to the clan-chief. I make him his nephew rather than his son.

The Strath of Halladale, where the gathering in our story takes place, is a wild area of the Highlands that sits in the heart of Mackay territory. The River Halladale begins its journey in the wilds of the Knockfin Heights, deep in the heart of the Flow Country, and then runs north for some twenty-two miles before entering the sea in Melvich Bay. The river flows through wild moorland, craggy cascades, gravely flats, larger slow-flowing pools, and farmland. Today the river is a popular fishing spot.

The Mackays of Farr did reside at Farr Castle (also known as Borve Castle). These days, only the ruined shell of Farr Castle remains. With a stunning position overlooking the sea, the castle was used in ancient times as an outpost for raiding other clans. It is said that a Norseman called Torquil may have built the castle.

Castle Gunn (also known as Gunn's Castle and Clyth Castle) is situated on a rock above the sea, eight miles south-west of Wick, Caithness. It was once a splendid and strong castle. Sadly, virtually nothing remains of it these days.

I hope you have enjoyed my notes. I really enjoyed researching the history and landscape of this wild and beautiful corner of Scotland.

STOLEN HIGHLAND HEARTS CHARACTER GLOSSARY

The Mackay clan
Angus-Dow Mackay (Mackay clan-chief)
Cait Mackay (Kennan's wife)
Chrissa (servant at Farr Castle)
Connor Mackay (Mackay chieftain—laird of Farr Castle)
Domhnall Mackay (Connor's uncle—deceased)
Duncan Mackay (Robert Mackay's brother)
Estelle Mackay (Mackay clan-chief's wife)
Farlan (blacksmith at Farr Castle, married to Maeve)
Fern (Jaimee's maid)
Gil (Farlan's apprentice)
Hugh Mackay (Mackay chieftain—laird of Loch Stach)
Jaimee Mackay (Connor's sister)
John Mackay (laird of Aberach—Mackay clan-chief's nephew)
Keira Mackay (Connor's wife)
Kennan Mackay (Connor, Morgan, and Jaimee's cousin)
Maggie Mackay (Morgan's wife)
Morgan Mackay (Connor's brother)
Niel Mackay (Mackay clan-chief's son—imprisoned)
Robert Mackay (Mackay chieftain—laird of Balnakeil broch)
Robin Mackay (Mackay chieftain—laird of Melness broch)
Rory Mackay (former chieftain of Farr—deceased)
Rose Mackay (Connor and Keira's daughter, named after Connor's mother)
William Mackay (Mackay chieftain—laird of Dun Ugadale)

The Gunn clan
Alexander Gunn (Gunn clan-chief's eldest son)

Fynn Gunn (Gunn warrior)
George Gunn (clan-chief)
Maddoc Gunn (sheep farmer and wool merchant)
Moira Gunn (Maddoc's wife)
Sorcha Gunn (Gunn clan-chief's deceased wife)
Tavish, Roy, Blair, Evan, and William Gunn (Alexander's younger brothers)

The Ross clan
Athol Ross (the chieftain's man-servant)
Graeme Ross (Ross chieftain)
Rhianna Ross (Graeme Ross's niece—eloped with a warrior named Callum)

Other characters
Aileana Munro (Maggie's maid)
Campbell Munro (Maggie's first husband—deceased)
Cullodina (healer at Farr Castle)
Father Lachlan (chaplain at Farr Castle)
Mother Jean (Prioress of Iona nunnery)
Ramsay Oliphant (Oliphant clan-chief)
Robina Oliphant (the clan-chief's daughter)

ABOUT THE AUTHOR

Award-winning author Jayne Castel writes epic Historical and Fantasy Romance. Her vibrant characters, richly researched historical settings and action-packed adventure romance transport readers to forgotten times and imaginary worlds.

Jayne has published a number of Amazon bestselling series. In love with all things Scottish, Jayne also writes romances set in Dark Ages Scotland ... sexy Pict warriors anyone?

When she's not writing, Jayne is reading (and re-reading) her favorite authors, cooking Italian feasts, and going for long walks with her husband. She lives in New Zealand's beautiful South Island.

Connect with Jayne online:
www.jaynecastel.com
www.facebook.com/JayneCastelRomance/
https://www.instagram.com/jaynecastelauthor/
Email: contact@jaynecastel.com